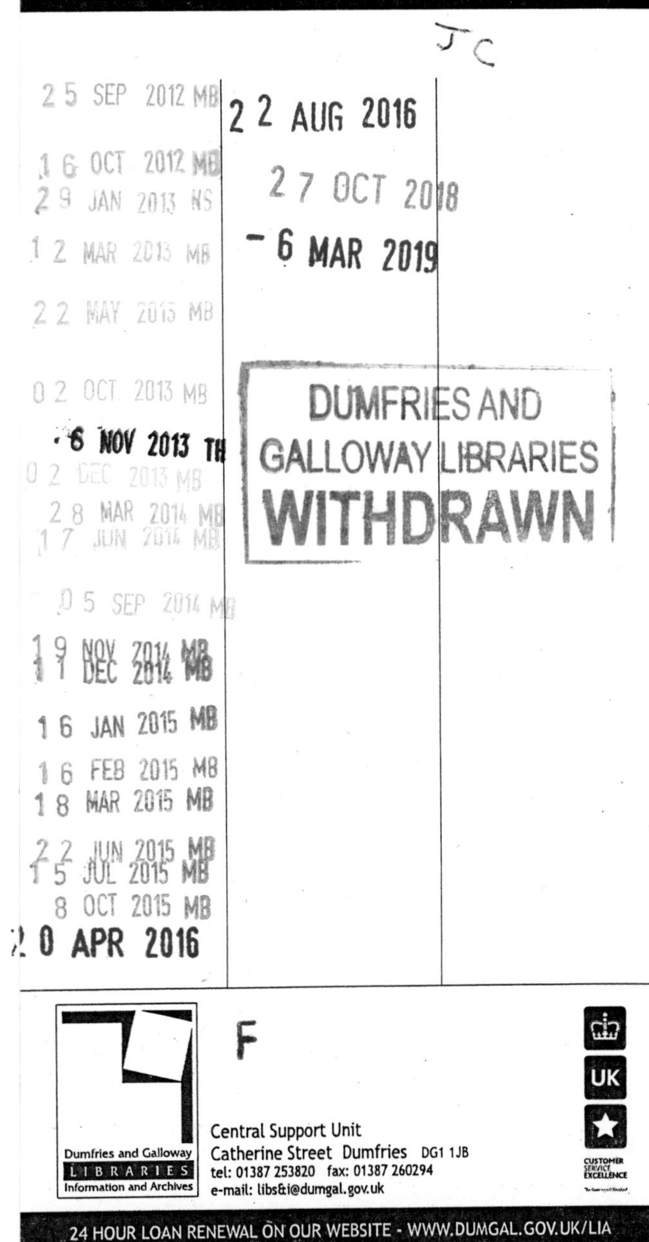

Susy McPhee was born and raised in Liverpool. She studied Russian and karate at St. Andrews University harbouring vague notions of becoming a spy.

Whilst waiting for MI5, the KGB, or the FBI to come calling, she trained as a Technical Author with ICL in Berkshire, and set about trying to inject life into what was traditionally not the most creative of disciplines. From such inauspicious beginnings her career led her into areas that came pretty close to her spy ambitions, including training rocket scientists in the former Soviet Union. She moved to Scotland from the South of England with her husband and three small daughters sixteen years ago.

Husbands and Lies

1 3 5 7 9 10 8 6 4 2

Published in 2009 by Ebury Press, an imprint of Ebury Publishing
A Random House Group Company

The Random House Group Limited Reg. No. 954009

Addresses for companies within the Random House Group can be found at
www.randomhouse.co.uk

A CIP catalogue record for this book is available from the British Library

The Random House Group Limited supports The Forest Stewardship Council
(FSC), the leading international forest certification organisation. All our titles
that are printed on Greenpeace approved FSC certified paper carry the FSC
logo. Our paper procurement policy can be found at
www.rbooks.co.uk/environment

Printed in the UK by CPI Cox & Wyman, Reading, RG1 8EX

ISBN 9780091928568

Acknowledgments

Writing this book has been a bit like being pregnant with my first child. Since its conception I've experienced every emotion from elation to despair. I've put on weight, slept fitfully, woken up nauseous, and never, throughout the whole process, been in any doubt that there was no going back. This book has emptied me. And then it filled me back up again.

Thanks to so many people for hanging on in there while I did the deed. To Alice Lutyens at Curtis Brown and Gillian Green at Ebury, first of all, for your enthusiasm, support, and belief in me, and especially for seeing something worthwhile in what I was doing and taking a punt on an outsider. I am a better writer because of you both.

Thanks to Lesley Campbell for nagging me to get on and write, for suffering the early drafts, and for constantly telling me I could write. To Kerry Bussell, Dale Hobbs, Lesley Mailer and Susan Harrison, brave women, sisters and friends, who have laboured through my efforts and come out smiling. Thanks to my mum, Joan Harrison, for her unfailing faith in me, aptly demonstrated by her complete lack of astonishment (and wholehearted delight) upon learning that someone wanted to publish my book.

Thanks to Helen Lewis-McPhee, who has kept putting her own dreams on hold to help me realise mine.

Thanks to Ed, Bob, Simon, George, Olly and my dad for letting me borrow their womenfolk for a bit.

Thanks to Roz Morrison for, amongst many, many other things, initiating me into the hitherto unexplored world of on-line dating. Thanks to Doctors Gail and Stephen Orme for keeping me straight on the medical facts (sorry, Stephen, for paying no attention when you suggested I make the on-call registrar a devastatingly handsome chap named Orme…).

Thanks to Carolyn, Lauren and David for putting up with their dad's cooking when I was too wrapped up in the plot to realise it was half-past ten at night and the only thing in the fridge was half a pound of Lurpak and a jar of Lazy Garlic.

Finally, thanks to Iain, my best friend and husband, for – well, everything, really. For giving me the space to do this. For letting me write in bed with the light on in the middle of the night. For loving every word I write. For understanding why this was so important to me, and reminding me when I forgot. For seeing into my heaped-up heart after Jane died, and unscrambling my loss with your love. This book is for you, with mine.

For Iain

Chapter 1

My mother taught me to lie.

Don't get me wrong. She never sat me down and said, 'Okay, Francesca, today's lesson is all about the art of the tangled web' or any such thing. She was far subtler than that, although as a rule the use of the word *subtle* in conjunction with my mother would demand the immediate addition of the 'as a brick' qualification. My mother rode roughshod through life on a tougher-than-rhino saddle leaving a trail of debris the size of Africa in her wake.

She taught me other things, too, of course, like where to hide when she was in one of her rages and how to hold the tops of my hand-me-down socks in place with a rubber band – early lessons that were dismissed with ne'er a nostalgic glance backwards once I left home and had shaken off the shackles of my childhood. The lying, though: that was another matter altogether. That one I practised. By the time I hit twelve I had it off to a fine art.

Which was just as well, really. Lord knows what kind of adult I'd have made if I hadn't learned to differentiate between compulsive honesty and an occasional well-placed falsehood. Sometimes, during the long, interminable days and nights of Alison's illness, lying was the only thing that kept me going.

Not least, of course, the lying I did to myself.

Alison. My best friend since primary school, when she'd punched Billy Waterman after he made me cry during times tables practice by showing me his willy under the table. She'd waited until playtime and then collared him by the girls' toilets, where she'd split his lip with a right hook that Frank Bruno would have been proud of. When an unexpected promotion brought me south from Staffordshire seven years ago, one of the deal clinchers had been that my new office was fifteen minutes from where Alison was living.

And now she was shackled to a hospital bed by a tangle of tubes and could barely lift a hand from the covers, let alone throw a punch. I caught a glimpse of her through the corridor window as I approached the side room that had been her home for the past month and a half, and a thousand horrible truths rampaged through my head. *So this is what it does to you. What's happened to your hair? Is your skin supposed to be that colour?*

I ignored them and set my mouth in a determined line lest they try to break forth anyway. 'You look well.'

'Liar.' Alison gave me a weak smile. 'I look like shit.'

'No, really – I think you look – well, you don't look so tired today. Your eyes look brighter.'

Alison regarded me closely. 'More than I can say for you, then. You look like you haven't slept in a fortnight.'

'I'm fine.' I dropped my coat over the back of the chair and drew it up alongside the bed.

'Sure? Max and Lottie okay?'

'Mmn? Oh – yeah. They're fine.'

Alison eased herself forward in the bed. 'Hon? You sure you're okay? Only you don't look okay to me. You look – grey.'

I regarded her for a moment, and felt tears begin to threaten. Oh, God. I always vowed before I came in that I wouldn't go getting upset in front of her. But watching your best friend being taken from you by degrees, deteriorating with each visit as the cancer that had been diagnosed five months earlier ate her up from the inside, was never going to be easy. Her concern for my wellbeing was humbling.

I pulled myself together. 'Grey, you think?' I gave a mock sigh and folded my arms across my chest. 'Yeah, well, Max was saying much the same thing the other day.'

She raised her eyebrows at the suggestion of my paragon of a husband saying anything so maladroit. '*Max* was?'

'Mm-hmn.' I looked at her innocently. 'We've just bought this new full-length mirror for the bedroom. One of those – chevalier things, you know. In an antique pine frame, to go with the dressing-table. It's got this little design kind of carved into the top of the frame.' I gestured with my hand, and she nodded encouragingly. Then I sighed heavily again. 'Anyway, I was just out of the bath, and doing the whole *scrutinising* thing in front of it – *big* mistake, by the way – and I said to Max, "Look at me. I'm fat, I'm wrinkled, I'm old, and I'm grey." I was waiting for him to disagree, you see.' Alison nodded again. 'And he didn't, so eventually I said, "For goodness' sake, Max, say something nice to me."'

Alison waited expectantly. 'And did he?'

I lowered my eyes. 'He said – well, he said—' I hesitated. '"At least there's nothing wrong with your eyesight."'

Alison gave a shout of laughter, and a nurse who was busy at a desk across the corridor looked over at us and smiled. Then Alison sobered again.

'No, but seriously, Fran. I think you're overdoing things.'

'I'm not.'

'You *are*. How could you not be? Full-time job. Husband and kid to look after – admittedly both cute, adorable, blah blah, but still a handful. Useless best friend who's about as much help to you as a chocolate teapot.'

'Less,' I said.

'What?'

'Less use. At least I could comfort-eat my way through a chocolate teapot.'

She stuck out her tongue. 'Sod off. Though I suppose it might fatten you up, at least.' She reached out and plucked at the sleeve of my jumper. 'Look at you. You're all skin and bone. Fat, my ass. *I've* got more meat on me than you.'

'Yeah, well.' I gave her a sidelong look, and one of the earlier truths I'd been trying to suppress slipped out before I could help it. 'At least I still have my own hair.'

She bit her lip to stop herself from smiling, and I felt the tears welling up once again.

'Come here,' she ordered, and patted the side of the bed. I slid reluctantly onto the edge of the mattress beside her, and she wrapped her wasted arms around my shoulders and leant her head in against mine for a moment, so that I could smell the fresh perfume that was so quintessentially Alison, the fragrance she had never lost despite the prolonged stay in hospital and the punishing weeks of treatment she'd undergone, which made me want to cry all the harder and cling on to her and scream at the gods to leave her be and stop their relentless quest to take her from me. Then she pushed me away and studied me at arm's length, narrowing her dark-shadowed eyes at me intriguingly.

'I want you to help me with something.'

I sniffed unattractively, feeling around unsuccessfully for a handkerchief, and she passed me a tissue from a box that stood alongside a vase of white freesias on her bedside cabinet.

'Go on.' I blew vigorously into the tissue.

She gave me one of her wicked looks, her eyes gleaming.

'You're not allowed to say no.'

'Oh God.'

'I'm dying. Would you refuse the wishes of a dying woman?'

'Yes!' I blew again. 'No,' I admitted.

She grinned at me conspiratorially, then gestured towards the cabinet. 'Open it. Top shelf.'

I did as I was bidden.

'There's a notepad on top of my clean PJs. Got it?'

'Uh-huh.' I lifted it out, and she took it from me and rifled through the pages. Then she handed it back to me, and I began to read aloud what she had written in her clear, rounded hand.

'"Thirty-something, closer to my fourth decade than my third, alas; never done any online dating before."' I raised my eyes to Alison. 'You're joining a dating agency?'

She gave a tired laugh. 'Not me, you cheeky bugger. I'm nowhere near my fourth decade.' She nodded at the page. 'Keep reading.'

I cleared my throat. '"One careful previous owner (lady driver). Friends tell me I have a good sense of humour, that I'm trustworthy and fun, but then I pay them well to say all that stuff!"' I broke off and raised my eyebrows at her before continuing. '"I'm into good food, great wine and long lazy weekends in the country. Strengths: I can cook. And wash up afterwards. And iron my own shirts. Weaknesses: hopeless fashion sense. Besotted by my six-year-old daughter. Would love to meet lady with similar interests who isn't afraid of tackling someone with a wardrobe dating back to 1979, isn't repulsed by children, and enjoys at least the occasional glass of Cloudy Bay."'

'Well? What d'you think?'

I looked at her, confused. 'Um ... he sounds divine. But – don't you think it's a bit optimistic to be looking at going out on dates, given the circumstances?' I gestured at the paraphernalia of equipment surrounding her bed. 'I mean, where will you hide the drip? Can you even remember how to put on anything that isn't a pair of pyjamas? Not to mention, won't Adam mind?' And do I care if he does, I asked myself, though I didn't voice this last, uncharitable thought. Adam, Alison's husband, worked as a producer for the BBC. The first time I'd met him, when Alison had brought him round for dinner and a checking-over after she'd been on a couple of dates with him, I'd been struck by his likeness to Max, and a bit dazzled on discovering that he routinely wined and dined some of Hollywood's finest. He was full of funny anecdotes about the lesser-known habits of the movers and shakers in the world of television, and I'd found myself seduced by his easy charm. Between the cashmere sweater and the fancy cufflinks he was wearing, he was like a glamorous version of Max, who wasn't wearing a sweater but who had rolled the sleeves of his shirt up above his elbows, and whose fingernails bore traces of the engine oil he'd been unable to scrub clean after he'd come in from work that evening. He had teased me after Alison and Adam had left at the end of the night, telling me I'd never be able to cope with a man who spent longer in front of the mirror than me. My admiration had been short-lived, however: the next time we were out together at a party, Adam had made a pass at me and had laughed in the face of my self-righteous indignation when I turned him down, calling me a prude. Since that time I'd harboured feelings of protectiveness towards both Alison and Max, neither of whom I'd ever told, and a desire to run a hot kebab skewer through one of Adam's eyes every time I saw him.

Alison looked hard at me now, her eyes glittering.

'What?'

'That *is* Adam.'

'What?' I felt stupid and slow all of a sudden.

'Adam and Erin.'

'What?' I said again.

'Fran!' She gave an exasperated sigh. 'I need you to say something other than just "What?" all the time.'

'But – I don't—'

'Yes, you do, Fran.'

I looked hard at her. My mouth felt suddenly dry. She continued to grill me with her eyes.

'You've written a dating CV for your husband,' I said eventually.

'Mm-hmn.'

'Because ...?'

She sighed. 'Please don't make me spell it out for you.'

'Spell it out for me.' I could feel a great surge of anger welling up inside me.

'Oh, Fran.' She reached out to take one of my hands, but I pulled away from her. She shrugged.

'Okay, then. I don't want Adam left moping on his own for the rest of his life. You should hear him when he's in visiting. Believe me, it's not like when you come in.' She broke off, and ran a hand distractedly across what was left of her ravaged hair. Then she rubbed her face with both hands for a moment, as though looking inside herself for the right words.

'I live for your visits,' she finally admitted, emerging from behind her hands. 'I love it when you come in: you make me laugh. You let me say things like "I'm dying", without giving me those great reproachful looks Adam's so good at. You poke fun at my hair, at the state I've become, without making me feel you're trying to protect me from some awful truth that everybody else already knows about but that I'm supposed to pretend I'm oblivious to. You tell me I'm less use than a chocolate teapot and make up stupid stories about looking at yourself in front of a mirror—'

'I do stuff like that to make you laugh!' I said, still angry. 'That doesn't mean I've become reconciled to losing you. It doesn't mean I haven't given up hope that they'll find some miracle cure. There are new advances in medicine every day now, and you've got to stay positive. You're not allowed to give up hope! You never know: the next treatment—'

'Stop it, Fran,' she admonished. 'Don't lie to me. Not you, too. There won't *be* any more treatments. You know that.' She reached out for my hand again, and again I refused her advances. She sighed patiently. 'Of all the people who surround me every minute of every day – the nurses, the oncologists, Adam, Erin, my mum – you're the only one who treats me any way that even approaches normal. When Adam comes in, I'm not allowed to mention the cancer. He doesn't know how to cope with it. He used to ask about the tests, the treatments, you know? But he stopped doing even that eventually. The answers were never what he wanted to hear. I feel as though I'm letting him and Erin down because I can't defeat this thing and I'm just going to up and – *disappear* one day, and the thought of them being left on their own terrifies me. You *know* how hard this is. You're a wife and a mother as well. Lottie's the same age as Erin. Adam and Max are so alike they could be twins – aren't we always saying that? And yet you treat me just the same as you always did, as though you're sucking the juice out of every visit and you're not going to let this foul thing that's eating me up steal what's left of our time together. I couldn't do this without you. I need you to stay honest for me.'

She was so calm. I envied her that, even if I didn't agree with whatever mad scheme she was cooking up. Frankly, I suspected that Adam would be more than capable of taking care of himself in the future.

I picked up the notepad once again.

'"One careful previous owner?"' I raised my eyebrows at her.

'Too much of a cliché?' She wrinkled her nose at me. 'I didn't want to put "widower". It makes him sound about a hundred. Plus, it seems a bit tasteless to mention it in a dating ad.'

'Whereas asking your best friend to collude with you in producing the ad whilst you lie dying in a hospital bed is the very height of good taste, I suppose.'

She smiled at me heartbreakingly. 'I love you, Fran.'

I sighed in exasperation, refusing to acknowledge the treacherous tears that were once again threatening. 'What do you want me to do?'

'Well.' She clasped her hands together in front of her excitedly. I had to admit, she hadn't looked this fired up in weeks. 'Nothing with the ad yet, obviously. Except – well, I'm not sure if I've hit the right tone. I thought perhaps you could go on to a couple of online dating sites and get a kind of feel for them – suss out what people normally say, that sort of thing. And then print a few out so that we can go over them together. I mean, mentioning Erin might be a huge no-no. I don't want to put people off before they've given him a chance.'

'Erin wouldn't put anybody off!' I said indignantly. 'The child is a doll.'

She laughed at my outraged tone. 'Of course she is,' she agreed. 'But there might be some *amazing* woman out there who is perfect for Adam and Erin, but doesn't even know how great she'll turn out to be with kids and would run a mile at the prospect, but once she meets Adam and realises how fantastic *he* is, she won't *want* to run. D'you see?'

'Not even remotely. But what the hell.' I looked at her eager face. 'Okay, okay: so – *if* I agree, you want me to suss out the lingo and report back. Is that it?'

'Well, no. Sorry. *Afterwards*—' She looked at me meaningfully. 'I want you to join him up without telling him.' I started to protest, but she held up a hand to stop me. 'This is important to me, Fran, so please hear me out. I mean, give it a decent period of time – six months, say. No longer than that. I don't want him brooding.'

I bit back a snort. The thought of Adam brooding was hard to swallow.

'And then go through any responses, and see if you can't find him a nice girl to look after him and Erin,' Alison continued. 'I mean, *I'm* not going to be around to filter out the fortune hunters from the singing nuns.'

'But – how on earth am I going to do that? I can hardly pretend to be him, can I, when all these would-be perfect women start phoning up to arrange dates with him?'

'Oh – you'll think of something,' Alison said dismissively. 'You can say you're his PA, or something. Didn't you tell me you worked with someone who met his partner through a dating agency? A really pretty girl who works in advertising?'

'Modelling,' I admitted reluctantly. 'Greg Patterson. He heads up the system architecture team. They're getting married at the end of the month. Second time round.' Greg's first wife had left him in the middle of a rainy November day, hiring a van and clearing their carefully constructed loft apartment of every stick of furniture while he was at work. She hadn't left a note.

'Well, then,' Alison said, as if that solved everything. 'You can ask him for some hints and tips.'

'Alison,' I said, trying to sound patient, 'I am not going to a colleague to ask for hints and tips on how to set up my best friend's husband on a dating site. I mean, apart from the fact that he would think me stark staring mad, it would be completely unprofessional. Guys just don't talk about that stuff in the office, plus I'm his *associate*—'

'So how come you know all about how he met his fiancée?'

'He – I don't remember.' She raised her eyebrows at me. 'Okay, *okay*. He told me.'

'Well, there you are, then.' Alison looked smug. 'I'm sure he'll be full of good advice.'

I shook my head at her. 'I'll start with stage one,' I said. 'I'm not agreeing to anything beyond that at this point.'

'Tonight?'

'What d'you mean, tonight?'

'I mean, will you go online and suss some agencies out tonight?' She tore the page out of the notepad and folded it in half before holding it out to me. 'Then you can report back when you come in tomorrow.'

'I might not make it in tomorrow,' I said loftily, gathering up my coat from the back of the chair. 'I do have a life, you know.' I looked at the piece of paper, which she was waggling at me, and eventually snatched it out of her hand and stuffed it into the pocket of my coat.

Alison grinned, unfazed, and with good reason. I hadn't missed a day since she was admitted six weeks earlier for intensive and apparently futile radiation treatment.

'Don't go anywhere,' I said, like I always did, dropping a light kiss on her cheek.

She winked at me, happy in spite of the tiredness that had begun to show in her features.

'I might,' she replied mischievously. 'I do have a life, you know.'

Chapter 2

When I arrived home from the hospital there was a gorilla on the landing. I could hear it stomping up and down outside Lottie's bedroom, making strange monkey-like noises and lumbering clumsily into the bookshelf before coming to a halt and banging noisily on her door. I stopped in the hall and listened.

'Who's there?' Lottie's voice, thick with delighted terror.

There was a pause, and a bit more snuffling and grunting. Then: 'I'm a great big gorilla with fat furry arms and huge white teeth. When you let me in, I'm going to hug your breath away!'

Lottie gave a squeal. 'Then I won't let you in!'

Silence. Then another knock on the door, softer this time.

'Who's there?' Lottie asked again.

'Whoooooo!' howled Max. 'I'm a very creepy ghost with a face as white as a sheet and chains that jangle and clank. When you let me in—'

'No!' cried Lottie. 'Not the ghost, Daddy! It's the witch next.'

'Oh. Right. Sorry.' Max cleared his throat, then spoke in a strangled falsetto. 'I'm a wicked old witch with a big ugly nose—'

'—a long pointed hat,' Lottie corrected.

'—a long pointed hat and – um, a hairy wart on my bottom—'

'—a wand full of magic,' Lottie interrupted again, giggling. 'She doesn't have a hairy wart on her bottom.'

'When you let me in, I'm going to turn you into a toad!'

'It's a frog, Daddy, not a toad, and I won't let you in!'

I smiled to myself and went through to the kitchen, which looked as though it had been invaded by a marauding army. Max had been a rock for the past couple of months, collecting Lottie each evening from the child-minder she went to after school, so that I could stop off at the hospital on my way home from work without worrying. Between them they had developed a companionable evening routine in which they prepared Lottie's dinner together, somehow managing to use every pan we possessed to rustle up fish fingers on peanut-butter toast or some other such culinary wonder, before a pre-bed bath that left the bathroom awash with wet towels and damp laundry. Their father-daughter time together ended with the complete re-enacting of Lottie's favourite book of the moment, a story that Lottie knew by heart, which was more than could be said for her father, who invented wildly every time he forgot one of the vital ingredients.

I began mechanically clearing up the debris from Lottie's dinner, rinsing out the pans and stacking them in the dishwasher while overhead Lottie was squealing that she wasn't going to let in the very creepy ghost who wanted to spook her. Then, when I'd tamed the worst of the mess, I brewed myself a coffee, retrieved Alison's piece of paper from the pocket of my coat, carried both through to the study and sat down in front of the PC.

Max hated everything to do with computers – a fact that had astonished me when I'd first met him, particularly as we were both attending a dinner thrown by the IT company I worked for. He'd come along as the guest of our head of HR, Melissa Llewelyn (known to her staff as Mel-Hath-No-Fury, or just The Fury for short), and I'd found myself sitting at the same table as them during dinner. Xenith were celebrating landing a lucrative contract with BT, and our MD Keith Hardacre was mid-flow harping on about what a big deal the new contract was, how it was going to take Xenith into a whole new era; and Max had caught my eye across the table and winked. I'd found myself blushing in mortification: aside from the fact that he was with The Fury, he was astonishingly good-looking and I'd been watching the two of them surreptitiously since the start of the evening, secretly covetous of the easy affection they appeared to have for one another. When he asked me to dance with him after the formalities of the speeches were over, I'd blushed again and muttered something about two left feet. He'd shrugged regretfully and taken The Fury up instead, and then at the end of the evening he'd cornered me by the cloakroom and asked if he could take my two left feet out for dinner one evening. I'd hesitated for a nanosecond before blurting out something about his being with The Fury, and he'd laughed again and said they were old friends, nothing more – an assertion strenuously contradicted by The Fury herself some weeks later when she found out that Max and I were an item.

'Old friends, yes,' she'd said in indignation when she collared me at the drinks machine, 'but I was working on him.' By the time we announced our engagement six months later she'd accepted defeat and moved on, though that didn't stop me feeling the odd twinge of guilt towards her for my part in the casual way Max had let her down.

In spite of his marrying someone steeped in the whole IT culture, computers continued to remain my husband's one blind spot. He had even stubbornly refused to introduce one into his business – a small but increasingly popular garage in Binfield in which he made a modest living restoring vintage cars. He had set up his workshop there when we'd moved down from Staffordshire. Not too far from some of the real vintage car aficionados, he'd said, and he'd been right. Draw a forty-mile radius around the place and you had the cream of Berkshire's gentrified all within striking-distance. The place had been buzzing almost from the day he opened the workshop doors. Eventually, finding that business was steady enough to justify his employing a second pair of hands, he had taken on a young mechanic named Guy, fresh from college and full of bright ideas for streamlining the business that included the purchasing of a state-of-the-art desktop so that they could store customer details, manage the stock efficiently and keep their accounts up-to-date. Reluctantly, Max had allowed himself to be dragged into the world of twenty-first-century technology, though at home he still refused to have anything to do with the PC.

As a result the study was my territory, and its calm wrapped itself around me as I sat down and unfolded the piece of paper Alison had given me earlier. I loved having a room of my own. As children, Angela and I had fought over proprietorship of the top bunk bed in a cramped ten-by-nine bedroom (she had won, claiming she outranked me in age). By the time I was eighteen and applying to university, one of the non-negotiable criteria for my place of study was that it had to be able to offer single accommodation, and over the next three years I had basked in the luxury of having a door I could close on the rest of the world. In that room I'd been able to create my own reality, and nothing had been allowed to intrude upon it. Since then, a room to myself had remained a priority. In fact, this tiny room, which was far from tidy and possibly even smaller than the bedroom Angela and I had reluctantly shared, had been one of the things that had persuaded Max and me to stretch our resources when we moved south.

I switched on the PC and stared unseeing at the screen as it booted up, trying not to brood on the injustice of a world that was determined in its meanness to carry off a thirty-four-year-old mother whose generosity of spirit wanted to do something to try to assuage her husband's grief after she had gone. Life wasn't meant to be like this. I could think of plenty of people who deserved her fate far more readily than she did: people who lied and cheated and didn't care who they hurt along the way. I gave myself a little shake and tried to focus on the screen. Brooding, I had learned early on, brought nothing but misery and was, as Alison had pointed out to me when she'd broken the news about the cancer, best left to the chickens.

I could remember with absolute clarity the afternoon she'd told me. It was the last time I'd felt completely happy; I just hadn't known at the time that I was. We'd taken Lottie and Erin into Windsor for shoes, and Lottie had thrown the mother and father of all tantrums because she wanted the same shoes as Erin and the shop didn't have her size. I'd been pink with embarrassment at the scene she'd caused, and Alison had shepherded us all out of the shop and across the bridge to the river at Eton, where she'd parked me on a bench with a flask of coffee and distracted the girls with a bagful of crusts she'd brought along for the swans. I'd sat watching the late afternoon sun dancing over the surface of the water and laughed as the girls shrieked indignantly when an over-bold swan came too close and made a grab for the bread Erin was holding, and Alison, who was sharing the bread between the two girls, looked across at me and smiled. Some part of my brain must have registered the significance of that smile, because I could still conjure it up every time I looked at her now with her ruined hair and her gaunt features. And eventually, the bread having been equally divided and distributed to the swans, she came over and sat beside me and looked out across the river towards the castle.

'Did you ever see anything so beautiful?' she'd asked me. She'd tilted her face towards the sun and closed her eyes for a moment before turning back to watch the girls.

'If anything were to happen to me, you'd look out for Erin, wouldn't you, Fran?' she'd asked unexpectedly, without looking at me.

'Of course I would!' I looked at her in consternation.

'Thanks.' She'd looked at me then, and smiled again.

'Well, I mean – you would do the same for Lottie, wouldn't you?'

She'd said nothing for a moment, and then eventually she'd leant across and squeezed my hand. 'Absolutely,' she'd said. 'Come on: let's get back.'

And only when we'd driven the twelve miles home and fed the girls and got them tucked up in bed together for the sleepover they'd been planning all week, only then, after we'd collapsed in the sitting-room with a cup of tea and I'd started to give voice to the question that had been forming in my head since she'd asked me about looking out for Erin, only as I started to say to her, 'You know when we were down at the river earlier —?' – only then had she interrupted me, and silenced me with that enigmatic smile.

'I've got cancer, Fran.' A look of utter disbelief had spread across my face. 'Acute endometrial cancer, to be precise.' She smiled at my expression. 'I know: I didn't believe it myself at first. Bit of a bummer, eh?'

'But – how? I mean – when did you—?'

'I went to see Dr Savage.' Dr Savage was one of the GPs at our local health centre. 'We've been trying for another baby, and it just wasn't happening. My periods were all over the place. And – after ruling out a lot of other things – she eventually decided to do a biopsy, just to check everything was okay, you know?'

'But – when was this?'

'Last week. I went in to see her again yesterday, and she

told me the results. There's a ten per cent chance they're wrong, of course ...'

'And a ninety per cent chance they're not?'

She nodded.

I swallowed. My tongue seemed to have grown thick in my mouth. 'Can they treat it?'

'Of course they can, though the treatment doesn't sound like a barrel of laughs.' She laughed anyway. 'And our chances of having more children look as though they just shrank to nil. But still.' She smiled again. 'We have Erin. I'm so grateful for that.'

'It's just that – when you asked me, down at the river—'

'Oh – I was just being maudlin. When you find out something like this, your imagination goes into overdrive, that's all. Sorry.'

I stared into my teacup in silence, until eventually Alison came over to sit beside me on the sofa and hugged me. 'Hey, come on! Chin up,' she said. 'I'm not dead yet! Dr Savage is referring me for a hysterectomy, and that'll be the end of it. I'm relying on you for some serious TLC once I get out of hospital. I shall expect home-made soup and flowers every day. I plan to be a very demanding convalescent.'

I gave her a rueful look. 'I'm useless at soup.'

'Then you will have to do what the rest of the world does: buy it in Tesco and lie,' she said. 'You *can* lie, can't you, Fran?' I nodded, smiling reluctantly at her in spite of the great knot that had formed in my stomach. 'Good. And in the meantime, don't you dare start brooding. Brooding's for the chickens.'

But the hysterectomy hadn't been the end of it. The cancer had spread to the connective tissue of the cervix, and neither the hormone therapy nor the gruelling weeks of radiation therapy had been enough to stop it marching relentlessly through the pelvis and straight towards the lymph nodes of the abdomen. And now here she was, busy making plans for her husband and daughter to try to ensure they wouldn't be left alone without someone to care for them after she'd been taken from them in the shittiest way imaginable.

It was hard not to brood.

I smoothed the piece of paper out in front of me and laid it on the desk next to the keyboard, and then turned as I heard a movement behind me.

'Hey.' Max came across and kissed me lightly on the top of the head. 'How're you doing?'

'Oh – you know. Same old same old.'

'How's Alison?'

'Oh, well – I thought she looked a bit brighter tonight.'

'Yeah?'

'For someone who's dying, you know.'

He leaned over and hugged me, hard.

'Monsters all dispensed with?' I indicated upstairs with my eyes.

'You'd better believe it.' He grinned. 'I don't know how she remembers every word of the book. I'm not allowed to get a single bit wrong.'

'I know. I heard you, trying to sneak the ghost in early and skip the witch.' I shook my head at him, pretending to tick him off.

'Do you have much to do in here?' He nodded towards the PC.

'Not much.' I laid my arm across Alison's literary efforts to hide them. I didn't feel up to explaining her scheme to Max just yet. 'Give me ten minutes.'

'Ten minutes it is, then,' he said, heading for the door. 'Fish fingers on toast all right for you?'

'Sounds – delicious.'

'Just kidding.' He smiled, crinkling his eyes at me. 'Lottie and I picked up some steak on the way home from school. And a rather fine Merlot to go with it. I take it that meets with Madam's approval?'

'Madam is delighted,' I told him, and meant it.

'Well, then. I shall go and rustle up something tasty to go with it,' he said, disappearing off towards the kitchen.

I smiled at his retreating back before turning back to the PC, allowing myself to bask for a moment in the security of a warm home and a loving family. Thank God, I thought to myself, that I have this. This is what makes the rest of it bearable. This is the bit I can cling on to when the rest of the world is falling apart. Max, I reflected, was like the door to that first room I'd had at university: behind the shelter of his broad shoulders I could shut out all the crap and build my own sanctuary against whatever life threw at me.

I brought up a browser window and typed 'dating agency' into the search engine, then clicked on the first link at the top of the list. I picked my way through the early questions about the height, age and alcoholic predisposition of my ideal man, and pretty soon I had a result:

twelve pages, in fact, of guys of medium height aged between thirty-five and sixty who didn't smoke but who drank occasionally. Alongside most of the names were tiny thumbnail photographs, though some of the aspiring husbands and lovers – presumably the really ugly ones – had chosen not to include a picture.

For no good reason, I picked someone who'd called himself 'bedbug', and scoured the advert to see what he had to say about himself. He was fifty-nine and claimed to be five foot eleven, lived in Newcastle and was divorced with two children. He described himself as a people-person who loved nothing better than to be out socialising with friends. He obviously had a sense of humour, because partner-wise he claimed that anyone with a pulse would do. However his open-mindedness was short-lived, as he went on to say that preferably she would be slim, attractive, not have let herself go, and aged between eighteen and twenty-five.

I almost choked on my coffee, and clicked on the thumbnail photograph alongside his sales pitch to enlarge it. He didn't look a day under seventy. Dirty old man. I copied the details, along with his photograph, into a separate document to print out and show to Alison the following evening. It would raise a smile, if nothing else.

I clicked back to the original list and selected another entry. This one's sales pitch was so short it was almost abrupt. 'Easy-going,' it stated. 'GSOH. WLTM lady 25-35 for frndshp, poss. marriage.' I checked out the photograph. He looked as though he'd sat on something sharp, and what hair he had was grown long and combed carefully over a bald pate. Beauty, it seemed, would be in the eye of the beholdee.

'Fran?' Max had appeared in the doorway. I almost leapt from my seat, and tried to block the PC screen with my body. 'Sorry, love: didn't mean to startle you. I just wondered whether you wanted a glass of wine in there while you're finishing off.'

'Er – no, thanks. I'll be done in a couple of minutes.'

'Christ: he's an ugly-looking bugger, isn't he?' he said, craning past my shoulder to look at the picture on the screen. 'So this is what women's internet porn looks like.'

I pushed him out of the way. 'It's not porn. It's – we're recruiting. I'm just checking through some CVs.'

'Oh, well, in that case, he should fit in just fine. If that bunch you work with are anything to go by, most blokes who go into IT are pretty nerdy-looking.'

'Well, we can't all be drop-dead gorgeous,' I said, standing up to usher him out of the room. 'Now, go!' I waved him away. 'The sooner you let me get on, the sooner I can be finished.' I sniffed the air. 'Can I smell burning?'

He shot off back to the kitchen and I returned guiltily to my sleuthing, clicking on another dozen or so candidates and adding a selection of the funny, the witty and the just plain awful entries to the document I'd created earlier for Alison's entertainment. Then, just as I was about to pack up and join Max in the kitchen, one of the thumbnail photographs caught my eye, and something about it drew me to a closer scrutiny.

'Footloose,' the header informed me. *'Member since September 2006.'*

Well, here goes, I read, *how to describe myself? I'm thirty-eight, six foot one, and divorced. No children, but would love some one day in the not-too-distant. I'm not too hideous-looking, or at least that's what my best mate said when I told him I was signing up. Dating lingo is not my forte: I thought GSOH was a men's magazine. Current love of my life is blonde and leggy; the only drawback is she has four of the aforementioned legs and her conversation isn't all that hot. Likes: country walks on windy afternoons. Dislikes: spiders. In fact, terrified of them. Hoping to meet an intelligent, sassy, outgoing lady who appreciates my admittedly weird sense of humour, for a see-how-it-goes relationship. Arachnophobes need not apply. (No point in having two people cowering behind the sofa.)*

The photograph wasn't the greatest quality in the world: it was slightly lopsided and looked as though it had been cropped from a bigger picture. All the same, you could still tell that this one was no dud. He had thick, dark hair and brown-black eyes. Chiselled features. Neat teeth. A crinkly smiley face that said reliable, trustworthy.

The same crinkly smiley face that had just finished pretending to be a gorilla, a witch, a ghost, a dragon and a giant, and that even now was rustling up something tasty in the kitchen to go with my steak.

Chapter 3

'Steak all right?'

I nodded without lifting my eyes from my plate. 'Mm-hmn. Delicious.'

That was a lie. It tasted like ash.

We ate in silence for a moment.

'How's your wine?'

I looked at him this time. I looked hard into his reliable, trustworthy face.

'It's lovely.'

Another lie. Every mouthful was vinegar.

I drank it anyway. My stomach felt as though someone were wringing it out.

'A funny thing happened at the workshop today.' He smiled, reminiscing. 'Guy had just—'

I pushed my chair back so sharply it fell over. 'Excuse me,' I said, and I bolted for the door. I just made it to the downstairs loo before throwing up in the toilet.

When there was no possible chance that a scrap of food or alcohol remained in my stomach, I stood up and flushed. Then I lowered the lid of the toilet and sat down, resting my forehead against the coolness of the sink for a moment before rinsing out a corner of the hand towel and using it to wipe my face. Once I'd composed myself a little I stood up shakily and peered at my reflection in the mirror above the sink.

Astonishingly, I looked pretty normal. No worse than after a bad day at the office, anyway. My eyes were a bit watery, but apart from that you couldn't tell by looking that my world had just fallen apart.

Max was waiting outside in the hall when I emerged. 'Hey,' he said, in that way he had. 'You okay?'

I nodded. 'Sorry about that.' Lies, lies, damned lies.

'My fault. I should have stuck to fish fingers.'

He led me gently through to the lounge and fussed around me for a moment, settling me into the sofa and placing a rug over my knees.

'For God's sake, Max! I'm not an invalid,' I protested.

He smiled at me enigmatically. 'I know. I'm just – you know. Glass of water?'

I hesitated, loath to accept, as though acceptance might form some kind of complicity. 'Yes, all right. Thanks.'

I watched as he disappeared through to the kitchen, my mind reeling. This was ridiculous. There had to be some mistake. It couldn't have been Max on that picture. Not my Max. He couldn't be playing around. He wasn't capable of the duplicity. When he came back in, I would just tell him outright what I'd found. *You're not going to believe this,* I would say, thus communicating to him the knowledge that I didn't believe it either, that I would never entertain the idea of his infidelity. And then I would show him the photograph, and I would realise that the similarity, whilst indubitably there, was saved by the slant of the eyebrows or a too-weak chin. The two of us would have a good laugh about it. I laughed silently now, rehearsing, chastising my over-active imagination.

But then, supposing he asked if that was what had

brought on the sudden reaction to his cooking? What if he didn't laugh it off, but took offence instead?

Stuff and nonsense. Of course he would laugh.

Unless—

I struggled hard, but the treacherous thought took form anyway.

Unless it really was him.

Before I could reach any firm course of action, Max was back with the water, which he handed to me before sitting down in the armchair opposite. His face wore an expression of suppressed excitement that I found hard to reconcile with my own inner turmoil.

'What?' I asked him, irritated.

'Hmn?'

'What on earth are you looking so smug for?'

'Oh – nothing. Sorry. I was just – nothing,' he trailed off lamely.

I put the glass down on the coffee table. 'Look – I'd better get on. I have a pile of paperwork to look through this evening.'

Max was on his feet in a flash, holding out a hand to help me up. I stared at him in astonishment.

'Max, what's got into you tonight? I'm perfectly capable of pulling myself up out of the sofa.'

'I know: it's just … well, you want to be taking things easy, that's all.'

'Why? I just threw up, Max. I haven't caught the cancer from Alison.'

I stopped, shocked at what I'd just said. Even Max looked crestfallen.

'Oh, God—'

'Hey, it's all right.' Max put an arm around my shoulder. 'You're just not yourself tonight, that's all. You didn't mean anything by it.' He gave my shoulder a gentle shake. 'You were like this last time, remember?'

I stared at him, baffled.

'Last time?'

'With Lottie. Don't you remember? You kept coming out with the most outlandish stuff, and blaming your hormones—'

'With – hormones? Oh my God.' I gaped at him. 'You think I'm pregnant.' In spite of myself, I started to laugh. 'That's funny, Max. That's really, really funny.'

'Well, you might be!' He looked at me, mock-pleading, mock-hopeful. 'The only other time in our eight-year-long marriage that I've ever known you to throw up was when you were expecting Lottie.'

'Listen, Max.' I turned to him and squeezed his arm hard. 'I am tired, overworked, and stressed. My best friend is dying. I am not pregnant. And if I were, you would be the last man on the planet I would be pregnant by. My body would automatically reject your low-life, snake-in-the-grass sperm. Now if you'll excuse me, I am going to finish this work.'

Max remained in the lounge watching me leave, still wearing that stupid grin on his face.

'Completely outlandish,' I heard him say happily to himself as I reached the door to the study. 'Just like last time.'

Chapter 4

I knew a brief, blissful moment of wellbeing born of sleep-induced amnesia as I surfaced in the morning, and then memory kicked in like a punch to the solar plexus, leaving me winded and gasping. Knowing yourself loved is the headiest kind of drug; fearing yourself cuckolded the worst trip imaginable. Cherished, you soar on the wind of a whispered promise. Deceived, the insidious poison of treachery seeps into your blood from a dank, festering darkness like some malicious pixie lurking in the corner of your consciousness, waiting for the venom to kick in so that it can gorge itself on your despair.

How we'd survived the rest of the evening in the same house together after I'd barricaded myself back in the study was anybody's guess. Away from the overpowering reek of his faithlessness, I had leant against the edge of the desk and drawn deep, gasping breaths, fighting to stop myself drowning in the quagmire of his betrayal. I'd sat before the blank computer screen in a time-frozen daze, not yet ready to turn it back on and confront the awful reality of his duplicity. When he'd interrupted my reverie, knocking on the door on his way up to bed some time after eleven, I had shouted through that I'd be right behind him. I waited for the muted going-to-bed noises to settle into silence. Then I pushed the chair abruptly away from the desk and reached behind me for a large storage box that sat on the bookshelf opposite the window, upending its contents onto the floor at my feet.

A cascade of memories tumbled to the carpet: baby photographs mixed up with pictures of Max and me on our wedding day; holiday snaps from a trip to Prague jumbled together with shots of Lottie and Erin on their first day at nursery, hand in hand and looking apprehensive but determined. I'd been saying for years that I would put them all into albums, but somehow there had never been time. Besides, part of me had liked the jumbled record of our time together: it had always seemed to reflect the happy chaos that had up until now characterised our lives. I found a heartbreaking picture of Max holding his new daughter close to his face and preparing to kiss her wrinkled brow. I hesitated over that one, feeling the numbing anaesthesia of disbelief nudging at the edges of my pain. It couldn't – *couldn't* – have been Max on that site. I'd made a mistake. He wouldn't have a clue how to scan a photograph, for starters. I almost laughed at myself. Almost.

And then I spotted it, peeking out almost coyly from behind another picture of Lottie and Max building a shaky-looking sandcastle together on the beach at Brighton.

As I'd thought, it had been cropped from a bigger photo. In the original, Max and Adam were leaning against the fireplace in our living-room. A litter of Christmas presents the girls had just finished unwrapping were strewn on the carpet at their feet. They both had their hands in their pockets and were grinning at the camera together, two buddies without a care in their faithful, happily-married, cancer-free world. I scoured their faces for some hint of the dark days loitering around the corner, but found none. On the back of the photograph, written in Alison's familiar, round hand: *Christmas 2006. Wouldn't you like one of these in your stocking???*

I felt unanchored, as though the rock that I'd believed was my marriage were nothing more than an illusion: one of those pictures that came free in packets of cereal and switched between two different scenes. Happy, secure family man. Cuckolding, two-timing shit. I flicked the two images back and forth in my head until I started to feel sick.

Eventually I eased myself stiffly to my knees and shuffled the photos back into the box, keeping hold of the one of Max and Adam. Then I shoved the box back onto the shelf and sat down again in front of the computer.

I found him faster this time round: I knew what I was looking for. Holding the photograph from the box up to the screen, I willed myself to find on closer inspection that it wasn't Max at all, but some footloose doppelgänger who truly didn't have any kids and who did have a dog and who was scared of spiders and, most of all, who was allowed to be out on the hunt to find the woman of his dreams. If wishing could have made things different, the man on the screen would have grown a moustache and lost half his hair since I'd spotted him earlier in the evening.

It couldn't. There he was: the man with the crinkly smile and the not-too-hideous face who claimed not to know what GSOH stood for. The man who loved kids and animals and was divorced. The man who was looking for a woman who would appreciate his weird sense of humour.

Well, it was obvious I would never fit the bill. This might be his idea of a joke, but I couldn't even raise a smile. I stood up abruptly and just reached the downstairs toilet before throwing up for the second time that evening.

I couldn't face joining him upstairs, going through the ritual of undressing and washing, performing the usual bedtime intimacies like rinsing out my tights or flossing my teeth in the en-suite knowing that he was lying a heartbeat away between fraudulent sheets waiting for me to join him. Instead I raided the bathroom cabinet for a spare toothbrush and took myself off to the spare bedroom, where I lay on top of the duvet staring at the ceiling, dry-eyed and panicking, and wondered what I was going to do.

I must have fallen asleep, eventually. I must, at some point, have crawled under the duvet, because all of a sudden it was morning and I was waking up and stretching extravagantly, and wondering what I was doing tucked up in the spare room wearing yesterday's clothes and why the house was so quiet. The double blow of realising that I'd overslept and that my husband was cheating on me struck almost simultaneously as I was throwing the duvet back, and I sat back down heavily onto the mattress, my heart racing.

I was at a loss to know what to do with myself. The simplest actions, such as showering and changing out of yesterday's work clothes, seemed like an insurmountable problem requiring an inordinate amount of energy and co-ordination that I simply didn't have. *Get up,* I chided myself. *Get a grip.* Instead I remained sitting on the bed, staring at the wall beside the door, trying to remember who I was.

After a while I gathered myself sufficiently to make it downstairs to the kitchen. Coffee would help, I told myself: the very ritual of brewing a pot would give me something to think about other than the prospect of Max in another woman's arms. The picture that this last thought conjured up caused the bile to rise up in my throat again, and I struggled to stop myself throwing up for the third time in less than twenty-four hours.

There was a note from Max propped up against the kettle. My hand trembled slightly as I reached for it. 'Morning, sleepy,' he'd written. 'Sorry to have abandoned you.' I paused over that particular phrase, reading more into it than I suspected he had intended. 'Don't be cross, but you were out cold this morning, and after last night I thought it was best to let you sleep in. I called your work and told them you're sick. I've got some stuff to drop in at the bank around eleven, so I'll pop home then to see how you're doing. Love you.'

He'd signed it with two smiling stick figures, holding hands, one tall and one small. The small one had a speech bubble coming from her mouth saying, 'Get well soon'.

I regarded the figures for a few moments, noting their clasped hands and their wide grins, and had a sudden picture of the two of them together at some point in the future, after Max had come to take Lottie away to spend the weekend with him and his new girlfriend. New wife, even. New wife and new baby. The images flooded in, uninvited, accompanied by an attack of vertigo so sharp I had to grasp hold of the edge of the kitchen table to stop myself from falling. Abruptly, I crushed the paper in my hand and dropped it into the bin.

Eleven, he'd said he would be home. I checked the clock: it was already after half-past ten. The thought of confronting him brought on a fresh attack of nausea.

I abandoned my plans for coffee; grabbing my jacket from the end of the banister, I fled the nightmare that my home had become to seek refuge in the sanctuary of the office.

It was a couple of minutes after eleven by the time I arrived. Maeve, the over-conscientious young girl I'd taken on a month ago to replace my previous secretary, Sean, an erratic, left-wing organisational nightmare who had serendipitously departed for fresh pastures, leapt to her feet as I was crossing the floor to my office. 'Mrs Howie!' She came hurrying after me. 'I thought – your husband telephoned and said you were sick.'

I paused at the door to my office. 'It's Fran, Maeve, and I'm fine. I was a bit queasy in the night, but I'm fine now.' I forced a smile.

I could feel her eyes appraising me, no doubt taking in the crumpled skirt and red-rimmed eyes. 'I'm fine, really,' I reiterated. 'Have they gone through yet?'

'They' were the rest of the department heads, who held an Exec meeting every Friday morning in the boardroom with Derek, head of Research and Development, to plan the following week's activities and allocate resources. 'They' were another reason for coming in, aside from the obvious one of avoiding Max: miss a Friday Exec and you were likely to find that Derek had put new milestones in place that meant you had to completely reschedule your team's activities for the following month.

'Just. If you're quick they'll barely have started.'

I grabbed a notepad and pen from my desk, shrugging myself out of my jacket at the same time, and Maeve's eyes widened. Yesterday's shirt had coped with being slept in even less well than the skirt. 'It's chilly in the boardroom,' she said tactfully. 'You might want to keep your jacket on.' She took hold of one of the shoulders and helped put the wrinkled shirt back under wraps. Mustering as much self-possession as I could, I nodded my thanks to her and hurried along the corridor to the boardroom.

Derek was already in position at the head of the table, gesticulating excitedly at a PowerPoint diagram he'd put together. '... massive corporate re-engineering project,' he was saying as I came through the door. '... ah! Good morning, Francesca.'

I nodded at him, keeping my eyes lowered. 'Morning. Sorry I'm late.' To my left, I felt rather than saw Greg pull out the chair next to his and I sank into it gratefully. 'You okay?' he murmured as I sat down, and I nodded without looking at him. 'New development environment,' he muttered as Derek took up his rhetoric once again. 'Hold the presses, ditch the old monolith ... I hope your trainers are up for a spot of training themselves.'

I frowned at him and tried to concentrate on what Derek was saying – or at least to give the appearance of concentrating. He pointed at various parts of the diagram. 'Key factors: asset management will be crucial.'

Asset management. I wondered irrelevantly how Max and I would divide our assets. *Stop it*, I told myself sternly, and I tried to refocus on what Derek was saying, but my mind couldn't let go of the image of some other woman in Max's arms.

'... Moving from a waterfall to an iterative development environment ...'

I wrote that down. *Iterative development environment.* The words blurred before my eyes. Then I laid my pen down on top of my notepad and wondered whether Max would say 'Hey' to her the way he said it to me. I chewed the inside of my mouth anxiously.

'... modular, reusable componentware that can be tailored to match every customer's specific configuration ...'

What would I say to Lottie? That was the worst of it. I couldn't begin to imagine what it would do to her if I had to tell her that her daddy and I were breaking up. I picked up the pen again and carefully wrote the words *modular, reusable componentware*, crossing the 't' with slow precision and trying to quell the queasiness in my stomach.

'... baseline an executable architecture early on ...'

My stomach tightened and I felt a sick wave of nausea wash over me.

'... your views. Francesca, let's start with you, seeing as this initiative is going to have the biggest impact on you.' Derek smiled at me encouragingly.

I looked at him uncomprehendingly.

'Francesca? Are you unwell?'

Bizarrely, my face felt wet. I reached up a hand and discovered, numbly, that tears were streaming down my face.

Alongside me Greg cleared his throat.

'Maybe we should take a quick comfort break, Derek,' he said smoothly. 'Grab a coffee, assemble our thoughts. Before we get down to the nitty-gritty.'

'Eh? Oh – absolutely. Good idea,' Derek agreed, shooting me a look of mild alarm. Around the table the other heads of departments began shuffling papers and pushing back chairs. Somewhere in the recesses of my mind I saw Brian McKinnon, head of deployment, raise his eyebrows at Alan Patterson, our system test manager, who gave a barely discernible shrug before disappearing through the boardroom door.

'Fran?' Greg had appeared at my elbow.

I looked at him blankly.

'Coffee?' He was looking down at me anxiously.

I didn't reply. My mind felt devoid of the capacity for speech.

He pulled out the chair alongside mine and sat down. 'Hey,' he said, reaching out and covering one of my hands with his own. And that was enough. Just the word, and the kind tone.

I broke down completely then and sobbed like a child.

Chapter 5

In the cut-and-thrust world of the corporate boardroom, there is a general unspoken understanding that, when it comes to conduct, anything goes. During my time with Xenith, I'd seen grown men fight over the last bacon roll at a breakfast meeting in a display of bad manners more appropriate to a school canteen than to the muted beech panelling of a multi-million-pound corporation. I'd watched the head of HR destroy the characters of previously valued employees during a downsizing exercise as justification for their selection. I'd witnessed clashes between warring department managers that had unleashed language so foul it would have made a docker blush.

I had never, in my seven years with the company, seen anybody cry. Not in the boardroom. I'd have drawn less attention to myself if I'd turned up for the review stark naked.

Outside the boardroom there was a hospitality area with easy chairs and low tables that sported an array of marketing collateral to entertain and entice prospective customers and business partners who might be visiting. Today, however, my colleagues had gathered there like a brood of hens whose feathers had been well and truly ruffled, and were conducting a hushed post-mortem on my professional meltdown.

'... probably female troubles,' Brian was suggesting as Greg opened the door and ushered me out. 'But then what can you expect when you put a woman into a position of responsibility? No backbone, you see. They can't handle the pressure.' There were murmurs of assent from one or two of the rest of the team.

'Oh, for God's sake, Brian.' Richard Sutherland, head of software development and a man with whom I'd had more than one heated discussion over resource allocation in the past, stepped into the fray. 'Don't be so bloody Neanderthal. There's only one bone you've got that Fran doesn't have, and in your case it's the one sticking out of the middle of your forehead.'

They fell silent as we passed, quelled by a look from Greg that I felt rather than saw, and I made a silent resolution that, the next time Richard came to me for resources, I'd move heaven and earth to accommodate him.

As we reached the sanctuary of my office, Greg wasted no time in coming to the point. He kicked the door shut behind us and looked at me searchingly. 'Was Brian right? Female troubles? Is that what all this is about, Fran?'

I sighed, rubbing my hands across my face before replying. I'd known Greg a long time. We'd joined the company on the same day and had gone through the same induction course together, imprisoned for a week in a bleak hotel in Maidenhead wrestling with the intricacies of Xenith's modus operandi and missing our respective partners. I'd been the person whose advice he had sought while his marriage was disintegrating around him. He'd cried at my desk in this same office more than once: hot, angry tears at his wife's casual departure; quiet, despairing tears when he realised she wasn't coming back. He'd kissed me once, too; an awkward, clumsy kiss at the end of a particularly desperate early-evening counselling session, and one for which he'd immediately apologised and for which I'd immediately forgiven him. Neither of us had ever referred to it afterwards, but the memory had left a residual bond between us – we were there for each other, and that was that. So he got to ask questions that, coming from anyone else, would have caused offence.

He reached across and pulled my hands from my face. 'Only,' he went on, frowning at me over our linked hands, 'it'd be the first time in the seven years I've known you that you've let something like that get the better of you. Not that there isn't a first time for everything,' he added, musingly.

I drew away from him to take a tissue from a box I kept on the window-ledge behind my desk, blowing noisily to buy myself a moment before answering. Greg pulled out the chair in front of my desk and swung himself into it, resting his forearms on the desk and leaning forward to resume his scrutiny of my tear-streaked face.

'You're overdoing things,' he decided, in an unconscious echo of Alison's words the previous evening. 'Apart from having the worst department in the organisation—'

'They're not,' I objected weakly, though he had a point.

'—the *worst* department,' he persisted as though I had not spoken, 'and a boss who has decided in his wisdom to implement a new development environment that will have massive implications for your team—'

'There's nothing new about this development environment.' I sniffed unattractively. 'You've been going on about it for months.'

'—six weeks before a go-live date with our largest client,' Greg swept on regardless, 'apart from any of that, you have a friend who's terminally ill, and a husband and kid to look after to boot.' He paused for a moment. 'I don't know how you do it: I'm surprised you haven't cracked weeks ago. I mean, look at you.' He did just that for a moment, and the frown on his forehead deepened. 'Actually, yes: look at you. Did you sleep in the office or something?'

I didn't answer.

'Come on, Fran. I'm worried about you. Is it your friend? Is she worse?'

'She's dying, Greg. How much worse can it get?'

He flinched, and I apologised. 'Sorry. Yes, she's still dying. No miracle cure yet. And no, that doesn't help matters.' I hesitated, looking into his eyes eventually, and seeing only kindness and concern. This was a man who knew about deception and lies – could have written a book about them – but still I faltered, loath to voice the inner fear that even now was twisting my stomach into a knot.

'Sorry, Greg: no can do. Not now.'

He pulled a face. 'Sure?'

I hesitated again. The drive to tell all, to pour it out, hand it over to another person, was almost overwhelming. But not now. Not yet. Not to Greg. I shook my head at him. Not while I still couldn't be sure.

'Okay, then. But you know where I am, right?'

I nodded. 'Absolutely.'

He pushed himself to his feet. 'Get you anything? Cup

of tea?' I shook my head. 'Gin and tonic? Soon be lunch time, you know. Sun's bound to be over the yardarm somewhere in the world.' I smiled at him weakly, and his face became serious again.

'Go home, Fran. You aren't well. Anybody can see that. Go home. Get some rest.'

'I will.' I glanced at the clock display on my computer. Eleven twenty. I thought of Max's note, his promise to come home to check up on me. 'After lunch, I promise. I just have some things to finish off here first.' I couldn't face him yet: the prospect of having to be under the same roof as him, breathing the same air as him, made me feel as though I were suffocating. I hadn't begun to work out how leaving things until dinner time would make that any easier.

Eventually, realising he was making no headway, Greg departed. As the door closed behind him I leant back in my chair and let out a deep sigh. I shouldn't have come in: Max had been right on that particular point. I wondered how long it would take me to rebuild my professional credibility with my male colleagues, who at the best of times were twitchy about women in senior positions, preferring them deferential and obedient to proactive and challenging. It was a fact that never failed to inspire outrage in me that during my own time with the company only two of us had made it to the lofty heights of senior management. We didn't have a glass ceiling so much as a reinforced concrete, wire-topped, bomb-proof barricade patrolled by armed guards with vicious, salivating hounds at their sides. I'd only made it through because I'd joined when the business was still in its infancy and there was nobody else with the right skills to take on the role. Latterly even having the right skills wasn't necessarily enough. My other female colleague had slept with the MD. Latterly that was no guarantee of advancement either. Alison used to describe me as an ambassador for the working woman, in the days before our conversation had become dominated by talk of scans and hair loss and, more recently, how best to protect what was dear to her when she was no longer around to protect it herself. Her support had been unfailing, and was all the more treasured because of the reactions of my own family to my work. Angela had been downright censorious, claiming that Lottie would grow up delinquent seeing so little of me – a comment that stung more than it should have because I harboured secret fears that she might be right. As for my mother, she had always been bemused by my decision to work when I had Max to take care of me. 'If your father had stuck around,' she had told me more than once, 'I certainly wouldn't have gone out working for a few extra pennies.' (Our father had walked out on us all when my mother was expecting me, the result of which was a general assumption on my part – reinforced by the occasional heavily laced comment from my mother as I was growing up – that it was somehow my fault, and an underlying and rarely acknowledged fear somewhere deep in my subconsciousness that one day Max would do the same thing to Lottie and me.) 'I don't understand you at all, Fran.'

And that, really, was the problem. She had never understood. Not my drive, at school, to do the best that I could. Nor my burning ambition, fiercely resisted but nevertheless pursued, to go on to university. My mother's attitude to educating girls was strictly nineteenth-century; she was far more comfortable with Angela's accomplishments in the domestic science class than with my carrying off the school maths prize. After Max and I had moved away it wasn't just the physical gap between us that widened. Even though, four years after our own move, both Angela and my mother had followed us south, we still communicated rarely, never easily, and always with more left unsaid than any of us ever felt up to voicing.

Which made it all the more strange that now, faced with my husband's likely infidelity, my best friend's inaccessibility and my own inability to sort out this sorry mess on my own, the one person I wanted to see was my mother.

Chapter 6

There was nothing to distinguish the small bungalow where my mother lived from its neighbours. Built of weathered reddish-brown brick, with too-new windows that sparkled incongruously like false teeth in an old woman's face, there was no particular feature in the architecture that caused it to stand out or incite alarm. If my heart were pounding a little as I drew up opposite, it was surely because of the strain of the past eighteen-or-so hours, when I had learned of Max's infidelity. I pulled the keys out of the ignition and stepped half-reluctantly from the car, locking it automatically behind me. It was odd being out and about in the middle of a working day. I felt as though I were skipping school.

The lay-by in which I'd parked gave onto a row of shops: some kind of hardware store where wooden bird tables jostled for priority over wicker baskets and sacks of pet food stacked on the pavement; a fish-and-chip shop that was doing a brisk lunch-time trade with some children from the local school; a small newsagent's with racks of newspapers hanging desultorily outside the door; an even smaller florist's, the buckets of flowers a chorus of colour against the grey of the afternoon. I hesitated for a moment, playing for time, then picked my way through the gaggle of children to the florist's, where I selected a bunch of red tulips from one of the buckets and stepped into the cool interior of the shop to pay for them.

'Nice enough day,' the assistant offered, rooting for change.

'Mmn,' I grunted noncommittally. The only nice thing about it was that it hadn't actually started raining yet, though the sky looked menacing.

'Local, are you?'

'No: I'm – just passing through.' On the counter, a display of gift cards offered manufactured messages to accompany the bouquets: 'Fondest Regards on your Birthday,' one of them suggested. 'Sorry for your loss,' consoled another. I blinked suddenly and smiled my thanks at the assistant as he dropped my change and a receipt into my hand.

Out on the tired street the schoolchildren had scattered like litter, picking their way haphazardly towards a dismal-looking building across a shoe-churned playing field. I drew a deep breath. Just passing through. Maybe that was what I should do – just pass through and head back to the office. Maeve could have the flowers: a little congratulations-on-your-first-month gift.

I shook my head. I'd come here for a reason, and if I didn't stick to it now, I never would.

There was a steady flow of traffic on the busy street, giving me the excuse to loiter for a moment under the meagre shelter of a crestfallen sycamore, trying to regulate my breathing and struggling to resist the urge to turn tail and retreat to the security of my car. And then, just as the traffic eased enough to allow me to step out to cross the road, the door of the bungalow opened with panic-inducing unexpectedness and my mother appeared on the threshold.

I shrank back behind what scant security the sycamore offered, clutching the tulips to my thumping heart, and watched as she came down the path. She looked younger than when I'd last seen her (on Lottie's birthday, ten months ago, I realised with a lurch); on that occasion she'd seemed strained and edgy. Her hair, which she had always worn in a rather severe perm, was looser today and topped by a jaunty red beret that framed her face and gave her expression a freshness I hadn't seen there before. The bias-cut, knee-length red coat she was wearing wasn't one I recognised: together with the hat it was a splash of colour in the greyness of the afternoon and, coupled with the spring in her step, it gave her the appearance of a chirpy robin. She looked – I struggled for a moment to find the right word. Nice. The kind of woman you'd want for a friend. I became suddenly and horribly aware of my own dark grey slept-in suit, and felt unapproachable and unfriendly by contrast. I withdrew a little further behind the sad little tree and watched her fumble with the latch on the gate.

The sudden tooting of a car horn caused us both to look around; a yellow Beetle was making its way down the road towards us, a hand signalling out of the driver's window. My mother stepped to the edge of the kerb and raised her own arm in a cheerful wave. The car pulled up in front of my mother, and she checked the road before stepping out to cross around the front of the car to the passenger door. For a moment I could have sworn that our eyes locked.

Then she pulled open the car door and ducked inside. The driver leant across to kiss her as she settled herself, and as they pulled away I could make out my sister behind the wheel, gesturing with her left hand as she changed gears and chattering animatedly. I stood for a few moments, watching the car disappear into the afternoon traffic, wondering why my heart continued to thump and struggling to overcome a feeling of something I couldn't quite pinpoint in the pit of my stomach.

'You okay?' A voice behind me caused me to jump. The assistant from the flower shop had appeared on the pavement and was regarding me quizzically. I realised with a flash of mortification that I'd been standing under the sycamore for a good five minutes, in full view of the shop door. 'You've been stood there for ages. You look like you're stalking someone.' He grinned to show there was no offence in his words.

I flushed, embarrassed. 'I'm just—' I gestured vaguely at the menacing sky. 'Looks like it's going to pour.'

'On foot, are you? I've an umbrella in the back you can borrow.'

My embarrassment deepened. 'No: that's okay, thanks. I've—' I inclined my head towards where my car sat not five yards away. 'I'm in the car.'

'Right.' He held out an ironic hand to the leaden sky, which was hanging on with obdurate resolution to any rain it had stashed away, and then turned back to me and shrugged, thrusting his hands into his pockets, a wry look on his face. 'I hope you make it back to your car before you get soaked.'

'Yes – thank you. Well: bye,' I muttered, resolving never to go near his shop again. He inclined his head towards me and I fled to the sanctuary of my car.

Once inside, I gripped the steering wheel tightly and tried to control the turmoil of emotions coursing through my body. Of course I'd been embarrassed. I'd stood, as the florist had helpfully pointed out, stalking my own mother for a full five minutes and then watched her drive off oblivious into the lowering afternoon without so much as raising a finger. Some part of me felt irrationally annoyed as well: annoyed that she'd looked so unlike I'd expected her to look; annoyed that Angela had turned up when I'd been about to – what? To take a first tentative step in covering the distance back to her. It was typical that Angela would show up and drag her off like that. They were probably going off for lunch somewhere, a cosy coven for two. I felt another lurch of that feeling in my stomach, the one I hadn't been able to figure out, and realised with dismay that it was jealousy.

If I'd been annoyed before, I was wild with myself now. The fact that they could incite such strength of feeling in me, after so many years, pushed me close to incandescence. Hadn't I always known what the two of them were like? Wasn't that the very reason I'd kicked the dust from my heels when I'd moved away? And now here I was, a grown woman with a child of her own, jealous of her horrible sister and her manipulative mother. Jealous of the easy, cheerful way they'd greeted one another – no furtive flower-buying and lingering under nasty little sycamore trees for them. Jealous – yes, and angry, too, at the way they'd so comprehensively cut me out of their lives that they could go out for cosy lunches together without a second thought for any hell I might be going through. Of course I knew I was being ridiculous, but somewhere deep inside me the little girl with the plaits and the straight-As report card was stamping her foot and shouting that it wasn't fair.

I blinked back angry tears and turned on the ignition. Outside the shop, the florist lifted a lazy hand as I pulled away, filled with self-loathing. I resisted the urge to turn the steering wheel and mow him down where he stood, but I glowered at him all the same and added him to the list of people I suddenly hated. I hated Greg for his well-meaning sympathy. I hated Max for throwing away everything we'd spent the past twelve years building together. I hated my mother for her stupid red coat and her jaunty hat. I hated Angela for her cocky wave and her ridiculous car. I hated Brian McKinnon and the rest of the smug, misogynistic bastards I had to put up with at work. I hated the suit I was wearing and the stupid shoes that cut into the sides of my feet. I hated Alison for being anchored by a tangle of tubes to a hospital bed when I needed her fit and well and able to help me make some sort of sense of my life, and I hated all the doctors in the hospital for not being able to cure her. Most of all, though, I hated myself. I was a disgusting, vile creature who was jealous of her own family and didn't have a kind thought for any other human soul, not even her best friend, who was dying of cancer.

I could hardly blame Max for being on the look-out for someone new.

Chapter 7

'What d'you want, Angela?'

'Oh – that's charming, that is. Not *how are you, Angela?* Not *how nice to hear from you, Angela.* Just *what do you want, Angela?* I didn't have to phone, you know.'

I pinched the bridge of my nose between my thumb and forefinger to try to stem the headache that had been threatening since I'd returned to the office an hour or so earlier. I had driven back in an ecstasy of shame, abandoning the tulips on the top of my in-tray the way my mother had been wont to discard my school reports on the kitchen worktop. They lay there glowing apologetically, as though accepting that the whole lunch-time fiasco was their fault. 'How are you, Angela?' I managed eventually through gritted teeth, wishing to God she'd never telephoned. 'How nice to hear from you.'

'Well, you might say it as if you mean it. As it happens, I'm fine. And you?'

'Fine. I'm – fine.'

'Well, isn't that nice? We're both fine. And how are Max and Lottie?'

At the mention of Max's name my stomach gave a by-now-familiar lurch. I'd been resolutely trying not to think about him all afternoon. Given my boardroom breakdown this morning and my aborted lunch-time peace mission, there had been plenty of other things for me to feel miserable about.

'They're fine as well – Angela, was there something you wanted?'

There was a silence from the other end of the phone, and for a moment I wondered whether we'd been cut off. 'Hello?' I tried experimentally. The line crackled in anticipation, and then she gave a small, impatient sigh.

'I'm still here. I just—' She dried up again.

'Angela, is something the matter?'

'She doesn't know I've phoned you,' my sister blurted unexpectedly. 'She saw you standing there, you know, under that tree. It *was* you, wasn't it? I knew it would be, the moment she described that awful suit.'

A wave of humiliation washed over me. 'If you knew it was me, why did you drive straight past? Why didn't you stop? Wouldn't that have been the normal thing to do?'

She gave a sharp laugh. 'Don't talk to me about normal! You spend the best part of twelve years barely having anything to do with us except when you can't avoid it, and then you expect a red carpet the moment you decide to show up with a bunch of sodding flowers. Besides,' she added, her tone marginally more conciliatory, 'she didn't mention that she thought it was you until after I'd pulled out, and then I was stuck in a stream of traffic until the roundabout. "I think I just saw your sister," she said, out of the blue, "standing under one of the trees in front of the shops, holding some tulips." And then she laughed and said she was probably hallucinating. But we did come back then, actually – we went right round the roundabout and came back to the house to check. And you'd gone. We couldn't waste any more time looking for you, supposing that it *had* been you hanging around under the trees: we were already late. We had a table booked for twelve-thirty. To be honest, I couldn't believe you'd remembered.'

That threw me. 'Remembered what?'

'Her birthday. You don't, usually.'

I winced in the heavy silence that followed, and after a moment she sighed laboriously.

'Oh, of course you didn't remember. Silly, silly me.' Another laboured sigh. 'Well, I suppose that makes the point of this call a bit ridiculous, really.'

'I don't – forget, exactly. It's more that we don't bother. Either of us, I mean. It's mutual.'

'Well, I don't see why it has to be like that.' Angela's voice was dismissive. 'You've only got one mum, you know, and she won't be around for ever.'

Dear God: she always knew exactly what to say to sting an already prickling conscience. 'Well, luckily for Mum, she has two daughters, and you have virtues enough for both of us,' the little girl with the straight As spat into the phone. I couldn't believe how pathetic I was being. 'Anyway, you mentioned a point ...?'

To give her credit, she didn't put the phone down on me, though I'd have deserved it if she had. Instead she produced another heavy sigh. 'Forget it, Francesca. It's not worth it. I just thought it might have been nice – we're having Mum over for dinner this evening, and I was going to ask if you and Max wanted to come over as well. When she said she thought she'd seen you, I allowed myself to believe you'd decided to grow up and let bygones be bygones, and I actually felt sorry – can you believe that? – that we'd missed you earlier.'

For a moment I was dumbstruck. The idea of Angela deliberately orchestrating something so thoughtful was unexpected. The timing, however, made her suggestion an impossibility. Just thinking about the effort of the performance that would be required of me to keep up the appearance of all being well between Max and me given current circumstances made me want to lie down in a dark corner and pull a blanket over my head.

'Um—' I began tentatively.

'I knew it.' She cut me off before I could say any more. 'I said as much to Phillip. "No point asking Francesca," I told him, "she'll be far too busy." You always are.'

'Angela—'

'Spare me the excuses, Francesca. Far be it from me to drag you away from your perfect life with your perfect job and your perfect little family. You've never had much time for—'

'Max is having an affair,' I blurted. I don't know what possessed me. But given that of the other three people closest to me, one was terminally ill, one was the source of the problem and one was only six, it wasn't as if I had a whole heap of confidants to choose from. Besides, I needed to do something drastic just to shut her up.

I heard her gasp down the other end of the phone line. 'What?'

I didn't answer.

'Francesca? Did you say Max is having an affair?'

'Look.' I took a deep breath. 'I've – I can't talk just now. I've got a meeting to get to. I'll—'

'Francesca, don't you dare cut me off. Max, having an affair? I never heard anything so ridiculous in all my life. The man's a saint: Lord knows how he's put up with you all these years. How do you know? Do you have proof? Did you catch them together?'

That last comment turned my stomach. 'I've got to go,' I said. 'Sorry.' I hung up before she could protest again.

The hand that replaced the receiver was sweating. As soon as I'd cut the call I drew a deep breath. I'd been right in my earlier instinct about not articulating my suspicions to Greg. Now that I'd come out with that statement to Angela the whole affair – I winced as my mind framed the word – had become even more of a reality. I felt unanchored again.

My desk phone shrilled loudly. Angela again, probably, indignant at having been cut off. I ignored it. Maeve was obviously out at lunch, because it continued to ring until my voicemail cut in.

'Frannie, it's me.' My heart lurched when I heard Max's voice. 'I came home at the back of eleven like I said I would and there was no sign of you. I've been worried sick.' I could hear him struggling to keep his voice level. 'I tried your office earlier on a hunch, and I couldn't believe it when that new girl answered and said you were in a meeting. I thought you were going to stay at home and take it easy.'

There was a pause, then he continued, his voice more conciliatory. 'Anyway. I suppose you must have been feeling better and decided to go in. I just wish—'

He sighed. 'What I mean is, well, you should be resting, that's all. These last weeks have been tough for you. You're exhausted.' He paused again, as though waiting for me to reply. 'I just want to help, Frannie, that's all. Just let me help.' I could feel the fresh sting of tears threatening. 'I'll see you later, okay? I'll get something in for dinner. Not steak or fish fingers, okay? Okay, then. Bye.'

Then there was a click, and he was gone.

I spun my chair around and looked out of the window. With typical March capriciousness the skies had lifted and the day had turned unseasonably warm, the rain that had been threatening earlier having taken itself off unexpectedly to fall elsewhere. A handful of office workers had spilled out of adjacent buildings to enjoy a late lunch on the grassy banks of the shallow man-made lake around which the business park had sprouted, sitting incongruously amongst the daffodils in their dark suits and smart shoes. On the lake itself, a female duck was paddling imperiously amongst the reeds, her little family of eight strung out behind her. Every now and then one of the eight would strike out in the wrong direction but the mother duck would continue on her majestic swimabout regardless, and a short while later the adventurer would realise its mistake and come paddling furiously back into line. I wiped the back of my hand across my cheeks and envied the mother duck for her uncomplicated self-assurance.

I'd always loved this view. I'd resisted initially when Derek had suggested I have my own office, fearing it would isolate me from my team, but he had insisted I needed more privacy than an open-plan desk would grant me. So I compromised by propping my office door wide open for most of the day, and by holding meetings at the desks of individual team members whenever it was practical to do so. The view, though – that had been one of the real perks – it meant I could turn my back periodically on whatever hassles were brewing on the other side of my desk and soak up the sight of the changing seasons a few short yards the other side of the window. It calmed me. Usually.

I don't know how long I sat there staring out of the window, but I was brought out of my reverie by a soft knock on the door.

'I got you a Thai chicken wrap,' Maeve said, 'and a smoothie. I didn't think you'd have eaten.' She stepped up to the desk and laid her offerings before me.

'Thanks, Maeve. You shouldn't have.' I tried a wan smile, and handed over a fiver for the lunch.

Maeve continued to stand there, looking uncomfortable.

'Is there something else, Maeve?'

She nodded uneasily. 'You've got a visitor. I bumped into her in reception, having a bit of a set-to with Julian. She didn't want to wear a visitor's pass,' she clarified. Julian was one of the office security guards. I raised my eyebrows questioningly.

'I brought her upstairs and put her in one of the meeting rooms,' she went on. 'But I don't think she's very happy.'

'Does she have a name?' I enquired.

'Oh, yes: sorry. Mrs Devlin.'

'Ah.' I nodded. 'You'd better show her in.'

Maeve disappeared reluctantly and was back a moment

later, a medium-built thirty-something woman at her side. She was wearing a brown corduroy skirt and a wraparound cardigan, from the top pocket of which trembled a plastic visitor's badge, and she was bristling with suppressed indignation.

'Hello, Angela,' I said with a sigh.

Chapter 8

My sister looked older than when I'd last seen her. Her hair, which had always been a luxuriant chestnut, was streaked by the first mutinous strands of grey, and there were dark smudges under her eyes. But then I was no one to talk. I felt as though I'd aged about a hundred years in the last twenty-four hours. She was still bristling as she took the seat I proffered. She nodded at the food perfunctorily.

'Too grand to get your own lunch, now,' she said by way of a hello. 'I saw that chit of a girl bringing it in to you.'

'Far too grand,' I agreed. I hadn't the energy to argue.

'God, Francesca, you look awful.'

'Thanks.'

She cast her eye around my office and sniffed disparagingly. 'Like trying to get into Fort Knox, coming here,' she grumbled. 'Can't see why. It's not as if you work for MI5 or anything.'

'I know.' Looking at her sitting there, so out of place amongst the business suits that normally populated these offices, I felt a sudden unexpected surge of affection for her.

'Nice view, though.' She nodded over my shoulder. 'A bit concrete, I suppose, but it could be worse.

I followed her gaze out of the window. The mother duck

had given up her regal tour of the lake and was enjoying an afternoon snack, courtesy of some of the workers. Six of her little brood milled around her excitedly.

'Two of the ducklings have disappeared,' I said absently.

'Have they? Well, anyway, Fran, I didn't come here to talk about baby ducks, sweet though they undoubtedly are.' She'd dropped the *Francesca*, I noticed. I turned back to face her.

'I know I may only be your sister,' she began. I opened my mouth to object, but she held up a hand imperiously. 'And we haven't been exactly close. But that doesn't mean I don't care. Which is why I'm sitting here, having run the gauntlet of that gorilla in the foyer and that prissy little secretary of yours, and then having been incarcerated in that horrible little room while she came to check that you weren't too busy to squeeze me in.' She paused to make sure I was taking on board the hardship she'd had to endure to see me. 'I have to say, your admission on the phone just now gave me a bit of a shock. I confess I may have seemed a bit – startled, when you said Max was having an affair, but I only meant to help – I *do* only mean to help. Which is why I've come.'

I acknowledged her good intent with a nod. 'I know. It's just – well, you're the only person I've said anything to.'

'Am I?' She looked pleased.

'Mm-hmn. And – well, voicing it – actually saying the words—' I stopped.

'I know,' she said briskly. 'You almost feel as though you're making the unthinkable thinkable. It was exactly the same when I found out about Phillip.'

I gaped at her. '*Phillip* had an affair?' The room wheeled around me: nobody, it seemed, was immune from the treacherous coils of infidelity.

'Well, not an affair, exactly, no. A dalliance, shall we say. Eighteen months ago. Something and nothing.'

Eighteen months ago. I felt a stab of guilt: I'd known nothing about it. 'But – how did you find out?'

'Oh – the usual way.' There was a usual way? 'Text messages arriving at all hours of the day, and him going all surreptitious when I asked who they were from. The phone ringing, and nobody speaking when I picked up. And he started working later in the evenings. He'd never done that before. Coming home close on eleven, telling me he'd already eaten – grabbed a sandwich, he'd say. *I grabbed a sandwich at the petrol station*. Of course I didn't believe him for a minute. You don't, do you? Not once you start to suspect.'

I swallowed, thinking of the suspicions I was now harbouring towards Max, and hearing my own unattractive future in her words. 'What did you do?'

'I followed him.' My jaw dropped open. 'There was a pattern, you see. Wednesdays and Fridays. So I got one of the women from the babysitting circle in one Friday evening. I diverted the phone to my mobile, and I went and staked out his office.' In spite of myself I smiled at the terminology. *Staked out*. Coming from my sister, it sounded so clandestine.

She scowled at my expression. 'There was nothing funny about it, Francesca.' Suddenly we were back on formal name terms. I rearranged my features. 'Sorry.' I nodded at her. 'Go on.'

'I told you. It was something and nothing.'

'Tell me the something, then.'

She huffed and puffed for a moment, and finally decided to continue. 'Well. I got this babysitter in, like I said. It's not easy, getting someone in at that hour of the evening, let me tell you. The kids hadn't even had their tea. I had to give her double points.'

My face crumpled in confusion. 'Double points?'

'It's babysitting circle currency. I suppose you've never been in a babysitting circle, have you? No: thought not.' She gave a disparaging sniff. 'We earn points by looking after other people's kids, and spend them when someone looks after ours. Anyway, never mind that. I went and parked outside his office, alongside one of those Jeep things, to make it hard for him to see me if he happened to look in my direction. And then I just sat and waited. My mobile rang at six-thirty. He was going to be late, he said. They had a rush job on.' Phillip worked at a printing works in Camberley. 'I could see the bastard coming out of the front door of the office as he was speaking to me. He got into his car and headed off towards the retail park. Of course it was peak hour and the traffic was horrendous, but I stuck a couple of cars behind him all the way to Tesco. He pulled up outside the main entrance, and she was waiting for him there. She couldn't have been much more than twenty. She let herself into the car and leant over and kissed him. Not just a peck on the cheek, either.' Angela's expression was studiously deadpan. 'And then he whisked her off down the A30 and after about ten miles he pulled in at that fish restaurant near Egham. Loch Fyne – do you know it?'

'Max and I went there last year for our wedding anniversary.' I swallowed bile again and wondered, in the light of last night's discovery, how we would celebrate this year. Splitting up our CD collection, probably.

'Hmnph,' she snorted. 'I've been wanting to go there for ages, but Phillip kept saying we couldn't afford it.' You had to strain to catch the bitterness in her tone, but it was there. Eighteen months wasn't long enough, I supposed, to have healed the wounds. I wondered how long it would take.

'Did you go in after them?'

She shook her head. 'I wanted to be sure, you see.' I nodded. I could understand that particular sentiment. 'I sat in my car in a dark corner of the car park, under one of the trees, and I watched them. They were in there the best part of an hour and a half. He kept cutting up little bits of whatever was on his plate and feeding them to her. It was revolting. I'm surprised some of the other diners didn't object. In the end I got fed up and called him on his mobile, and asked him if he wanted me to stop by the office with a sandwich.' She grinned suddenly. 'You should have seen the expression on his face. Total panic. He said not to leave the kids: he'd get something at the services on the way home. "If you have room," I said to him, "after your fish." I hung up then and drove home.'

I gaped at her, dismayed that I hadn't been there for her, that she'd gone through all of this on her own. This was the girl that used to fight me for all the best bits of Lego. Just how big a gulf had we allowed to open up between us?

'He got in five minutes behind me.' She picked up her story once again. 'I hadn't even had time to see the baby-sitter out. He skulked in the kitchen until she'd gone, then he came through and said, "It's not what you think." I said, "What do I think, Phillip?" and he said he could see how it looked, that it didn't look good, and that it wasn't good; but that it was nothing more than a flirtation. Nothing had happened between them. They hadn't had sex, that was what he meant.'

The words hung in the air between us like ragged washing pegged out in smog, and my stomach gave another twist. 'Did you believe him?'

She shrugged. 'I don't know. It didn't seem to matter, one way or another. It was a question of trust, you see. I knew he'd been lying to me. And he'd taken her *there*, as well. We hardly ever went out, just the two of us, and he took her to the one place he knew I really fancied trying. I hated him for that. And I didn't trust him any more. Whether or not they'd had sex seemed almost irrelevant. Once the trust's gone, you never really get it back.'

'But—' I found myself searching for something to clutch at, some Athenian thread, however fragile, that I could follow out of this labyrinth of faithlessness into which I'd been so casually thrust. 'You're still together.' My heart had started to hammer in my chest. 'You – you seem happy enough.' I stumbled clumsily to a halt. Was she? I'd seen so little of her, I wasn't really in a position to make that kind of judgement, and somewhere inside my chest a shard of guilt pierced the soft flesh of my anguish. In any case, was happy enough good enough?

Angela paused before replying. 'Yes, we are.' She gave another shrug. 'You learn to live with it. You have to. Either that or you break up. And I didn't want that. There were still good sides to our marriage. We were happy, most of the time. I wasn't prepared to throw away the last eleven years of my life just because my husband had had his head turned by a flighty checkout operator.'

I looked at her in astonishment. 'A checkout operator?'

She nodded. 'I know: so mundane, isn't it? It might have been easier to get my head around if she'd been some drop-dead gorgeous glamour model with come-to-bed eyes. But no: she was a greasy-haired girl in a nylon overall who wore too much eye makeup and bit her nails. In Tesco. That's why he'd gone by there. He was picking her up. I went in the following week myself. Piled a trolley full of shopping. Ice cream. Stuff from the deli. Then I queued at her checkout. And as she was popping the things through the scanner, I emptied a bottle of bleach into her lap.' She smiled reminiscently. 'Of course, I apologised. Said the lid must have come loose. Though you know what these security tops are like. You can barely get them off when you're wanting to clean the toilet. I asked her if she needed a change of clothes, because there was just a chance she'd left her knickers in my husband's car the previous week, and I could run and check if she liked.'

I gave a gasp. 'You didn't!'

'Of course I did. Nothing to lose, you see. It's amazing how liberating that can be. I walked out after that, cool as a cucumber, and left all that ice cream just sitting there melting in the trolley.'

I felt like bursting into applause. I never knew there was so much fire in Angela. 'But what about you and Phillip?' I faltered again, looking for clues that might offer some hope for Max and me. 'How did you move on from it all?'

'We never spoke about it after that one night when I'd followed them to the restaurant. He tried to bring it up once or twice, but I would cut him short. I wasn't going to allow him the luxury of thinking I'd forgiven him just like that. I was very bitter. Quite a cow, actually, now I think about it.'

'But you got beyond it,' I insisted.

'We did. I'm not saying it was easy. Phillip started behaving like a model husband. Coming home punctually at six every evening. Helping the kids with their homework. Buying me little gifts – perfume and stuff.' She hesitated. 'Only behind it all, every now and then, I'd catch this look in his eye. This – despair. Like he was constantly wondering, *is this it?* And I realised that I hadn't been entirely blameless. I'd allowed myself to become frowsy and boring. Sitting at home all day every day, cleaning the bloody cooker. Some days I didn't even bother to get dressed. The less I did, the more exhausted I used to feel. I wasn't like you – some hotshot executive with a life.' She gave me a sour look, which I chose to ignore. 'No wonder he went out looking for a bit of excitement.'

I trod down on the myriad reasons I had given my own husband for straying – the late nights at the office; the irritability I'd been wearing like a shroud since Alison's admission to hospital; the fact that I hadn't had the energy or the inclination for anything approaching intimacy in weeks. 'You were probably a bit depressed, Ang. Looking after three kids all day while your husband worked late every evening.'

'Ah, well. Water under the bridge now. We picked up the pieces. Learned to live with the fact that maybe we didn't know each other quite as well as we'd always thought. I started making a bit more effort – with Phillip, of course, but mostly with myself. It wasn't that hard, actually. I mean, you can become quite skilled at living a lie. As time went on it got easier, and it felt less like I was trying and more like that was who I really was.'

I thought about what she was saying. Could I do that with Max? Pretend that everything was all right between us? Pin a smile on my face and keep telling myself that I was happy, really, even though it felt as though he were holding my heart in his hand and squeezing all the life out of it?

'Anyway.' Angela interrupted my musing. 'I didn't come here to talk about me. Seeing as you wouldn't talk on the phone, I figured I'd better come down in person. Out with it.' She tried a tentative smile to soften her next question. 'What's big bad Max been up to?'

I gave her a wan smile in return. *Big bad Max.* That was just the sort of thing Alison would say, and I found myself transferring some of the warmth I was more used to feeling around her onto my sister, wondering again how it was we'd become such strangers to one another.

'It's difficult to know where to start.'

'Oh, rubbish. People always say that. Just spit it out and stop making a meal of it.'

And so I told her. I began with Alison, explaining how she found out about the cancer, and how I didn't know what to do or say, but how I knew that nothing I did or said would make any difference anyway. I described the months of treatment, every new test offering a fresh, tantalising glimmer of hope before being snatched away. I told her how Alison had been taken into hospital weeks ago for intensive radiation therapy, and how even that had apparently failed and now we just seemed to be playing a waiting game. I threw the afternoon to the wind and talked for over an hour. Angela sat and listened in silence. I described Alison's mad scheme to her: explained how my best friend wanted to make sure that the two people she cared about most in the world weren't left alone for too long after she'd gone. I confided to her what Alison had asked me to do, and she tutted and said that nobody ought to try to control another person's life like that. I was going to object, to fight Alison's corner, and then I didn't, because I realised that, deep down, that was just how I felt myself. I told her how I'd gone home and checked out the dating sites and how, finally, I'd made my awful discovery. And finally I stopped, wrung out, and waited for her to tell me I was being a fool.

'Poor you. You've really been through the mill, haven't you?'

I gave her a wry look.

'I wish – well, you should have been able to call me. I know: we haven't had that much to do with each other, and I suppose it's a bit much suddenly dropping back into one another's lives heaped up with emotional needs and crying for help.'

We were both silent for a moment.

'Still, we *are* sisters.'

I acknowledged that with a nod. 'I know.'

'Probably why it's so bloody difficult. We never got beyond the being-in-competition-with-each-other phase.'

'Were we in competition with each other?'

'Oh, Frannie, of course we were! We fought over everything, not just our toys. Though I gave up in the end.' She looked at me ruefully. 'You were just too damn good for me.'

'I was?'

'Of course you were. Mummy's little darling. Such a smarty-pants at school. Off to university. She never stopped bragging about you.'

I stared at her. 'But – I always thought Mother didn't give a tuppenny toss for my studies. She was too busy admiring all those goodies you brought home from the Home Economics class.'

She smiled wistfully. 'I did my best, that's true. If ever a girl deserved a prize for effort, I was that girl. Mother just made a fuss of my paltry offerings to try and hide her disappointment in me. Why d'you suppose she insisted you come home from university for my wedding? She had to, you see. She had to go along with the charade that my life counted – that I was just as important as you were.' She gave a sigh. 'Ah, well. Ancient history now.'

'Is it?'

'Of course it is.'

'I missed my graduation ceremony, you know.'

'Oh, for God's sake, Francesca! Give it a rest. What the

hell does it matter whether you made it to your bloody graduation ceremony? Haven't you got more important things to worry about?'

I bit my lip. She was right, of course. I'd almost forgotten, in the midst of our discussion, what had prompted it in the first place.

'Doesn't look too good, does it?'

I shook my head. The afternoon had taken on an unreal quality, like the backdrop to someone else's life. I felt as though I'd been accused of some heinous act for which I was now being punished, and had to resist the urge to cry out that they'd got the wrong person.

'But he hasn't actually done anything – not as far as you know?'

I shook my head again.

'Well, then.'

'Well, then – what?'

She tutted again. 'Really, Francesca. Sometimes I despair, I really do.' She looked at me as though I were a simpleton. 'Right now you aren't sure about anything, are you? I mean, apart from the photograph, you've no real evidence to go on.'

'No, but – well, I think the fact that the photo's there at all is pretty damning.'

'Well, yes, it could be, of course. But there might be some entirely rational explanation.'

'Like what?'

'Oh – I don't know,' she said airily. 'Maybe somebody else put it there for a joke. Then she narrowed her eyes at me. It's definitely Max, you say? You're absolutely sure?'

'One hundred per cent.' I shook my head at her in despair. 'God knows, I wish I weren't.'

'Then why don't you just go to him and say, *Oh, by the way, darling, guess what I found on the internet?* Confront him with it. See what he has to say for himself.'

I looked at her miserably. 'I know that would be the sensible thing to do. It's just – I can't. I *can't*,' I repeated, as though she had argued the point with me. 'I don't know why not.'

'Oh, of course you can. All you need to do is—'

'Angela, I *can't*!'

'It never does any good in the long run—'

'I can't face it, all right?' I jumped up and began pacing around the office. 'I just can't do it.'

She was staring at me, astonished at the vehemence in my tone. 'Because ...' she prompted after a moment.

I could feel perspiration on my forehead. I drew a breath and licked my lips. 'Because – what if he leaves me? He's done it before, you know. He was with someone when he met me. What if he walks out on Lottie and me to be with someone else, like our dad did to you and Mum? What then? What does that make me? Some kind of walking man-repulsion unit?'

Her mouth fell open. 'Frannie, Dad's leaving wasn't your fault.'

I gave a snort. 'Oh, sure it wasn't. I can *remember* being blamed for it. Those comments Mum used to make—'

'What kind of comments?'

'I don't know—' I waved an arm around vaguely. 'Stuff like, "No wonder your father buggered off" and "You were the last straw, Francesca." I can remember her saying them.'

'Oh, my God.' Angela's face hadn't lost its look of utter astonishment. 'I can't believe you thought she was blaming you. I suppose that's why you're always so—' She stopped suddenly.

'Always so what?'

She made a dismissive gesture with her hand. 'You know. Distant. Uninvolved. I used to wonder what we'd all done wrong.' She sighed. 'She was just tired, Fran. Tired, and fed up, and poor, and struggling to bring up two small kids on her own after he left her. She didn't mean it was your fault. She was just letting off steam, saying stuff to vent her own anger and frustration.'

'It wasn't fair of her.' I could feel tears threatening: I felt like a five-year-old all over again. 'I blamed myself. I *still* blame myself.'

'Oh, for God's sake.' Angela's tone was becoming impatient. 'Show me the mother who hasn't occasionally yelled at her kids when they've done nothing wrong. Everybody fucks up, Fran. Even you.'

'I'm not saying I don't!' I hated how defensive I sounded. 'It's just – I feel as though, the moment I say anything to Max, that'll be it. My life, such as it is right now, will cease to be.'

'Oh, don't be so melodramatic.' It took a sister to be so dismissive. 'Your life, such as it is right now, has already ceased to be, because you suspect your husband is cheating on you. Never mind what screwed-up and, let me add, completely delusional preconceptions you're carrying around from your childhood. What you need is to take some decisive action. No good having you wallowing around in this festering pit of uncertainty.'

Festering pit. That just about summed it up.

She swept on. 'If you're determined not to confront him outright—' she looked at me for confirmation, and I shook my head '—then it seems to me that there's only one thing for it.'

'What?'

'Well, you must stake him out. Just like I did with Phillip. Then you'll know.' She looked hard at me. 'You do *want* to know, don't you?'

'Yes. No.' I hesitated. 'I'm not sure.'

'It's no good living in cloud cuckoo land. You've got to face facts.'

'But – how do I stake him out? It's not as if I can get in the car and follow him if he's having cybersex with some chit of a girl in Georgia.'

'Hmm. Well, that chit of a girl in Georgia could turn out to be a sixty-four-year-old pervert living in Bracknell. You hear all sorts about these chat rooms and whatnot. It's a nightmare for parents. I hope you don't allow Lottie to use the web unsupervised.'

I blinked at the sudden change in direction our conversation had taken. 'No, of course I don't – though she is only six, remember.'

'That's as maybe. They learn very young these days. Ralph is only nine, and last week Phillip caught him trying to download the words to one of the South Park songs. You can't be too careful. Anyway.' She gave herself a little shake. 'We're getting off the subject. It's quite obvious what you're going to have to do.'

'What?'

'I can't believe you haven't thought of it already. Answer the advert, of course.'

Chapter 9

By the time Angela and I had finished our heart-to-heart it was almost three. I walked her down to reception and past the gauntlet of security guards back to her car, which she'd left in one of the visitor spaces right beside the front door to the office. Before she climbed inside she hugged me fiercely for a moment.

'Phone me,' she instructed. 'Any time. I mean it. I want you to promise me you'll let me know how you get on. And remember—' She held me at arm's length for a moment, then shook her head at me. 'Daft cow.' Then she pulled me in for another hard hug. 'You're not on your own. You never were.' Before I could answer she pushed me away and unlocked her car.

As she swung out of the car park I watched her disappear around the corner with genuine regret. It was a nice feeling amidst all the other feelings I'd been having for the past twenty hours or so, and I nursed it to my chest like a fledgling bird that had fallen from its nest, determined to take from it what comfort I could.

Whatever fragile solace I had found in Angela's visit vanished as soon as I returned to my office, where another voicemail from Max was waiting for me, the message light on my desk phone flashing self-importantly as though gloating over the prospect of sharing bad news. His tone this time was brusque. 'Fran,' he said. 'Call me when you get this. Please,' he added as an afterthought. I deleted it without returning his call, and spent the next hour fighting down the panic that threatened to overwhelm me by working through the schedule of upcoming work for the department and trying to figure out how we could fit in some team training before the new development environment was implemented. Eventually, at four o'clock, I gave up and left, retrieving my coat and handbag from the back of my office and telling Maeve I was taking some flexitime and going home early.

'You shouldn't be taking it as flexitime,' Maeve chided, frowning disapprovingly at me over the top of her glasses. 'You should be claiming sick leave.' She looked at me meaningfully.

'I'm fine,' I assured her. 'I just have one or things to do, that's all.'

All the way home my head buzzed with the deception I was about to embark upon. Nothing in my mother's early instruction in the art of lying had prepared me for this: we were in a different league altogether.

I can still recall the moment when I discovered the world wasn't black and white. I was six at the time – Lottie's age – and up until then I had been convinced of my mother's infallibility in all matters, which probably accounted for my unquestioning acceptance of her frustration-laden comments about my role in her husband's desertion of the three of us. Tired, fed up and poor she may have been, but like most kids of six I never saw that. I craved her approval like an over-eager puppy.

She might be a bit free with her hands and shout and yell more than other kids' mums, but she was still my undisputed champion. There was nothing she didn't know, nothing she couldn't explain, no crisis she couldn't sort out one way or another. My mother, in short, was closely related to God.

Her undeification was as unexpected as it was unsettling.

She had nipped out one afternoon to catch up with a neighbour who'd been visiting and had left her glasses behind, and she'd left me in Angela's dubious care for ten glorious minutes (you could do that sort of thing in those days). And while she'd been out I'd made merry with the biscuit tin, cramming Jaffa Cakes into my greedy little mouth as though my very survival depended upon it. Her face puckered in disappointment when I strenuously denied being within fifty yards of the kitchen, in spite of the fact that my face was liberally smeared with evidence to the contrary and Angela was bouncing up and down and saying gleefully, 'I *told* you she would kill you.' 'You really are the last straw,' my mother had said with a sigh, adding in what I would come to recognise as a spectacular display of hypocrisy, 'It's wrong to lie, Francesca.' She was rummaging in the kitchen drawer for the leather belt she kept there. 'If you lie, the ground will open up and swallow you. Now, hold out your hand.'

Later that night, when I was sure I could still feel the twinges from the thrashing she'd given me (you could do that sort of thing in those days as well), the doorbell had rung while Angela was in the bath and she had frozen like a rabbit caught in the headlights of the proverbial oncoming truck. 'Oh God: it's the insurance man,' she had said, horrified, and she'd dived behind the sofa. 'Francesca, get over here. Don't let him see you. No: on second thoughts, go and tell him I'm out. Go on: put the door on the chain. Tell him you don't know when I'll be back.'

I'd hesitated, the thrashing still fresh in my mind. Maybe this was some kind of test. 'But – you said it's wrong to lie,' I finally said. There. That would be bound to please her. That would show her I wasn't slow on the uptake. I gave her a half-expectant smile.

A hand shot out from behind the sofa and she caught me squarely on the side of the head. 'Don't answer me back, you cheeky little madam,' she spat. 'Go on: do as you're told.'

And so I took myself off, rubbing my smarting head, and lied through my neat white milk teeth to the insurance man, and once he'd disappeared around the corner at the top of the road my mother emerged from behind the sofa and fetched me one of the few remaining Jaffa Cakes for being such a clever girl. Lying, she explained to me, was not really lying in some situations, such as when the insurance premium was due and you only had twenty-two pence left in your purse.

My instruction in the finer points of lying was further advanced when we were out shopping in the village some time afterwards, en route to collecting Angela from her dancing lesson. Since the Insurance Man episode I had started to scrutinise my mother closely for other inconsistencies. (Finding out that the one person you'd always believed infallible had feet of clay was proving something of an unsettling experience, and I was desperate for some sign to prove I was wrong and the incident with the insurance man nothing more than a momentary aberration.)

We'd been traipsing around the shops for what felt like an eternity, and had just emerged from the greengrocer's when we ran into Mrs Boucher who ran the Sunday school. 'Doreen!' the woman had exclaimed. 'Agnes!' my mother had in turn cried, dropping the shopping bags on the ground at her feet. They'd touched cheeks and made that kissing noise women make that means they're pleased to see you but they don't want to ruin their lipstick. 'How lovely to see you. How are you?'

They preened themselves and prattled on for fifteen minutes or so, each exclaiming and laughing at the other's wit, while the bag of potatoes I was carrying grew heavy in my arms. Eventually they took their leave of one another amidst another flurry of cheek-touching and kissing noises and fervent promises to see one another in the immediate future. Then my mother stood smiling and waving at the woman's retreating back as she disappeared into the dry cleaner's, before gathering up her shopping bags once again.

'God: I can't stand that woman,' she said as she turned to go, looking back and giving her a final wave and a smile. 'Sanctimonious cow. "Ooh, we must have a cup of tea some time,"' she mimicked. 'No, thank you very much; I'd rather eat my own head.' She set off at a fair lick down the street. 'Come *on,* Francesca. Stop gawping and get a move on. We'll be late for Angela.'

The following day, Sunday, Mrs Boucher came up to me as our class was drawing to a close and I was just putting the finishing touches to a picture I'd been colouring that showed Jesus on a donkey riding through a crowd of adoring people who were all waving leaves at him. The donkey hadn't turned out quite as I'd hoped: some rather over-enthusiastic work on my part with the black wax crayon had left him sporting what looked like a rather luxuriant moustache. But Mrs Boucher was nothing if not discreet, and she made the appropriate admiring noises that one knew to expect from Sunday school teachers, thus confirming to me that my mother was not the only liar in the world masquerading as a champion of the truth. 'So, Francesca,' she said once she had left off cooing over my bearded monstrosity, 'I am having a small group of ladies over for tea on Thursday afternoon, at about two o'clock. Do you think you could be a very clever girl and tell your mummy?'

I don't know if it's in the job description for Sunday school teachers to be patronising. It's certainly not in the job description for six-year-olds to be duplicitous. I gave her a wide-eyed look.

'My mum said she would rather eat her own head,' I lisped.

She froze, still clutching my nasty piece of artwork. 'I – I beg your pardon?'

'My mum said she would rather eat her own head,' I enunciated, as clearly as I could.

Mrs Boucher's mouth dropped open. It wasn't a particularly attractive sight. Then she pressed her lips together tightly and clenched both fists, which, frankly, didn't do very much to improve my poor picture. Finally, she dropped the paper back onto the table and stalked off towards the kitchen.

When my mother arrived to collect me a short while afterwards, she greeted Mrs Boucher with her customary insincerity, and was somewhat bemused, not to mention put out, when Mrs Boucher gave her a cold nod and a frosty, 'Doreen', before turning her back on her and busying herself folding up some damp tea towels. My mother backed off looking bewildered, and came to help me into my coat, crouching down in front of me to fasten the buttons with a puzzled frown on her face.

'What's got into *her* today?' she asked, talking to herself rather than to me. Then she suddenly shot me a sharp look, and jerked the lapels of my coat towards her, causing me to stumble forwards so that our faces were inches apart. 'Did you say something to her?'

We were eye-to-eye, and I could feel her gaze burning its way into my heart. I knew all about hearts. Jesus could see straight into them, and so could my mother. There was nothing you could hide in there that either one of them wouldn't be able to see straight through to.

My mum said she would rather eat her own head.

I'd never, until that moment, been considered anywhere near the brightest candle on the Christmas tree. But the Lord in his mercy took it upon himself to bestow upon me the gift of understanding, and in a moment of blinding clarity that must have rivalled Paul's Road to Damascus experience, I suddenly recognised the awful reality of what I had done, and I knew I was for it.

'You said something to her, didn't you, you little wretch?' My mother jerked the lapels of my coat again.

'I didn't!' The words sprang unbidden from some dark corner of my soul, and I waited for the ground to open up and swallow me. One or two people stopped and turned at the sound of my indignant denial.

'You didn't? Are you sure?' My mother smiled at the onlookers and unclenched her hands from the lapels of my coat, smoothing them back into place with a reassuring pat. Then she turned her eyes back onto me and continued in an undertone, her face still fixed in a smile. 'Because if you're lying to me, young lady – and I'll know if you are – so help me, I'll batter you so hard you won't be able to sit down for a week.' She cast another beatific smile at our unanticipated audience.

Is it lying to say one thing with your mouth and another with your eyes? My mind was a whirl of confusion. I remember being lulled by my mother's words and smile, while at the same time my stomach was twisting itself into a knot at the thought of what she was about to do to me. Some stubborn streak I'd obviously inherited from her made me stick to my guns.

'I'm not lying!' I lied. 'She's been in a grumpy mood all day. She even shouted at Joy before.' Joy Sneddon, darling of the Sunday school, was the vicar's daughter.

'She did?' That threw my mother. 'What for?'

Oh, God. This lying business was harder than it

looked. I was starting to sweat. 'Um – because she wouldn't help tidy up the crayons.' For pity's sake: that was pathetic. She would be bound to see straight through that one. Everyone knew nobody would ever tell anyone off at Sunday school for not tidying up the crayons. It was practically the law. I ploughed on, hoping to pull some kind of rabbit of falsehood out of a hat. 'She kept colouring her picture after it was time to stop.' Actually that was me, hence the bearded quadruped, but hey. At least it had the ring of authenticity about it. I was beginning to find my stride. 'Mrs Boucher said Joy was a very selfish little girl. And Joy started crying,' I added for good measure. I stopped, astonished at my new-found talent. The lies were positively spewing from my lips.

My mother considered for a moment. 'Hmnph,' she said finally, easing herself upright. 'Oh, well. Must be the time of the month, or something.'

It was, if I remember correctly, Sunday the twenty-second of March, which I supposed at the time to have some mysterious connotation unknown to me, other than being Palm Sunday. However the crisis seemed to have passed, and as I followed my mother out of the hall it suddenly occurred to me that she'd lied to me yet again when she'd said she would know if I was lying, because she'd fallen for my story hook, line and sinker. And even before the beads of perspiration had dried on my brow, I realised that I'd uttered a lie myself – a veritable stream of them, in fact – in what was practically the nursery to the House of God, and got away with it.

This business with Max, though – it was a whole different ball game. Could I do as Angela had suggested – set a trap to catch him out? And would I know what to do with his faithlessness once I had ensnared it?

Chapter 10

I was in a state of nervous excitement mingled with stomach-churning dread when I turned the car onto the driveway outside the house around a quarter to five. Max wouldn't be back for at least another hour: he wasn't due to collect Lottie from the childminder until six.

Angela had told me that if I wanted to contact Max through the site I would have to register with the agency myself. She suggested I set up my own user profile as it would lend credibility to whatever I wrote to Max. It was easy, she assured me: people did it all the time. I'd voiced scepticism, at the same time speculating as to how she knew so much about it, and she'd rolled her eyes at me and told me she wasn't a complete ignoramus. I wondered aloud whether she'd flirted with the idea of registering herself at some point in the aftermath of Phillip's dalliance, but she snorted at that idea and told me she'd seen a Channel 4 programme on web dating. Online romance was, she warned me, a minefield, providing rich pickings for married men who fancied a bit on the side. You could say anything you liked about yourself and nobody would be any the wiser. We were back with the sixty-something-pervert-from-Bracknell scenario before we knew it. 'But, of course,' Angela had reassured me, 'this time we'll be using the power of the web for our own nefarious purposes.' Which made it all right, I supposed.

I hurried through to the study and switched on the computer, my heart hammering in my chest as it booted up. My hands shook as I opened up the dating agency site, and I had to breathe deeply to steady myself, telling myself over and over that I was doing the right thing. I knew I'd never be able to live with the uncertainty that last night's discovery had dumped into my lap: it would eat at my heart like a disease, as surely as the cancer that was killing my friend was deploying its filthy army through her body and destroying her from the inside. No: I would gather the weapons of certainty and right, and I would conquer this nightmare. Either that – I bit down on the thought – or kill off my marriage completely.

Angela was right: registering was a breeze. Five minutes' typing and you had the pick of Berkshire's bachelors, free for the taking if you left aside the forty quid signing-on fee. Except that they weren't free. Not all of them, anyway. Not Mister-No-kids-I-thought-GSOH-was-a-men's-magazine Max Howie, that was certain. A curl of anger began to unfurl in my stomach, sending a wave of hatred towards Max coursing through my body, and I welcomed the feeling with relief. Hate I could handle. It was the devastation that was killing me.

Setting up my own user profile was harder. 'Attractive lady,' I typed, and then stopped. That made me sound like someone who went to church and wore twinsets in soft pastel hues. I deleted it and tried again.

'Fun-loving girl seeks funny guy for fun times—' I stopped again. This was harder than it looked.

I paused for a moment, and another wave of rage washed

over me. 'Cuckolded wife with bastard husband seeks revenge.'

I deleted that one as well.

I sneaked a look at what some of the other women who had registered with the site had said about themselves, and realised very quickly that pretty much anything went. One hopeful had typed everything like a text message, as though she were paying by the letter for her entry. Another had written five paragraphs giving chapter and verse on her likes, which included people with nice eyes, and her dislikes, which included her mother. I resisted the urge to copy and paste what she'd said and ground my teeth with frustration. I couldn't do it. I was sitting there, an intelligent woman with a not-too-bad degree and a well-paid, responsible job, and I couldn't think up a way of selling myself on the web.

I picked up the phone alongside the computer to call Angela, and realised with a lurch of shame that I didn't know her number by heart. I fished my address book out of the top drawer of the desk and looked it up.

'I can't do it,' I told her as soon as she answered.

'What d'you mean, you can't do it? Ralph!' She broke off suddenly. 'Put that down. Sorry,' she said to me. 'The kids are just in from school. Anyway. Don't be so lily-livered. Of course you can do it.'

'I can't!'

'Then confront him with what you've found.'

I considered that for a moment before dismissing it. 'I can't do that either.'

'Francesca.' Angela's tone was calmly patronising. 'At

the moment you aren't even sure if the account is still active. He could have set it up before the two of you met, and then forgotten all about it.'

Could he have? A small germ of hope began to take root in my stomach before being dashed as I recalled the date on the back of the photograph. God: the uncertainty was killing me. I took a deep breath and steeled myself.

'Okay: I'll do it. Only – I can't think of what to put.'

She gave a harrumph. 'Well, what did Max put?'

'Hold on—' I looked at the screen. 'I don't think I can go back to his profile without closing down this bit. Oh – just a sec.' I put the receiver down and scrabbled in my handbag, retrieving the printouts I'd made the previous evening. Suddenly, taking them in to the hospital to give Alison a laugh seemed not quite so funny as it had when we'd first discussed her plans.

I found the one of Max and smoothed it out, picking up the receiver once again.

'Still there?'

She tutted. 'Of course I'm still here, Francesca.'

'Okay. First of all, he says he's divorced and doesn't have kids. I mean, the cheek of it! How can he just – annihilate Lottie like that? Let alone wipe out ten years of marriage?'

'Francesca.'

'What?'

'Just read me the advert.'

'I was!'

'Word for word. No commentator's opinions. I am warning you,' she finished, I hoped not to me.

'Oh – all right. It's just—'

'Word for word, Frannie.'

I tutted, then sighed and cleared my throat. 'Okay.' I took a deep breath. 'Ready?'

'Yes.' I think that came through gritted teeth.

'There's no need to be so – sorry. Okay.' I cleared my throat again. '"Well, here goes." That's him, by the way, not me. That's how it starts.' Down the phone I discerned a strangled cry.

'Just – *read*. If I have to tell you one more time, there will be no TV this evening.'

'Right.' I paused. 'Right.' I took a deep breath, and then launched myself into Max's duplicitous advert before the awfulness of what he'd done crippled me once again. '"How to describe myself? I'm thirty-eight, six foot one, and divorced. No children, but would love some one day in the not-too-distant. I'm not too hideous-looking, or at least that's what my best mate said when I told him I was signing up."'

Angela gave a snort. 'Bit full of himself, isn't he?' she observed.

'I thought you wanted this word for word.'

'I do. Carry on.'

I read the rest of the advert as quickly as I could, falling over the words in my haste to be shot of them, and then stopped abruptly as though I'd run right up to a cliff edge, swaying giddily and studiously avoiding passing comment.

'Is that it?'

'Yes.'

'Read it again. Slowly.'

I did so, realising about halfway through that she was taking notes.

'Okay: here's what you say,' she said a moment after I'd stopped. '"Strong, sassy lady seeks fun-loving man with WSOH—"'

'"WSOH"?'

'Weird sense of humour.'

'Oh – okay. That's good. I like that.'

'After that you can put in brackets, "you know who you are" or something like that. Anyway: "—man with WSOH for intelligent conversation, nights out, nights in etc." That's it. Keep it short. Keep it witty. Keep it to the point.'

I scribbled frantically. 'Actually, you know, I'm not sure what sassy means. And I strongly suspect Max doesn't either.'

'"Thank you, Angela, for your help,"' my sister prompted.

'Thank you, Angela,' I said meekly.

'It means a smart Alec,' she clarified. 'So you should fit the bill perfectly.'

I winced.

'I've got to go,' she said abruptly. 'Ralph is rubbing butter into his sister's hair, and she of course is doing nothing to stop him. Really, I sometimes think I gave birth to pair of simpletons.'

'Angela?'

'What?'

'I just – thanks.'

'You're welcome.'

I cut the connection and typed up what Angela had said, then went straight to Max's profile.

'Email this member?' a chirpy little button on the screen

suggested. I hesitated for a moment, and the hammering in my chest set off afresh. I felt as though I were wavering at a crossroads, none of whose destinations held any appeal. I wanted to turn around and hammer on the door that led back to yesterday's Fran, the one who had believed herself to be unhappy because of a sick friend, but who hadn't known the half of it.

I couldn't, of course. The door was not just locked: it had been bricked up and sealed with the smooth, unyielding render of my husband's deceit.

I clicked the button and began to type, stabbing the keyboard viciously as though it were personally responsible for Max's treachery. 'Hello, Not-Too-Hideous,' I hammered. 'It sounds as though I could be just your type, as I'm blonde and leggy, like the current love of your life. Unlike her, though, I have plenty to say for myself, and lots that I would like to say to you.' Never, I reflected, had I written a truer word. 'Why don't we meet up some time for a drink?' I hit that last question mark with a force that sent a sharp pain shooting up my finger.

I pressed the 'Send' button, and waited for the ceiling to fall down on my head. When it didn't, I logged off and went through to the kitchen, where I poured myself an unsteady glass of wine from the bottle we'd failed to finish the previous evening. I studied it for a moment before drinking, and gave a sigh. 'When did my life get to be so complicated?' I said aloud to myself.

'Round about the time you stopped returning my calls.'

I wheeled round. Max was standing in the doorway. He stepped into the kitchen, dropped a couple of carrier bags on the table, and then came over and planted a kiss on my cheek.

'I didn't hear you come in.' I looked behind him. 'Where's Lottie?'

'Rainbows,' he reminded me. 'It's Friday, remember.'

'You're home early.'

'So are you.' He looked at me quizzically. 'I rang your office today. Three times.'

'I know – sorry. I forgot to call you back.'

'I thought you were going to stay home and rest today.'

'No. I – well, I felt better after you'd left. And there was a meeting I couldn't miss.'

'Couldn't, or didn't want to?' His eye fell upon my glass of wine. 'Should you be drinking that?'

I frowned at the glass. 'Why shouldn't I?'

'I just thought – you know.'

'No: I don't, Max. You'll have to explain.'

'It's just that—' He looked sheepish all of a sudden. 'Nothing.' His expression softened. 'Sorry. Didn't mean to give you the third degree. Why don't you go through and put your feet up, and I'll make us a brew?'

'I don't need to put my feet up.' The prospect of a cup of tea made me feel queasy all over again. 'I saw Angela today,' I said abruptly, to distract myself.

He looked taken aback at the switch in the conversation. 'As in Angela, your sister?'

'Mm-hmn. She came to my office.' I could hear the accusing note in my voice, and fought to suppress it.

'What for?'

Because I'd just told her you were cheating on me. 'Lunch.

We had lunch together.' It wasn't a lie, exactly: at some point during our heart-to-heart I'd managed to consume the wrap and the smoothie, and Angela had watched.

'Sounds very chummy.' He was watching me warily.

'She told me some stuff. About Phillip.' I struggled to keep my tone level, to resist the urge to heap a thousand accusations onto his duplicitous head. 'Apparently he had a bit of a fling a couple of years ago.' I watched his face for any sign of guilt. 'With a checkout operator from Tesco's.'

Max tutted, and crossed the kitchen to put on the kettle. 'Stupid sod. What's he want to do something like that for?'

'Well, I suppose he was bored, maybe. People do get bored, you know. When they've been married a while. They get bored and they do stupid things.' The accusing tone was back, and I clenched my fists in an effort to calm myself.

Max gave me a strange look. 'So how come she just told you this now?'

'What?'

'Well – you just said it was a couple of years ago. How come she only told you about it today?'

I turned back to the sink and busied myself with the dishcloth to hide the fact that he'd flustered me. 'I don't know – we haven't seen much of each other, I suppose. This was the first opportunity.' It sounded weak, even to me. 'Look—' I turned back to face him. 'I don't really want tea just now. I'm going to get over to the hospital to see Alison.' His face fell. 'That way I can be back a bit earlier than usual and we can have dinner at a civilised time, for once.' Angela was right, I realised in dismay: it was easy to start living a lie.

He shrugged resignedly. 'Okay. Only, try not to be too late. We never seem to spend any time together these days.'

'Right – well, I'll see you later.' I reached up and kissed his cheek. A Judas kiss. All part of the deception.

As I pulled up outside the hospital a wave of exhaustion overcame me, and I leant my arms on the top of the steering wheel for a moment, resting my head on them to try to steady my thoughts before going in to confront Alison with my discovery. The thought of explaining it all for a second time was making my head ache. At this rate I would need a day off to recover from leaving work early.

Alison was asleep when I walked into her room. I pulled out the visitor's chair and sat down quietly beside the bed, wondering what on earth I was going to say to her when she woke up. Maybe I could make light of it to her, as I probably should have tried with Max. I began to regret not taking Angela's first piece of advice and confronting him outright. At least I wouldn't still be wallowing in – what was it she'd called it? – the festering pit of uncertainty.

I let my gaze wander across the room, which overlooked a small garden laid out with rose bushes and benches where patients in better shape than Alison could take the air. Crossing to the window, I laid my forehead against the cool glass and watched an elderly woman in a hospital gown make her way down one of the paths between the rose bushes, leaning heavily on the arm of an equally elderly man. She was hooked up to a mobile drip on a stand, which the old man carried in the hand he wasn't using to steady his companion. They shuffled slowly along the path towards one of the benches, and the old man eased his charge gently onto the seat, fussing with the drip before resting his hand on her arm and lowering himself down beside her. The elderly woman laid a gnarled hand over his and smiled at him, and he reached across and placed his free hand against her cheek. It was an intimate gesture that for some reason made me feel depressed. Max and I would never become like that, now. He'd grow old with somebody else. I felt the sting of tears threatening and shook my head at myself and sighed, then turned back to the bed to find that Alison had woken up and was regarding me solemnly. I tried a smile.

'Hey.'

'Hey yourself.' Her voice was little more than a whisper.

We regarded one another in silence for a few moments. Her breath sounded laboured. Then she suddenly inhaled sharply, as though normal breathing weren't enough to give her the oxygen she needed, and a small frown crossed her face.

'What's up?'

'Not a thing.' I managed a better smile this time.

She shook her head tiredly at me. 'Leave it out, Fran.'

I swallowed. She knew me so well, could read me so easily. I couldn't begin to imagine a time when she wouldn't be around. I shook my head to clear the smarting that had set up in my eyes.

'I cried at work today.'

'You don't look far off crying now.' She gave a short, rasping cough. 'I like it much better when you're rude to me.' She closed her eyes and breathed in sharply again.

'Alison—'

'Don't mind me.' Her face was grey. 'I had another radiation session this morning.' She opened her eyes and gave a weak smile. 'If the cancer doesn't kill me, I think the treatment might.'

I didn't know what to say to that. Today wasn't the day for light-hearted non-sequiturs.

'Here: give me a hand, will you?' She started trying to push herself to a sitting position.

'No – look: stay where you are. You need to rest.'

She grunted. 'I've got plenty of time to rest. You're here. I want to sit up.'

God, she was stubborn. I crossed to the bed, hooking my hands under her wasted arms to help her up. There was nothing of her.

Once we'd got her settled to her satisfaction, she leaned back against the pillows and gave me a searching look.

'Let's have it, then.'

'Really – it's nothing. I've just had a tough day, that's all.'

She sighed. 'Don't make me work for it, Fran. I haven't got the energy today.'

I bit my lip. 'Something's – happened. Sort of.'

Her eyes widened in alarm. 'It's not Lottie, is it?'

'No, no,' I soothed her. 'Nothing like that. Lottie's fine.'

'Well, then.' She settled back against the pillows again. 'So what is it?'

'I did what you asked me to do.' She looked at me quizzically. 'I went onto the internet. Remember?'

'Oh – that.' She gave a half-smile. 'You think I'm mad, don't you?' She gave another rasping cough. 'It's all right:

you don't have to answer that. You're probably right.' She closed her eyes again briefly, and then abruptly snapped them open, blinking once or twice as she tried to focus on what I'd just told her. 'And?'

I rummaged in my bag for the printouts and handed them to her, with Max's profile carefully placed at the bottom of the pile. She took them from me and began reading through them silently. She never smiled, as I'd thought she would, at the hairdo on the balding guy who looked as though he'd sat on something sharp. Her expression never flickered when she read about the fifty-nine-year-old who was looking for someone between eighteen and twenty-five. She read through every one of the profiles I'd printed off without a word. And finally she reached the last entry: the not-too-hideous divorcé called Footloose with the weird sense of humour.

She studied the picture for a moment, and then looked back across at me.

'Oh, Fran.'

Her gaze flicked between me and the picture, and she shook her head as if to deny the reality of what she was seeing.

'There isn't any mistake, I suppose?'

I handed her the other photograph I'd found: the one that showed Max and Adam in the living room.

'Two Christmases ago,' I said. 'It says on the back.'

She turned the picture over and studied the writing, frowning at it for a good few minutes before handing it back to me. Her expression was inscrutable.

'I don't know what to do.'

'Nothing.' Once more she shut her eyes. 'Don't do anything.'

'But—'

'*Nothing*, Fran,' she said with sudden force, opening her eyes and leaning towards me urgently.

'But I can't just do nothing. Not now that I *know*. Besides, I thought you wanted me to—'

'Forget it. I should never have asked you. Just – leave it. Forget the whole stupid idea.'

'Alison, you can't mean that.' If I'd felt as though the rug had been pulled from under me when I made my discovery about Max, Alison's reaction caused the floor to disappear as well. 'I've just found out Max is probably cheating on me—'

'You haven't.' She cut across me. 'All you've found is a ridiculous advert that's God knows how old and probably isn't even Max at all—'

'Of course it's him!' I interrupted her indignantly. 'You saw the photograph. There's no mistake.'

She closed her eyes again, shutting me out, and leaned back against the pillow. 'Oh, Fran. Don't go looking for trouble. If Max were having an affair there would be more evidence than one stupid photograph on a dating site. Just forget it.'

'I think—' I broke off, chewing nervously at the inside of my cheek. 'Well, it's a bit late for that.'

'Oh, God.' It came out on a whisper. 'What have you done?'

'I – um—' I winced. 'I answered the ad. I set myself up with a profile and I emailed him.'

She was quiet for a moment, thinking. 'When?' As if that might make a difference.

'This afternoon. Just before I came in to see you. I set up my own user profile so that he'd think I was a bona fide singleton, and I emailed him. It was Angela's idea,' I added a touch defensively.

'Angela? As in the sister you never see? Since when did you start following her advice?'

I felt a hot flush of defensiveness towards Angela. 'She was only trying to help. She said it would be the only way I could be sure.'

'Oh, no.' I was horrified to see that her eyes had filled with tears. 'Oh, I wish you hadn't done that, Fran.'

'Why?' My heart had begun to hammer in my chest. 'What's wrong with that? If he's cheating on me I can nail him properly. I *need* to know, Alison.'

'Sometimes it's better not to know.' The tears began to course down her cheeks, and she made no move to wipe them away.

I stared at her in astonishment, feeling as though I were spinning through a vortex of confusion where none of the key players in my life were behaving as they should have been. 'I can't believe you just said that.'

'I mean it!' Her voice rose higher, her distress increasing. 'You don't know what kind of can of worms you might open. Sometimes you're just better off shutting your eyes and getting on with it.'

She wouldn't talk about it any further, and my pressing her only pushed her to further distress. Before long she was weeping properly and deaf to my attempts to console her.

In the corridor outside the room, a nurse looked across at us from the nursing station. 'Hey,' I said, soothingly. I leaned across and touched her arm. 'Shouldn't it be me who's crying?' I might as well not have spoken.

'I'm afraid Mrs Beckett isn't at her best this afternoon.' The nurse had appeared in the doorway. 'Perhaps you'd better come back tomorrow.' There wasn't a hint of censure in her voice: just efficient practicality. 'The radiation therapy usually leaves her feeling pretty rotten.'

'I'm sorry, Alison: I just—' I felt helpless. Worse than that: I felt responsible.

'Really, it's not your fault. It's the treatment.' The nurse cut in front of me and began making soothing noises. 'Come on, now, Alison. No need for all these tears.' Alison's distress only increased.

The nurse looked at me over her shoulder while continuing to try to calm Alison. 'It really would be better if you went. I'll look after her.'

I picked up my handbag and the printouts, which were lying on top of the bedcovers. Then, ignoring the nurse's fussing around, I leant over and kissed the top of Alison's head. She gave no sign of having noticed.

'I'll see you tomorrow,' I said, like I always did. 'Don't go anywhere.'

It was only when I reached the lift that I realised she hadn't answered me.

Chapter 11

Alison's reaction had shocked me. I'd expected her to be shaken by my discovery. But I hadn't expected it to unleash such an outpouring of distress. Somewhere along the line I'd assumed she would buy into the whole stake-out philosophy, help me plan my strategy, work out what I'd say when I eventually confronted Max. I'd relied on her support, I realised, even if I hadn't necessarily expected her approval. Which was probably unfair of me. She had enough to cope with, without taking on my problems as well. I chided myself for not handling things better, and over the following few days each of us studiously avoided mentioning anything to do with online dating during visiting time.

A week went by and I heard nothing from Max. Web Max, that is. Real Max kept following me around the house, asking me over and over if there was something wrong. He had started looking broody and miserable. It was weird: there was no doubt that I wasn't my normal self – hence the reason for his persistent quizzing. But now that I'd taken action, and in spite of Alison's alarm, I found myself feeling oddly empowered, as though I were the one harbouring a secret and not Max. Bizarrely, mixed in with the feeling of strength was something that could have been guilt, as though I were afraid he might be about to catch me out doing something I shouldn't. And at the same time my stomach churned almost constantly with the fear that Alison had spotted something I'd missed. I felt exhilarated, at fault and terrified all at the same time. It was a heady mix.

I would watch Max when he wasn't watching me, which he did most of the time wearing a puzzled little frown, and think to myself that I didn't really know him at all. After a time I suppose all marriages settle into some kind of rut: a comfort zone where you stop making monumental efforts to please and just – relax. Where you put your feet into your husband's lap at the end of the day and he rubs them without either of you having to say a word. Or he raises an eyebrow at you and you shrug, and both of you know that means a bit of a roll in the hay at bedtime. If anyone had asked me a fortnight ago about the kind of relationship I had with Max I'd have sworn it was rock-solid, that we understood each other perfectly, that half the time we didn't even need to speak for each of us to know what the other was thinking. Now, though, when I managed to sneak a look without him actually catching my eye (which I was avoiding at all costs), I couldn't equate the man I thought I knew with the fabrication with whom I was currently trying to set up a date. I would shake my head in wonder and Max, seeing the slight movement, would ask me once again if there was anything wrong.

We skirted around one another over the weekend, during which the edges around my two Maxes began to blur, so that I was no longer sure where one stopped and the other started. On the Saturday morning, which was our usual time for taking Lottie to the water park in Bracknell, he suggested he take her on his own so that I could have a lie-in. I didn't know whether to feel cross with him for splitting up our little family or touched by his consideration. When they returned two hours later, Lottie was chattering with her usual post-Coral Reef excitement. Seeing them together, as they recalled with glee the moment during the morning when Lottie had braved one of the flumes for the first time, I forgot all about the secret my husband was keeping from us both, and for a brief moment we were normal again.

I spent far longer than I was welcome for in the hospital with Alison on the Sunday, hiding out and trying to stay upbeat and positive, She tried to look interested in whatever irrelevant topic I introduced, but there was something missing, some spark that had been there before in spite of her illness but that had disappeared after her meltdown that Friday evening. Some of the time she didn't seem to be listening at all, and once or twice she confirmed my suspicions by falling asleep while I was mid-sentence. The second time that happened I settled for sitting beside her bed just staring into space for long enough periods to earn me some sidelong looks from the nursing staff. And then she woke up suddenly and asked me abruptly, 'Have you heard from him yet?'

We'd been so vigilant in steering clear of the topic that I'd like to have said I had no idea what she was talking about. Of course that wasn't true. I knew instantly. As she'd known I would.

'Erm – I haven't checked.'

Her face clouded. 'I don't think you should. I think you should just go back on to the site and delete your profile.'

'But *why*, Alison? I don't understand.'

'You're playing with fire. Putting innocent lives at risk.'

I smiled in spite of myself at her earnest tone. 'That's a bit drastic, isn't it?'

'*Please,* Fran. Do it for me. And if not for me, do it for Lottie.'

She looked so worn out, so drawn. I began to think that at this rate it wouldn't be the cancer or the drugs that would kill her. It would be the stress of what I'd inadvertently dropped onto her plate.

I sighed. 'All right. If it matters that much to you.'

'Thank you.' The relief in her tone was unmistakable. 'And don't have it out with Max, either. Promise me you won't.'

'But then I'll never know—'

'Sometimes it's better not to.'

I looked at her sceptically.

'Trust me, Fran. Please.'

She wouldn't talk about it any further, and we returned to safer ground. As our non-conversation continued, however, it became obvious that she hadn't the energy for it. I stood up to take my leave.

'Don't forget,' she said, gripping my hand with surprising strength.

True to my word, on Sunday evening I took advantage of Max having taken Lottie across for tea with his parents, crying off joining them by feigning a headache, to log back onto the dating site so that I could do as Alison had asked.

I was thoughtful as I settled in front of the PC. Somewhere along the line all the joy seemed to have been sucked out of our little household. It felt like a slow kind of torture: a sort of suffocation by degrees where the air around us didn't contain enough oxygen to sustain us all, as it always had in the past. Maybe Alison was right: maybe sometimes it was better not knowing.

'You have a new message,' the message board on the site told me as soon as I logged in. My stomach somersaulted. *Ignore it,* a voice inside me advised. *Ignore it and delete the profile.*

I hovered over the Edit menu option, which provided the route to update or delete the profile, and another voice inside my head piped up, *But then you'll never be sure.*

My palms were sweating. Several minutes passed during which I did nothing, although my heart felt as though it were galloping out of control. Then I made my mind up and I ran the cursor down the Edit menu to highlight the Delete option. *Delete this profile?* The system asked me. *OK/Cancel.* I pointed the mouse at 'OK'. And hesitated. And it was in that moment's hesitation that I knew I was sunk.

'Sorry, Alison,' I whispered to myself, and hit the 'Cancel' button.

'Dear Sassy,' the message began, and I cringed. 'Well: wow! I'm really excited that you contacted me! You have the advantage of me, though, because you haven't posted a photo of yourself on the site! I mean, at least you know what I look like!' The plethora of exclamation marks set my teeth on edge: there was a flippancy about them that made me feel that Max was treating the situation like some kind of huge joke. 'You sound like a lot of fun, but it's hard to tell from one email!' I gritted my teeth and tried to stay focused. 'Put me out of my misery and send me a picture – let me know you don't have two heads or something! Yours hopefully, Footloose.'

I leaned back from the PC and took a deep breath. That was that, then. The account was active, and my loving husband had taken the bait.

My hands were shaking as I started to type my reply. 'Dear Footloose,' I began, and then stopped. I needed to unearth some more of the anger I'd found lurking around the fringes of my despair earlier, eventually harnessing my irritation at his appalling punctuation to give me the courage to plough on. 'I don't have two heads and you won't be disappointed, but you're going to have to trust me on this one.' There was no way on God's earth he was getting a picture. 'I'm sure you would be much more interested to see me in the flesh.' *Particularly when you spot the stake I am about to drive into your cheating heart,* I thought. 'Something tells me sparks would fly if we got together.' I clicked 'Send', and then almost leapt from my seat as the telephone started ringing like a siren beside me.

'Hello?'

'Hey, it's me,' Max said. 'How are you feeling?'

'Oh – er, fine, you know. Head's still a bit ...' I trailed off.

'Right. Well, Mum asked me to give you a call to find out if you'd like her to send over some lavender water. She reckons it's the only thing for a headache.'

I took a deep breath to calm my pounding heart. I felt as though he'd caught me red-handed. 'Er – no, thanks. Tell her no. I think it's – lifting a little.'

'Good: that's good. I expect you've probably nuked it with something much stronger than lavender water anyway. But still: you know Mum and her little foibles – oh, bugger!'

'What's the matter?'

There was a rustling noise from the other end of the line. 'I've just – hold on a mo—' He put the receiver down with a clunk and I could hear him scrabbling around. After a minute or two he picked up the receiver once again. 'Sorry about that: I'm through in the study and I just knocked a pile of Dad's papers onto the floor.'

'Well: I'll see you later—' I broke off as the PC sounded forth a little pinging alarm, signalling new mail.

'Yeah: we shouldn't be late.'

'Bye.' I hung up quickly.

I stared at the screen in disbelief.

'You have a new message,' the message board was telling me for the second time that evening.

I couldn't quite take it in at first. He must have been online at the same time as he was on the phone to me. Talk about double-dealing! I couldn't believe his audacity. All that posturing about not liking computers in the home, and he was straight onto his parents' PC while his daughter was in the next room and his parents thought he was being a dutiful husband by telephoning and offering me lavender water.

I clicked on the envelope to display the mail. 'Dear

Sassy,' he'd written, and I winced again and wished I'd picked a different pseudonym. 'Well, far be it from me to turn a lady down. Dinner? When and where? And should I pack a fire extinguisher?'

I stared at the mail in horror. Dinner? When? And where? The two-timing, conniving little shit actually wanted to go ahead and meet me. Well, not me, exactly, but whoever he thought the mysterious 'Sassy' was.

I checked my watch again. Seven-ten. They would be home in twenty minutes, and I really couldn't face them. I logged off and switched off the PC, then took a piece of paper out of the printer and scribbled a note on it. 'Headache back with a vengeance,' I wrote. 'Hoping to sleep it off. Don't wake me.' Then I took myself off upstairs and raced around getting ready for bed so that I could feign sleep once they were back.

I heard the two of them come in a couple of minutes after I'd gone to bed, spilling into the hallway and chattering animatedly. I followed their giggling progress up the hall to the kitchen, where the noise became suddenly more muted as Max took in my fictitious illness and hushed Lottie's chirruping. Shortly afterwards the door of the bedroom opened softly, and I felt rather than saw Max looming over the bed. I lay motionless, and after a moment the door shut with a sigh. Later in the evening, after sleep had actually overtaken me for a blessed couple of hours, I heard him come in again and stand over me.

'Fran?' he'd said on a whisper. 'You awake?' Oh, God. Just hearing him whisper my name like that made me want to reach out and cling to him and beg him to tell me that it wasn't true: that he'd never in a million years even think about going behind my back. Instead I grunted and turned over, and after a minute or two he went back downstairs. By the time he came to bed I'd managed another couple of hours of oblivion, so that – typically – as soon as he settled himself in his half of the bed and fell asleep my eyes sprang open and I spent the rest of the night staring up at the ceiling.

I read somewhere once that, the minute you begin to suspect your partner of infidelity, the relationship is as good as over. Once the trust has been lost, it can't be recaptured. I found myself recalling this unwelcome bit of wisdom at various points during the long night. Should I just call it a day now? Wake Max up and have him pack a bag and leave straight away? It seemed bizarre to remain lying next to him with this knowledge that had come between us, even if he was oblivious to the fact that he'd been rumbled. And what would I say to Lottie? Should I tell her? Would she hate her daddy? Did I want her to? Or should I make something up, so that she still loved him? It was all so confusing.

I reminded myself that Angela and Phillip had somehow weathered Phillip's little fling. There could be life after infidelity, evidently. I chided myself silently. Of course there could. If every relationship fell apart whenever one or other partner strayed from the marital path, there would barely be a marriage left intact. People were fallible. There would always be individuals greedy enough or unscrupulous enough to take what they wanted in life, always convinced that the grass was greener in somebody else's marriage, and there would always be someone weak enough or stupid enough to let them. I couldn't say whether I felt more admiration or scorn for Angela's ability to get beyond what Phillip had done. All I knew was that, right now, I envied her.

I turned to look at Max as he slept. I could just put a pillow over him right now: by the time he woke up to struggle it would be too late.

He must have sensed me looking at him, because suddenly his eyes opened and he smiled a sleepy smile at me. 'Hey,' he said, his voice thick with sleep, and my stomach did a little flip. 'How are you doing?' Then he turned over and fell straight back to sleep, and I resumed my ceiling-staring.

Eventually a measly, watery dawn broke over Berkshire. Feeling grubby with tiredness, I got up early and went for a shower, trying in vain to scrub away the grittiness that seemed to have worked its way under my skin during the interminable night. I dressed in a dream, and went downstairs to fix breakfast for Lottie. By the time Max appeared, two cups of coffee had done their worst and I was starting to feel slightly less surreal.

'Morning.' He leant over to kiss me as he headed for the coffeepot – an action that took me so much by surprise that I wasn't quick enough to move out of range. 'How's the head?'

I stared at him. How on earth did he do it? How could he spend the previous evening arranging clandestine dates behind my back, and then behave so – *normally* – the following morning?

'Fran?'

'Oh.' I gave myself a mental shake. 'Okay. Thanks,' I just remembered to add.

He looked as though he were about to say something else, but then changed his mind. We ate breakfast without exchanging another word, while Lottie chatted happily about a new game she and Erin had invented for playing at school during their lunch break. When the strain of being there grew too much for me, I picked up my handbag from the table and made to leave, mumbling something about an early meeting.

'Kiss, Mummy,' Lottie demanded imperiously as I was about to leave the kitchen.

I planted a kiss on her silky head, and headed for the door.

'And Daddy,' she instructed.

For a split second, time stopped. I found myself looking Max properly in the eye for the first time that morning, searching for some clue as to what was going on inside his head. At the same time he met the look in full, his expression quizzing me silently. We were like a couple of poker players, each trying not to show their hand until they were sure of their advantage.

I bent and dropped a light kiss on his cheek, then left the house without a word.

Chapter 12

'Fran!' Greg's head appeared around the door of my office, and I started guiltily. 'Good weekend? Nice to see you've showered today.'

'Go away, Greg,' I said tiredly.

With typical insouciance, he took my discouragement as an invitation and swung the rest of his body after his head into my little office, hitching himself up so that he was perched on the edge of my desk.

'Spill,' he said, nodding at me encouragingly.

'I can't. Not just now. I'm – it's not ...' I waved my hand around helplessly. I'd logged onto the dating site as soon as I'd hung my coat up, and had been about to check my account when he put in his untimely appearance. My secret burned out of the screen like an accusation, and I needed him out of my office fast before the pair of us wound up getting scorched.

'Oh, come on. You can't have anything on your schedule that won't wait half an hour while you unburden yourself to an old pal.'

It wasn't as if he were being deliberately nosey – your work PC was public property as far as the company was concerned – but as he leant across the desk to peer at my online diary it was as if the world had slowed to half-speed and the air in the room had become unnaturally thin. 'Let's have a look,' I heard him say from a thousand miles away, and suddenly I was drowning under the weight of the burden I was carrying, choking on the bitter taste of Max's furtive scheming, complicit in the deception myself for not having the courage to confront him when I'd first stumbled upon the evidence of his inconstancy. I gripped the edge of the desk and resisted the urge to throw myself against the arm that was even now turning the screen towards him and beg Greg to save me.

He frowned as he took in what he was seeing. 'That's the dating site that I met Cheryl on,' he said, puzzled. Then he lowered his head towards me and looked at me admonishingly from under his eyebrows. 'Fran. What the fuck are you up to?'

Absurdly, I had a sudden urge to laugh. And then just as abruptly, I slumped in my chair and dropped my face into my hands. I could feel the blistering heat of his disapproval burning into the top of my head.

'It isn't what you think,' I said at last, my voice muffled by my fingers. I lifted my head to look at him, and winced at the incredulity in his face. 'My friend Alison wanted me to – well, to look into something for her. A sort of research thing.' I could tell from his expression that he didn't believe a word of it. I couldn't blame him: 'It's for a friend' ranked alongside 'The dog ate my homework' as the oldest excuse in the book. 'No, truly, she did.'

He frowned. 'Alison? Isn't that your friend who's in hospital?'

'Mm-hmn.' A blush spread across my face and down my neck, and I ducked my head away from his uncompromising gaze.

'And she's asked you to do some research on dating sites?' He pushed himself off the edge of the desk and stalked towards the window in disgust. 'Come off it, Fran.'

'She did! She wanted to know the sort of thing that men write when they're trying to "sell" themselves.'

'Why?' He leaned in to the screen again, as though it might tell a different version of events if he looked hard enough.

'Because—' I broke off. 'Never mind why.' I swung the PC screen away from him. 'She just did.'

Greg narrowed his eyes at me. 'You don't have to join the agency yourself to do that.'

'Yes, well …' I hesitated. 'I – um, needed to join up to do the research thoroughly.'

He looked at me sceptically. 'Let me get this right.' He began pacing the floor of my tiny office. 'Your friend Alison, who is terminally ill in hospital – she *is* still terminally ill, isn't she?'

'Greg, don't—'

'I'll assume that yes, she is still ill. So: *she*—' he pointed at a picture on the wall, as though Alison were standing there in person '—wants *you*—' he swung his finger round to point accusingly at me '—to do some research into how men advertise themselves on dating sites.'

I nodded uncertainly. 'I realise how crazy it must sound—'

His face cleared suddenly. 'She's trying to fix him up, isn't she? Her husband, I mean. She's trying to fix things so she gets to choose who he hitches up with after she's gone.'

'It's not like that—' I protested weakly.

'Oh, my God, Fran: that's sick. That's—' He dropped his hands to his sides. 'That's the most disgusting thing I've heard in a long time.' His eyes hardened. 'Don't tell me you're going along with this fiasco?'

'She doesn't want to *choose,*' I said defiantly. 'She just wants to make sure he doesn't mope for too long afterwards.'

'Mope!' Greg's tone was aghast. 'The poor sod's wife is dying, and he's not allowed to *mope*? Christ, Fran, I'd have thought you'd have had more compassion.'

I could feel tears threatening, and blinked them away.

'There's more, isn't there?' he swept on relentlessly. 'Oh, come off it, Fran. You've got "guilty" written all over your face. And I think I've known you long enough to be pretty sure you're not the sort who plays away.' He folded his hands across his chest. 'So come on. Out with it.'

'I can't.' A lump had formed in my throat.

He gave me a thoughtful look. 'Are you in some kind of trouble?'

He looked at me expectantly, his eyes glittering.

'I'm not budging until you tell me what you're up to.' He resumed his perch on the edge of my desk.

I sighed. Then I reached out reluctantly and retrieved the mouse. I clicked and brought up Max's little fictional profile.

Greg frowned at the screen. '"Well, here goes,"' he started to read aloud. '"How to describe myself? Thirty-eight, six foot one, no children ..."'

'Greg.'

'Hmn?'

'Please don't read it all out loud.'

'Oh. Right. Sorry.' He continued to scan in silence, and finally he twigged about the photograph. He scrutinised it for a moment without speaking. I watched as realisation dawn on his face and he turned to look at me.

'Ah.'

He had met Max on half a dozen occasions, mostly at different company bashes, though in another lifetime he and Claire had once come over to the house for dinner. The two of them had hit it off straight away – surprisingly well, considering Max spent all his time tinkering with other people's motors whilst the closest Greg had ever been to an engine, or so he'd told us, had been the trip he and his classmates had taken to the transport museum in York when he was twelve. I bit my lip, unable to add anything constructive.

'Oh, Fran.' Greg's face was wreathed in sympathy. 'You think he's seeing someone else.' It wasn't a question so much as a statement.

I nodded, and the now-familiar tears began to course down my cheeks onto the desk.

'And – don't tell me – you've joined the agency yourself to try to catch him out.'

Another nod.

He pursed his lips. 'Are you sure you know what you're getting yourself into?'

I gave a despairing laugh through the tears. 'No! But what else can I do?'

'Erm – ask him to his face?'

I shook my head vehemently. 'I can't do that. I just can't. My sister said the same thing, but – I need to know. For my own peace of mind, I need to be sure. Otherwise—' I broke off.

'Otherwise what?'

It was a good question, and for a moment I wrestled with the turmoil that was spinning around dizzily inside my head. Otherwise the spectre of his betrayal would haunt our marriage, taunting us, draping its filthy tendrils over every precious memory we'd built together, suffocating the air out of them, destroying all that had ever been good between us and robbing us of any kind of a future. I'd never be able to look Max in the face again without wondering, and I knew myself well enough to be sure I could never live with that kind of uncertainty. It was a pretty big otherwise; not one I was up to framing in a coherent answer, and so I said nothing.

Greg continued to regard me quizzically, and seeing that I wasn't about to come up with an explanation he pressed his lips together and gave a small nod. 'So you thought you'd set him up.'

'He's set himself up!' I cried indignantly. 'He was the one who put his details up on the World Wide bloody Web!'

Greg held up his hands appeasingly. 'Okay, okay! Keep your hair on.' He gave me a considering look. 'Have you been in touch with him? Electronically, I mean.'

I nodded, crestfallen. 'He wants to meet me for dinner.'

'And then, what?'

'Well, *then,* hopefully, once it's all out in the open I'll find that it's some kind of joke that's backfired and we can have a good laugh about it and put it behind us,' I said uncertainly.

There was a short hiatus while neither of us said anything. Then Greg pushed himself off the edge of my desk. 'Well, I think the whole thing stinks. You should just have it out with him. The atmosphere in your house must be a nightmare right now.' He paused, and his expression softened. 'Let me know how you get on. And if you need someone to talk to, I *am* Mr Online Dating 2007, don't forget.'

'I won't. And thanks for sparing me the lecture.'

I paced the floor restlessly after he'd left my office, riddled with uncertainty. Maybe he and Angela were right: I should just bite the bullet and have it out with Max. I considered this option, rolling it around inside my head like a taste I'd never come across before. Yes: on the whole, that was the mature thing to do. I nodded to drive the point home to myself. I could just pick up the phone right now, and tell him I was coming over to see him.

Though, of course, then he could just lie his way out of the situation – he was clearly more accomplished in the art of deceit than I'd ever given him credit for being – and I'd never get to the bottom of things.

My head was beginning to ache with the strain of trying to figure out the best way forward. No matter which way I cut the cake, none of the pieces looked very appetising.

I stepped across to the desk, still wavering. I even got as far as reaching out my hand and grasping the receiver. And then my eyes fell upon the dating site once again, and just as I'd done after Alison had pleaded with me to delete my profile, I found my hand refused to co-operate with me. It reached of its own volition for my mouse instead, and brought up the email I'd received – or rather, Sassy had received – the previous evening.

I studied it for a few minutes. So we were to have dinner, were we? I felt a familiar fluttering in my stomach. That comment about the fire extinguisher, too – it was sharp, witty. Cyber Max was flirting with me: something in-the-flesh Max hadn't done in years. I could almost have enjoyed the sensation if it hadn't been for a sinking feeling in the pit of my stomach. My husband might be flirting with me, but he thought I was someone else.

I did eventually pick up my desk phone, and punched in a number. Angela answered on the second ring.

'Angela Devlin speaking.'

Relief at hearing her calm, practical voice flooded through my body. 'Angela, it's me.'

'You shouldn't say that, Francesca. It's not good telephone etiquette.'

'What?'

'You shouldn't just say, "it's me" like that. You should give your name. "Me" could be anybody.'

'But you knew it was me!' I protested as the relief curled up and withered. 'You said my name.'

'Yes: but I might not have. And then I would have been at a disadvantage, because you would have known who I was, but I wouldn't have known who you were.'

Holy cow, I thought. *Was she always this pedantic?* I clenched my teeth and tried to remember why calling her had seemed like a good idea.

'Okay: sorry. It's Fran speaking.'

'I know that now. I was just pointing it out to you for future reference.'

'Right.'

'So—?'

'Sorry?' What else had I neglected to say?

'You rang me, Fran. I'm presuming you have news.'

'Oh – yes.' I'd forgotten for a moment, lost amongst the minefield of protocol that governed a telephone conversation with my sister.

'Well?' Her tone was elaborately patient, as though she were speaking to a very small child. I had to resist the urge to scream in frustration and hang up. After all, aside from Greg she was the only confidante I had right now.

'Um – I sent him an email.'

'And?' The tone hadn't altered.

'He emailed me back.' I gave her a brief summary of Max's flirtatious email. 'He wanted a photograph. I hadn't put one on, of course. That would have given the game away.'

'I suppose it would,' Angela concurred. 'Although you could always have used a fake one.'

'But – he'd know as soon as he saw me on the date that I wasn't the same as the photograph,' I objected, and I heard her sigh laboriously.

'Well, that would hardly matter, would it? The whole idea is to spring a surprise trap when he turns up to meet you. No: a fake photograph would have been a good move. He might smell a rat without a picture. Someone young and stunningly attractive. Someone you think would be his type.'

'*I'm* his type, Angela.' I felt old and frumpy all of a sudden. 'At least, I used to be.'

'Oh, well: too late now,' Angela continued briskly. 'What else did he say?'

'Not much, really. I mailed him back and told him he'd probably prefer me in the flesh.'

'Oh – excellent. I like that. Just a hint of debauchery. Very good.' I swelled a little. It was nice knowing I'd done something right for a change. 'And have you had a reply to that?'

'He wants to meet me for dinner. He asked if he should pack a fire extinguisher.'

'What a peculiar thing to say. What on earth would he need a fire extinguisher for? I must say, Fran, that sounds rather odd.'

'Actually, I thought it was rather witty,' I countered, feeling oddly defensive of Max all of a sudden. 'It was in response to my comment about how sparks would fly if we got together.'

Angela sniffed. 'Oh. Well, you should have said so.' *I just did,* I thought rebelliously. 'Anyway, you can't meet him for dinner.'

'I can't?'

'Absolutely not. You never do dinner on a first date.'

'Why not?' Angela's logic was starting to make my head spin.

'If you go on a blind date with someone, you might take an instant dislike to them. Supposing you can't stand them? Supposing they pick their teeth when they're eating, or talk incessantly about their collection of Matchbox cars or something. You don't want to be stuck with someone like that through dinner. Lunch is much more containable. You can be done and dusted in half an hour and you never need to see them again if you loathe them.'

'Angela.'

'What?' she said, her irritation spilling out of the earpiece.

'This is Max we're talking about. *Max.* I can stand him. He doesn't pick his teeth and he doesn't collect Matchbox cars.' Actually, that wasn't strictly true. He did have a very small collection of vintage models that his mother had been buying him periodically since he opened the workshop eight years ago. They were on show in the small reception area next to the office.

'Well, yes, I know that. I was speaking more generally. It's the principle that's important. You don't want him smelling a rat. Although of course dinner does set the scene better for the denouement. Have you fixed a place yet?'

'No, of course I haven't fixed a place! I am busy trying to arrange a clandestine dinner date with my unfaithful husband, masquerading as the woman of his fantasies, whilst at the same time running his home, bringing up his daughter, and holding down a full-time job. You'll have to forgive me if I'm a little slow off the mark.'

'You were the one that wanted a career,' she countered, disregarding my sarcastic tone. 'I suppose motherhood wasn't *fulfilling* enough for you.'

'Angela—'

'Anyway,' she swept on, happy now that she'd had her

dig, 'be that as it may. With regard to a suitable venue, you should probably keep it as far away from your normal stamping ground as possible. You don't want to be running into anybody you know. And go for a hotel with a really decent restaurant attached, or a really decent restaurant with a hotel nearby. That way you can hint that something more than sticky toffee pudding might be on the menu for dessert if he plays his cards right. See how he takes that suggestion. And choose somewhere expensive. You might as well get him to splash out. Plus it will give you an idea of how serious he is.'

'How will it do that?'

'Well, think about it. If he gets cold feet at the suggestion of an expensive place and proposes the Harvester in Bracknell, for instance, you'll know this is just a bit of fun for him, and you'll be able to have a good laugh to yourself and move on. You could even have a bit of fun yourself afterwards – suggest the same restaurant next time he decides to take you out to dinner. Let him know that you know, without the hassle of a showdown. That way you could clip his wings and hang on to your dignity at the same time. And it will be much easier to forgive him if you know it isn't serious.'

Would it? Was it easier to forgive a bit of fun than a deep, passionate affair? Were there degrees of infidelity? I imagined Max professing to me that he'd fallen in love with someone else, and felt a physical tearing in my heart at the prospect. Yes: Angela was right. A bit of fun would hurt. But not so much as the total rejection of being replaced in Max's affections by another woman.

I nodded to myself slowly. Everything – or at least most – that Angela said made sense. 'Any ideas?'

She thought for a minute. 'There's a place called Babylon that ought to fit the bill. One of the women from the babysitting circle was there for her husband's company Christmas do there last year. I've never been, of course. But she said it was very posh. Very discreet. Perfect for an assignation.'

'She said that?'

'Well, no: of course she didn't, Francesca. Don't be so finicky.'

'Babylon, you say?' It rang a distant bell somewhere deep in my memory.

'In the West End. It isn't a hotel, but that doesn't really matter. There are plenty of hotels round about.'

I frowned into the phone. 'I can't place it. Is it near the cinema?'

She gave a snort, as though I were deranged. 'I thought you were supposed to be sassy. Not the west end of Bracknell. I'm talking about London.'

'London!' I was horrified. 'We can't go up to London! We haven't been there in years. He won't know where it is.'

'Of course he will. Everyone knows where London is.'

'Not London! The restaurant. Babylon.' Saying the name again, I remembered suddenly where I'd heard about it before. Adam had taken Alison there last summer for her birthday: apparently he used it all the time to entertain the great and the good who orbited the lofty heights of the BBC.

'He'll find it if he's keen.'

'We'll have to get a babysitter.'

'I'll do it,' Angela volunteered.

'Really?'

'Well, you can hardly ask his mother, can you? It'll have to be done more surreptitiously than that. We'll play the detail by ear, but in principle, yes, I'll come and babysit. I'll tell Phillip it's for someone in the circle.'

I trod down hard on the knot of anxiety in my stomach. 'Okay, then. When, d'you think?'

'Oh – as soon as possible, I would have thought – tomorrow evening, if you can. No point hanging around.'

'What?' I was horrified. 'Why? Wouldn't it be better nearer the weekend?' I felt sick at the prospect of such an imminent confrontation.

'No, it wouldn't be better. Firstly, Babylon will probably be booked solid on a Friday night. It's that sort of place. Secondly, you already sound as though you're about to pass out: there's no way you'll be able to stand the tension until Friday.'

I sank my head into my hands. 'This is all such a pig's ear. It's all very well us scheming away over the phone. I'm the one that has to go out there and face the music.'

'Oh, don't be so pathetic, Francesca.' Her tone was brisk again. 'I've lived with the uncertainty too, remember. It kills you. The sooner it's over and done with, the better. Now, get out there and – you know. Kick some arse, or whatever the expression is.'

I felt a great wave of gratitude mingled with something like humility sweep over me. Really, she was remarkable, this sister of mine. She *had* been through it: what's more, she'd had to do that alone. I'd known nothing and been unable to provide her with any support. But here she was, shoring me up unstintingly when the chips were down. Suddenly I couldn't understand why we'd spent such a large part of our adult life avoiding one another.

'And, Francesca?'

'Yes?' I asked her affectionately.

'Wear something feminine. Not your usual pseudo-Nazi Commandant stuff.'

'What pseudo-Nazi Commandant stuff?'

'That awful dark suit you had on last week.'

I glanced down at the pinstripe trouser suit I was wearing. 'That was work gear,' I said indignantly. 'I wouldn't wear it on a date!'

'And get your hair done. You looked like you had birds nesting in it.'

I ground my teeth in frustration, and remembered why we'd rarely sought out one another's company. The gratitude and affection were wearing thin.

'Call me when you've got things organised, then. Right?'

'Right,' I answered. 'And – er, thanks.'

There was no answer. She'd cut the connection as soon as she'd had my concurrence.

Brisk, bossy, no-nonsense Angela. She was wasted as a housewife, I reflected, and born about sixty years too late. With skills like hers, Chamberlain could have used her in the battle against Nazism. Hitler would have lost the will to live within a week.

Chapter 13

'Mummy, what's a Daisel Fly?'

'A what?'

'A Daisel Fly.'

'Um, I don't know, Lottie.' Max was working late this evening, and so I'd collected Lottie from the childminder on my way home from a flying visit to the hospital, where I'd spent a pointless half-hour sitting beside Alison's bed while she slept, my head full of Angela's proposed plans for my husband's undoing. We were driving home listening to a CD of songs from one of the old musicals – Brigadoon, I think it was – that Max's mother had bought for Lottie after the two of them had watched the film together one weekend when she was staying over with his parents. She insisted we play it whenever we were in the car together and was singing along now, perched on her booster cushion in the rear of the car, and looking as though she hadn't a care in the world.

'Well, why is it in the song, then?'

I tried to concentrate. 'Which song?' A black BMW cut across my exit from the roundabout and I braked sharply to avoid hitting him. The car behind gave me an irritated blast on its horn. Ah, me. Six o'clock traffic in beautiful Berkshire. You couldn't beat it.

'This one. You know. He says, "With bonnie Jean my Daisel Fly".'

I focused on the tape for a moment. 'Go home, go home,' the chorus were singing. 'Go home with bonnie Jean.' I thought back rapidly through the rest of the song. Wait a minute: there! I had it. My face split into a huge grin. I loved kids. Just when you thought there was nothing left to smile about, somehow they cut through all the crap and gave you hope.

'It's "days'll fly", Lottie. Days will fly. He means the days will go by very quickly because he loves her so much.'

'Oh.'

I tried to imagine what kind of picture the song had conjured up in Lottie's head when she'd envisaged the words as 'Daisel Fly'. With bonnie Jean my Daisel Fly. Cyd Charisse with bulbous eyes and a couple of antennae. Did flies have antennae? It wasn't a particularly attractive thought.

'Mummy?'

'Mmm?'

'Are you Daddy's Daisel Fly?'

'Of course I am.' Was I?

'Do the days go by really quickly because you love him so much?'

'Absolutely.' Well, it was half-true, anyway. The days were positively flying past at the moment. I barely had time to think. Trying to have an affair with your husband so that you could catch him out having an affair was damned hard work.

'Will you love him till the day you die?'

Good God: did the child never give up? This was like being interrogated by the Gestapo.

'Will you, Mummy?'

I pulled onto the driveway and switched off the ignition, and the tape was mercifully silenced.

'Right: out you jump.'

'But will you?' Lottie wasn't budging.

'Of course I will.' Of course I would. And that was the bugger of it all.

Max wasn't expected home before seven, so there was plenty of time for me to bait the trap, as it were. As soon as we were through the front door I went straight to the study and logged onto the site. 'Babylon, West End, 8.00 p.m. tomorrow night,' I typed.

I hesitated just for a moment. This was it, then. No turning back. But I had to know, one way or another. At least this would put an end to the uncertainty. I pressed my lips together and clicked the 'Send' button.

My email alert pinged almost immediately. 'How will I know you?' my lethal, lying husband, who was supposed to be updating the books for his accountant, was now asking. So much for him not using the work computer, then.

This time I didn't hesitate. 'You won't. But I'll know you.'

Chapter 14

The views from Babylon's rooftop restaurant were spectacular. Outside on the balcony, with all of the capital spread out beneath me like a jewelled blanket and the noise of the city drifting mutedly upwards, I smoothed my hands down the front of the very chic dress I was wearing and tried to bring my stomach under control.

I had told Max this morning that I was out with a party from work, celebrating a deal we'd pulled off with Vodaphone. It was a real coup, I'd said: the company was pulling out all the stops to show its appreciation and had booked out the ballroom at the Grosvenor in London. No partners, sorry. He'd looked at me miserably and said 'fine'. Not 'Darling, that's wonderful.' Not 'Congratulations! Have a great time.' Not even 'Can't you smuggle me in under your coat?' like he'd asked about the last company do I'd attended. Just 'fine'. I'd almost felt sorry for him, until I remembered that he'd started the whole fiasco in the first place. And any vestiges of sympathy were quickly dispensed with after he'd turned round and said that I'd have to organise a babysitter because he wasn't going to be in either.

'Why? Where are you going?' As if I didn't know.

'Guy and I are staying on late at the workshop to finish off the paperwork.'

Oh, please. Couldn't he do better than that?

'Well, you could have told me sooner. I can't just organise a sitter with – what? – twelve hours' notice.'

'You mean the way you gave me so much warning about your little – jaunt?'

My mouth dropped open. Boy, he was good. I was starting to feel bad, and he was the one in the wrong. 'It isn't a jaunt!' I said hotly. 'It's a work function. You know I hate them.'

'Then don't go.'

'I have to!' This was ridiculous. How come he was twisting the whole thing round and making *me* feel like the guilty party? 'I'm a member of the senior management team. You don't get to just not go. And anyway,' I added as an afterthought, 'I'm quite sure I told you all about it last week.'

Max gave me a hard look and left the room without replying.

True to her word, Angela turned up at six. I was nervously spraying on perfume upstairs when the doorbell rang. By the time I came down Lottie had let her in and was scrutinising her shyly over the lid of a packet of dried raisins Angela had just given her ('So much better for her than sweets.') She turned to inspect me as I reached the bottom stair.

'Hmn. Not bad,' was her verdict. 'The dress is a bit short, and you've an awful lot of cleavage on show. But then I suppose you want to look a bit slutty.'

I bit my tongue. Slutty! My lovely dress – Max's favourite, a deep purple silk affair with a plunging neckline

– swung loosely and satisfyingly around my hips. I must have shed a few pounds during these last few days with all the stress of trying to manage a duplicitous husband. My feet were encased in dark purple strappy sandals that were a nightmare to walk in but gave me height and made my legs look longer than they were. All the armour was in place. I had thought it didn't look half bad until Angela came out with her verdict.

'You remember Auntie Angela, don't you, Lottie?' I said, focusing my attention on my daughter to avoid stabbing Angela in the eye with one of my stilettos. 'She's going to be looking after you this evening.'

'Of course she remembers me.' Angela followed me into the living-room, where I started upending all the cushions on the sofa looking for my mobile. 'I gave you that nurse's outfit for your birthday. Remember?' Lottie nodded at her shyly.

'You know your trouble?' she asked, turning her attention back to me. 'You take on too much. You should make more time for yourself.' She meant well, of course, but how on earth did one go about making more time, when every second seemed to be taken up by the demands of other people? The impatient honking of the taxi that I'd ordered to take me to the station saved me from having to respond to this last homily. 'I'll see you later,' I said briefly to Angela. 'Thank you for looking after Auntie Angela,' I added to Lottie, dropping a quick peck on her cheek before making my escape into the night.

And now here I was, standing alone on the balcony of

what I had to admit was probably the poshest restaurant I'd ever visited in my life, nervous as hell and waiting for a secret assignation with my husband. I'd left work early (again) and spent ages getting ready. I'd showered and shaved and plucked and buffed myself until my skin was positively glowing, and then had to powder my face to take away some of the shine. Tom, the hairdresser who despaired over my hair every three months or so, had squeezed me in at the last minute after I'd called him up in my lunch hour and explained that it was an emergency. By the time I was ready to hit the town I reckoned I looked as good as I'd ever look, despite Angela's comment about my dress.

A cool breeze that swept across the night sky brought my arms up in goose bumps, and I shivered and went back to wait inside the restaurant. I had arrived deliberately early, wanting to give the place the once-over and get myself firmly settled on the moral high ground before Max arrived. It wasn't easy: the waiting area, which was down a few steps to the left, was completely boxed in by a wall of aquaria full of colourful fish that drifted languorously back and forth in their watery prisons. Sofas and easy chairs lined the walls in front of the fish. It looked a bit like an up-market dentist's waiting-room. I'd planned to be standing mysteriously with my back to the restaurant entrance when my fraudulent husband arrived, so that just for a minute he might not know it was me. The balcony would have done on a warmer night, I supposed, but as it was the goose bumps didn't go with the rest of my outfit.

To the right of the door there was a small bar area with high stools. Gingerly – negotiating a bar stool in stilettos proving trickier than I had anticipated – I eased myself into the stool farthest away from the door and sat facing the main restaurant eating area.

The maître d', who had already asked me twice if he could show me to a table, clicked his fingers at a rather good-looking bloke behind the bar, who had a margarita poured and in front of me almost before the words were out of my mouth. He placed a small dish of salted almonds on the bar in front of me, alongside a small display stand that contained a stack of business cards advertising the restaurant. I took a large gulp from my glass and picked up one of the cards. Like the rest of the place it was a bit over-the-top: where most places would have settled for a straightforward piece of card Babylon had gone for something that folded in the middle, like a short, squat greetings card. The usual contact information was tucked away on the back of the card, while the front contained a single sentence: 'talk with me'. Not even so much as a capital letter, the omission of which set my teeth on edge. I was beginning to think I'd have been more at home at the Harvester.

Inside the card was a series of teasers obviously meant to stimulate sparkling discussion amongst the restaurant's clientele. 'What have you regretted the most from a drunken night out?' the first question asked. I rather thought I might be about to find out. 'If you had the chance to meet anyone in the world, dead or alive, and ask them one question, who would it be and what would you ask them?' Hmn. How about, 'Why did you put your picture on a dating site, Max?'

I checked my watch surreptitiously. 8.15. I sighed and slipped the card into my handbag. Max was late. I twisted round in my seat and glanced at the door to the restaurant and just as I did so I spotted a lone figure outlined against the glass.

For a moment I was sure it was Max. And then the door opened and Adam, Alison's husband, walked in.

I nearly fell off the bar stool in shock. Quickly I swivelled round so that my back was to him, my heart thumping, praying that he hadn't noticed me. And then I felt a hand on my shoulder, and a voice in my ear.

'Fran! I thought it was you. What on earth are you doing here?' He looked me up and down, checking out the dress and the shoes, and clicked his tongue in appreciation. 'And dressed to kill, I see. Who's the lucky man?'

I affected lofty surprise. 'Adam! What a coincidence. I'm waiting for Max, as it happens.'

'Max! As in Max, the man who lives in a pair of oily overalls? Are you sure?'

'Of course I am.' God, this man really knew how to needle me.

'I just wouldn't have had this down as being Max's kind of place, that's all. I'd always thought of him as more of your Harvester kind of chap.'

I gritted my teeth, even though I'd recently had much the same thought myself. 'Well, that just goes to show how little you know of my husband,' I said. 'Anyway, why are *you* here? Shouldn't you be in visiting your wife?'

He cast his gaze around the restaurant, which was moderately busy. 'Been and gone,' he said vaguely. 'I'm meeting a colleague for a business dinner. Horribly dull, really: he's one of those chaps who has no conversation other than how much his stocks have gone up in the past month. We use this place all the time – we have an account here. The food's good but, generally speaking, the company leaves a lot to be desired.' He looked me up and down again. 'Frankly, I'd much sooner have dinner with you: you look good enough to eat. Tell you what: if old Max doesn't show, I'll get rid of Boris the Bore and you and I can hit the town. What d'you say?' He grinned at me lasciviously.

I checked my watch again, irritated. 8.20. Where the hell was he? It was bad enough him making secret trysts behind my back. The least he could do was to turn up on time. Unpunctuality was little short of bad manners, and here I was stuck with Adam the sleaze, who was hitting on me in spite of the fact that he'd left his wife's hospital bedside barely an hour earlier.

'Yes: why not?' I said. 'We could hit the town, as you say. Take in a nightclub or two. And then we can tell Alison all about it tomorrow.' He had the decency to look momentarily disconcerted before recovering swiftly. 'How nice for you that you can still manage to get out for your business meetings,' I continued. 'Who's looking after Erin? Still with Alison's parents, is she?' Even to myself I sounded small-minded and spiteful.

'Don't be nasty, Fran: it doesn't suit you.' Adam scanned the restaurant once again. 'Ah: I think I see my colleague.'

Across the other side of the restaurant a balding man who looked to be about fifty was signalling across in our direction. Adam nodded to him in response. 'I'd better get over there. Have a good evening.' He bent and dropped a chaste kiss on my cheek. 'I hope you manage to track down your tardy husband.'

I watched him cross the restaurant floor, and then jumped as my mobile started to purr in my bag.

'Hello?'

'Francesca?' There was a sigh from the other end of the line. 'I do wish you would learn to use the telephone properly. "Hello" could be anyone. It's Angela. Has he turned up yet?'

'No he bloody well hasn't,' I seethed into the phone. 'What time did he leave?' Max hadn't arrived home before I'd left.

'Not long after you,' Angela said. 'He just came in, said a quick hello to Lottie, asked after Phillip, changed out of his overalls and took off again.'

'What was he wearing?'

'Jeans, I think, and an old rugby top.'

'But—' I looked back into the restaurant. 'This isn't exactly your jeans and rugby top sort of place.'

'Well … maybe he took a change of clothes with him to throw me off the scent. I mean, he'd have had a hard time explaining himself if he'd got himself all togged up for an evening at the workshop, wouldn't he? And actually, now I think about it, he did have a little rucksack with him. I don't know what was in it, though.'

'That must be it! He's obviously taken his posh outfit

with him. He usually keeps his hill-walking stuff in that rucksack – he must have emptied it out and re-packed it so that he could get ready for his sordid little rendezvous at the workshop, without arousing your suspicions. The lowlife.' I checked my watch again: it was coming up for 8.25. 'Look, Angela, I'm not going to hang around much longer. He's nearly half-an-hour late, and frankly I think I deserve better than this.' I checked myself. What on earth was I saying? Of course I deserved better than this. That was the whole point of this sorry fiasco: so that I could take the moral high ground. Well, I'd certainly managed that. The trouble was, there wasn't much you could *do* on the moral high ground if the enemy didn't even have the decency to show up so that you could shoot at them.

I retrieved my coat from the solicitous maître d', who assured me that he hoped to welcome me back to Babylon very soon. I doubted that. Somehow the whole sordid experience wasn't one I was anxious to repeat. I slunk out of the restaurant feeling dirty and dishevelled and oddly flat, and all the way down in the lift I kept wondering what I would do if, when I stepped out into the foyer, Max was standing there waiting to go up to the restaurant.

He wasn't. The foyer was depressingly empty, although outside on the street a black cab was just disgorging its passengers, an elegant couple who were entwined around one another and obviously set for a romantic night on the town together. I hated them by default. Not enough to spurn the gift of the taxi they were just vacating, though. I climbed in and sat back while the driver whisked me over to Waterloo, where I caught an earlier-than-anticipated train back home.

As I was scrabbling in my purse for the cab money I came across the card I'd absently put in there earlier in the evening: the little business card from the Babylon. I opened it up while the cab driver was pulling onto the taxi rank. 'What's worse,' the third question on the inside wanted to know, 'getting stood up by your date, or getting turned down for a date?'

Well, I was pretty sure I knew the answer to that one.

By the time I arrived home it was almost ten. Max was still out: the old Cresta that was his pride and joy was missing from the driveway. Where the hell had he gone? Maybe he hadn't been able to locate the restaurant, as I'd thought. Or maybe – what if there were more than one Babylon in London? Oh, God – I should have been more specific. Poor Max. I could just see him trawling across the city in a cab, lurching from one restaurant to another frantically trying to track me down.

Poor Max? Did I actually think, poor Max? What I meant was, serve him right, the little shit.

Angela must have heard my key in the lock, because before I got to turn it she was wrestling the door open from the inside. She took one look at my drawn features and pulled me inside. 'Brandy,' she said knowledgably. 'You look as though you've been put through the spin cycle.'

'I feel it,' I said, kicking off my lovely purple stiletto-heeled shoes. 'I can't believe I've been stood up. How could he do that to me?'

Angela looked at me in amazement. 'What?'

'I put on my best dress just for him,' I said, starting to snivel. 'It's his favourite.'

'Fran. You're in shock. Here: get this down you,' said Angela, tipping amber liquid into a glass until it was half-full and handing it to me. I took it off her and downed it in one, like they do in films, then promptly fell into a coughing fit. That never happened in the films.

'Oh, Angela,' I started to wail, once the coughing fit had passed. 'He doesn't love me any more. He couldn't even be bothered to turn up and be unfaithful with me.'

'Don't be so ridiculous,' Angela said. 'It's a good thing that he didn't turn up. He probably thought better of it and changed his mind. Maybe he's come to his senses. I mean, it wasn't you he was standing up, was it? Not you, Francesca Howie. He was standing up that woman we made up. Sappy, or whatever her name is.'

I stared at her. Of course he was. Oh, how dim could you be? Suddenly I felt filled with love for Max for his willpower in resisting temptation. I was proud of him. Not every man would have been as strong in his shoes.

Unless, of course, he'd just got the wrong restaurant.

The bastard.

'You should get off to bed,' Angela told me, breaking into my thoughts. 'You look positively grey. And we can't have you looking anything less than perfect. It's all too easy to let yourself go in these situations. Next thing you know you'll end up with some disgusting bug and then where will you be?'

I sighed wearily. 'Thanks so much for watching Lottie. Was she any bother?'

'None at all. She tried telling me she's allowed a chocolate spread sandwich after she's done her teeth, but I stood firm. You don't normally give her sweets before bed do you, Fran? They'll ruin her teeth.'

I was too exhausted to take offence. 'Only at the weekend,' I said, then smiled tiredly at Angela's indignant expression. 'Just kidding. Oh—' I suddenly remembered. 'Guess who I saw tonight?'

'Where?'

'At the restaurant.'

'Who?'

'Alison's husband. I was just sitting at the bar, waiting for Max and trying to look sophisticated and aloof while perching on this ruddy bar stool, and suddenly there he was behind me. Apparently the bloody BBC have an account there.'

'Hmnph,' Angela snorted. 'I'll bet he eats there all the time. In fact, I'm willing to wager he's never cooked a single meal for himself. Probably doesn't even know how to turn the cooker on. Most men are pretty useless when it comes to that sort of thing.' She turned and hugged me tightly and unexpectedly before slipping her arms into her coat. 'Get some sleep.'

'I can't see that happening, somehow. Still, I appreciate the sentiment.'

While I was getting changed upstairs out of my lovely purple silk dress, I knocked my toe on something that was sticking out from under the bed. I bent down to see what it was. Max's hill-walking gear was all spilled higgledy-piggledy on the floor, and I'd managed to stub my toe on one of his boots, which was caked in dried mud from his last foray into the countryside.

I took my pillow and went off to the spare room to cry myself to sleep.

Chapter 15

At work the following morning I took a sneaky peek at the dating website, closing the door of my office first so that nobody could catch me at it. The little yellow 'new mail' envelope was waiting for me.

'The trouble with cold feet is that they can take an awful long time to thaw out when you go home alone, don't you find? D'you want to try again?'

Cold feet. He'd got cold feet about our date. I didn't know whether to laugh or cry. What was he – some kind of namby-pamby drip? I mean, he was supposed to be a mid-thirties singleton looking for a smart and sassy lady, wasn't he? What was all this about cold feet?

I didn't know where he'd been, though, if he'd really had cold feet. He hadn't arrived home until around eleven-thirty. I'd heard the car tyres scrunching on the gravel, the slam of the car door and his key in the lock of the front door. He'd moved around a bit downstairs – I followed the sound of his movements between the kitchen and living-room – before creeping up the stairs to bed. He'd opened our bedroom door and then paused before crossing the landing and opening the door to the spare room. Light from the landing spilled across the bed and I kept my eyes closed, feigning sleep. I heard him sigh heavily before closing the door quietly and crossing the landing back to our bedroom.

He was gone by the time I woke in the morning. I'd overslept again: there was no alarm clock in the spare room and in my confusion and exhaustion I'd forgotten to set the alarm on my mobile. By the time I finally dragged myself up to consciousness the house was empty: once again Max had dressed Lottie and taken her to school while I'd lain in bed oblivious. This time there was no note leaning against the kettle waiting for me, no cheerful stick people telling me to get better soon.

The house didn't feel like our home any more. Oddly, it felt as though nobody actually lived here any longer, even though on the surface nothing had changed. It had held its breath the evening I had discovered Max's details on the dating site, and in just under a fortnight it seemed to be drawing a last gasp before its heart finally stopped beating and our relationship was officially declared dead.

I showered and dressed as quickly as I could and escaped to the office, where some semblance of normality settled onto my shoulders as I parked up and walked through the front door.

We had, I mused, reached a sorry state of affairs when rushing into my office to log onto a dating site constituted normality.

I turned my attention back to the email and had a stab at composing a reply.

'Don't worry: we all get cold feet sometimes! It didn't matter a bit.'

Too accommodating. Made me sound like a proper little doormat. Hey, sure, you've walked all over me once. Feel free to do it again. Please. Be my guest.

I deleted that one and started afresh. 'Frankly, I don't think much of being kept hanging around in a strange restaurant half the evening.'

Too whiney. Come on, Fran. Think smart and sassy. What was it that the card from Babylon had said? I pulled it out of my handbag and began to paraphrase. 'Well, I'm not sure what's worse: getting stood up by your date or getting turned down for a date. What do you think? If I turn you down now, does that mean we're even?'

There. That would do. Kind of jokey, a bit witty (he wasn't to know it wasn't my wit), and it put the ball firmly back in his court. I clicked 'Send', and then clicked onto Outlook to schedule the first of my one-to-ones with the technical trainers. Before I'd had a chance to start checking their availability, my email alert sounded.

'I don't know about it making us even, but then I'm a bad loser. Lunch tomorrow: meet me at the Natural History Museum, 1.00 p.m.'

Oh, God. He must think I was based in London. I couldn't get away in the middle of the day. Could I? For that matter, how on earth could Max hope to leave the workshop on a whim, when he was supposed to be in the middle of tax returns? Surely he'd have a tough time explaining to Guy why he was disappearing for what would constitute the best part of the day at their busiest time of year?

I took a quick look at tomorrow's schedule. Thursdays were never the most hectic day of the week – that award definitely went to Fridays and the R&D Exec review – and tomorrow's schedule actually looked particularly quiet. I had a nine-thirty interview, but that would be unlikely to last longer than an hour and a half. If I took a half-day's leave I should be able to make it up to London by one, though it was stretching the company policy of flexible working to the limit. It would certainly make life less complicated, meeting at lunch time instead of during the evening: I'd never get away with trying to conjure up an excuse to Max for being out and dressed up for the second night in one week. The last thing I wanted to do was to raise his suspicions. He had already been behaving pretty oddly.

I braced my shoulders and began to type. '1.00 it is. I hear there's a spectacular arachnological display on at the moment. Will I meet you in that section?'

Back came the reply almost by return. 'Central Hall, Cromwell Road entrance, you heartless little witch.'

The rest of the morning passed without incident. At twelve Greg stopped by my office at just the same time as Maeve, who had taken to popping in before she went for lunch so that she could check whether I wanted her to pick me up a sandwich while she was out. She blushed as they bumped into one another in the doorway, and gestured him inside. The blush deepened when he insisted she pass through ahead of him. 'Sorry,' she said, flustered. 'I was just checking whether I should bring you something back for your lunch.'

Greg grinned. 'Got your staff running round after you now, have you, Fran?' I glowered at him. He was starting to sound like Angela.

'Mrs Howie is very busy,' Maeve reproved. 'She doesn't have time to go out. Sometimes she barely has time to eat.'

'Is that right, Mrs Howie?' Greg queried. 'Well, that's a shame. I came by to see if you'd like to join me for a bite over at the Italian place, but obviously if you've too much to do ...'

'Oh, no: that's a very good idea,' Maeve cut in. 'Much better than a sandwich.' She nodded at me encouragingly.

I looked from one to the other. 'Well, thank you, Mr Patterson. As it happens, Miss Loxley is right. I am far too busy to knock off for lunch. My schedule this afternoon is solid.'

'Yes, but not before two,' Maeve pointed out helpfully.

I glared at her. 'My first appointment is at two. But I have preparation to do before then.'

'What?' Greg was now asking.

I switched my scowl to him. 'I'm doing one-to-ones with all the technical trainers, if you must know. I need to check what the three I'm seeing this afternoon have been working on over the past six months.'

'Oh, I put all that information into a spreadsheet last week,' Maeve said, helpful as ever. 'If you like, I can print it out and leave it on your desk while you're at lunch.'

'In which case,' Greg said, reaching to unhook my coat from the stand beside the door, 'there's no reason why you can't come out with me. Is there, Miss Loxley?' He smiled winningly at Maeve, who almost fainted with delight, and then shook the coat out and held it up to me.

'You're a pair of bullies,' I grumbled, sliding my arms into the sleeves. He grinned impudently at me and Maeve skipped off happily, no doubt to do some more interfering elsewhere.

Greg and I crossed the car park to his Alfa Romeo, and he held the passenger door open to me with a great show of chivalry. Once I was seated he shut the door and loped around to the driver's side.

'So: what gives?' he asked as he slid the car into reverse and started to back out of the parking space.

'Which particular bit of my life are you looking for an update on?' I asked him. 'The professional meltdown nightmare, the dying friend nightmare, or the bastard husband nightmare?'

He laughed. 'Nothing like having a choice, is there? Though, to be honest, nobody's talking about the boardroom fiasco any more. Not since Brian buggered up the O_2 deployment last week. He might not have shed actual tears at Friday's meeting but, let's face it, he did so much whining and snivelling he might as well have done.'

Laughing at Brian's misfortune covered the time it took us to drive the short distance to the restaurant, where we were greeted like old friends by its owner, Antonio, and furnished with two large glasses of Barolo in spite of my protests about having to work in the afternoon.

'Right,' said Greg, once Antonio had disappeared into the kitchen, 'let's have it.'

I took a deep breath. 'I set up a date with him.' I watched carefully to gauge his reaction, but he kept his features studiously unreadable. 'I created my own user profile on the website – minus picture, of course – and I emailed him. And he took the bait: he asked me out for dinner. I spent ages getting ready, though according to my sister the result was more slutty than sophisticated. I hauled myself off to a fancy restaurant in central London, waited half-an-hour for him to show, during which time Alison's husband turned up and started sleazing all over me, and then I got fed up and went home. He's emailed me this morning saying he got cold feet, and asked me to meet him at the Natural History Museum for lunch tomorrow.'

Greg studied me for a moment. 'And you're going, of course.'

'Of course. I've put in for a half-day's leave. I told Derek it was a family emergency, which wasn't far from the truth. He practically fell over himself to approve it – I think he thought I might start crying again if he turned me down.' I pursed my lips. 'Come to think of it, I probably would have.'

Greg pulled a face. 'You haven't reconsidered, then?'

'There's nothing to reconsider.'

'It's not too late to have it out with him.'

'No.' I shook my head vehemently. 'It's too easy for him to bluff his way out of it, to say he only did it for a dare, or that someone else set him up. I've gone over and over this a thousand times, and I just have to do this.' I picked up my wine glass and tipped it up, watching the wine bleed back down the side of the glass when I set it upright again. 'If I can catch him out actually turning up for a date, then I'll know for sure. And I need to know for sure, Greg. I can't bear this half-knowledge.' I picked the glass back up again without drinking, wrapping both hands around the stem and staring into the wine as though it might contain answers.

Greg covered my hands with his own. 'This is killing you, isn't it?' I nodded without speaking. He sat thinking for a moment. 'You know, I have to go up to London myself tomorrow.' I raised my eyes and looked at him in surprise. 'No: really, I do. I've booked the afternoon off, too. I'm meeting Cheryl at three – she's got a lunch-time shoot and can't get away before then – and we're going up to Hatton Garden to choose wedding rings. So – I could come with you, if you like. For moral support,' he added. 'I could loiter behind one of the exhibits.'

I thought over his offer. The idea of moral support did sound rather attractive. At the same time, I wasn't sure I wanted anybody around when Max eventually turned up. *If* he turned up, that is.

'Of course, I could just bugger off once he shows up,' Greg continued, as though he'd read my mind. 'Unless you'd rather I hung around.'

'No – I think buggering off sounds like the better plan,' I said. 'Once I confront him, I won't need moral support. Though I might need someone to stop me from killing him.'

'Right: that's what we'll do, shall we?' I nodded. I liked the sound of 'we'. Suddenly I didn't feel so alone. I smiled gratefully at Greg.

'Okay, then.'

I could barely keep my eyes open during the afternoon – a combination, no doubt, of the trauma of the previous evening, a lousy night's sleep in the spare room, and the two very large glasses of red wine I'd drunk over lunch. Maeve, spotting my fatigue, kept a constant supply of strong, dark coffee coming during the afternoon, so that by five-thirty I was buzzing slightly from a serious caffeine overdose. I found myself dreading the evening visit to the hospital. I hadn't been in to see Alison since Sunday – hadn't been able to face telling her that not only had I broken my promise and not deleted my profile from the dating site, I'd also managed in the short time since I'd last seen her to organise – and attend – a date.

There was no sign of her when I arrived at her room just before six. Even more oddly, there were no flowers on the bedside cabinet, no get-well cards. The picture Erin had drawn, showing a stick person lying in a bed with 'Get well soon Mummy' written below it in a wobbly childish hand, had disappeared. The room had been stripped bare.

I stood stupidly in the doorway for a moment trying to make sense of what I was seeing. Where was the drip? Her slippers, which sat optimistically underneath the visitor's chair? Her magazines that she kept heaped beside the bed for what she called her 'good' days? It was as though someone had taken a board duster and wiped away all evidence of her ever having inhabited this small corner of the hospital.

A sound behind me caused me to wheel around, and I found myself face-to-face with the nurse who'd been there the evening that I'd made Alison cry. She was carrying a bundle of fresh linen.

'Oh, dear,' she said when she recognised me. 'Didn't anybody tell you?'

Chapter 16

'Are you all right?' The nurse touched my arm lightly as she passed me on her way out of the room having deposited the linen on the empty bed. 'You've gone as white as a sheet.' She crossed the corridor to the nurses' station and began looking for something on the computer screen that stood on the desk behind the counter. 'Here we are,' she said, frowning at the screen. 'Ward Eleven.'

'I'm sorry?' I felt disorientated.

'It's at the end of the corridor.' She shrugged at me. 'She wanted to move. You do get that sometimes. She said she'd had enough of being on her own.'

I stared at her. *Morag*, her name badge proclaimed her to be. I wanted to punch Morag in the face – I actually felt my fist starting to curl - though I tried to tell myself it was probably guilt that led me to believe she'd been deliberately ambiguous. 'There aren't really enough private rooms to go around, so we weren't going to argue too much.'

'Right – Ward Eleven, you said?' I uncurled my fist. My heart, which had set off at a gallop, started to settle back down.

'That's right, although I think she's having a bath at the moment. One of the auxiliaries has gone to give her a hand.' She gestured with her head. 'Just at the end of the corridor. You can wait for her in there if you like, though she might be a while.'

I walked slowly down the corridor to the ward the nurse had indicated. It contained only four beds, two of which looked to be unoccupied. A third bed bore a woman who was fast asleep, lying flat on her back and snoring quietly. So much for wanting company, I thought, pulling out the visitor's chair from beside what were obviously Alison's new quarters. Erin's picture had been Blu-Tacked to the side of the cabinet, and the get-well cards were back in evidence, ranged around the water jug and on the wall behind the bed. The pile of magazines was stacked on the little shelf below the drawer. I pulled one of them out and started leafing through it, not really giving it much attention. After a few minutes I tossed it onto the bed and sighed. It didn't take a genius to appreciate the reason for the timing of Alison's bath coinciding with my normal visiting time. It spoke volumes, too, that she'd given up the privacy of her own room and chosen to move onto a shared ward, where the opportunities for earnest heart-to-hearts were severely restricted. I felt shut out and hurt. And angry with her as well, because you weren't supposed to feel these things towards a friend whom you were in danger of losing permanently in the not-too-distant future. I even found myself wondering whether she was cutting me off deliberately so that the loss, when it finally came around, didn't feel so acute. The speculating was making my head ache.

I must have nodded off in the overheated room, lulled by the soft snoring of the woman in the bed opposite, because the touch of a small hand on my shoulder jerked me upright. 'It's Auntie Fran,' Erin exclaimed in delight. 'Auntie Fran, why were you asleep? Are you staying in the hospital as well as Mummy? Is she, Daddy?'

I rubbed my hand across my eyes and looked up to find Adam looking down at me amusedly for the second time in twenty-four hours. 'My, my, Fran,' he said to me now. 'We do seem to keep running into one another at the moment, don't we?' He raised an eyebrow at me.

'Mummy's got a new bed,' Erin told me excitedly. She was clutching a fresh bunch of white freesias to her dress. 'Look, Auntie Fran: here's the picture I drew her.' She pointed it out to me. 'She looks at it when she's in bed and it makes her feel better.' I smiled at her wanly. 'Mummy's having a bath,' she went on. 'Not a bed bath. A proper one. She had to get up for it: the nurse said so. So she must be getting better. Mustn't she, Daddy?'

'Erin, why don't you go and find the nurse again and see if she'll help you find a vase for those flowers?' Adam suggested, and Erin scampered off happily up the corridor.

'Does she have any idea her mother's dying?' I asked him as soon as she was out of earshot. 'Or are you keeping that as a surprise for her?'

Adam ignored my question. 'You've never liked me, have you, Fran?'

I pushed the chair away behind me and stood up angrily. 'This isn't about you,' I countered. 'It's about Alison. And Erin. Helping her to cope.'

'What would you have me do?' he asked, his voice level, his face close to mine. 'Spoil what little time they have left together by telling Erin her Mummy's going to leave her to live with the angels in heaven?' His face hardened. 'Stay out of it, Fran. You know nothing about it.'

Down the corridor a door opened and Alison emerged, swathed in a dressing-gown and leaning heavily on the arm of one of the nursing auxiliaries. Together they shuffled back towards the ward, reminding me depressingly of the elderly patient I'd seen shuffling along in just such a manner, the old man who was with her carefully holding her drip and stand out of the way so that she could reach the bench in the little garden.

As they approached the ward Alison looked up and spotted Adam and me standing together beside her bed. It might have been my imagination, but I could swear her face fell when she saw me.

They continued their slow passage into the little ward, and Alison stopped when she was level with me and turned to look me full in the face. *Did you do it?* her expression wanted to know. *Did you do what you said you would do?* She stared at me, her eyes accusing. Then behind us Erin burst back into the ward and saved me from having to answer.

'We brought you flowers, Mummy! The nurse is finding a vase.'

Alison held my gaze just a moment longer before turning to her daughter.

'Did you, darling? The white ones? The ones Mummy likes best?'

'Yes!' Erin bounced up and down beside the bed for a moment before Adam caught her around the waist and lifted her up. 'Hey, quieten down, tiger! Some people around here are trying to sleep.'

Over in the other bed, Alison's room-mate snored on regardless. The auxiliary fussed around, helping Alison back into the bed, straightening the covers across her legs. I gathered up my bag from the floor beside the visitor's chair.

'I'd better go. Give you guys a bit of peace.' I looked across at Alison. 'See you tomorrow, yeah?'

She looked up at me briefly from the pillows, and for a heart-rending moment I thought I saw something that looked like disgust in her eyes. 'Sure.'

'Alison—' I began, inwardly cursing the lack of privacy. Adam stepped forward proprietarily, Erin still in his arms, so that he was standing between me and the bed.

'Bye, Fran,' he said mildly, an expression of suppressed triumph flitting briefly across his face.

Chapter 17

'D'you suppose taking a proper bath instead of a bed bath is a sign that Alison's getting better?' I asked Max over dinner that evening. He looked up at me and frowned.

'She's got cancer, Fran. Remember?'

'I know – it's just, well, I'm pretty sure that she hasn't had the strength for a real bath in weeks. Practically since she was admitted, in fact.'

Bizarrely, we'd just enjoyed an incongruously harmonious meal together, with neither of us making any reference to the other's odd behaviour over the past week or so. When I'd come in from the hospital Max had been through in the kitchen stirring a large pot of chilli. The radio had been playing, and through in the living-room Lottie had been watching the tail end of Brigadoon, which she'd borrowed from Max's mother at the weekend. He'd looked up when I'd gone through to the kitchen, unsure of himself, trying to gauge my mood. And when I'd dropped into a chair and declared myself exhausted, he'd furnished me with my third glass of red of the day and told me dinner would be fifteen minutes.

Without consciously making a decision about it, I found my defences towards him starting to relax as the meal progressed, no doubt assisted by the anaesthetising effect of the wine, so that by the time we reached dessert – an apple pie generously donated by Max's mother, liberally topped with ice cream – I'd somehow managed to separate husband-Max from web-Max so thoroughly that I was able to ignore the sins of the second and enjoy an almost normal family meal with the first.

This must be how people coped who were married to the serially unfaithful, I decided. You just shut your eyes to the bits you didn't want to see, and after a while you stopped seeing them. No wonder the cuckolded got so upset when well-intentioned friends forced them to face the truth, dragging them reluctantly out of whatever reality they'd managed to create for themselves. Right now I was too exhausted to go on hating Max, and so I gave myself up willingly to the pretence that we were just a normal family enjoying a tasty mid-week meal together. I'd deal with web-Max tomorrow at lunch time, once I got to the Natural History Museum.

Lottie had been excused from the table as soon as she'd scraped the last traces of ice cream from her plate, and had hurried through to the lounge to catch the finale of her film before bath time. I'd dropped my question about Alison as soon as I heard the TV starting up.

Max sighed now and came round to sit beside me at the table, amidst the debris of our meal. He took the wine glass out of my hand and placed it down beside the bottle, then took hold of each of my hands in his in a gesture that called to mind the lunch I'd shared with Greg just a few hours earlier.

'I know this is tough for you,' he said, looking right into my eyes. 'But you have to face up to the fact that Alison isn't getting better.' He gave my hands a little shake without moving his eyes from mine. 'Believe me: I'd like nothing better than if that weren't true. But you yourself said weeks ago that the consultant had told her there was nothing further they could do, aside from some radiation to slow things down a bit. Didn't you?'

I nodded, not trusting myself to speak.

'So don't go clutching at straws, Fran. Alison doesn't need that. Does she?'

A lump had formed in my throat. 'No.'

He continued to regard me for a few moments. 'You look all in,' he said finally. 'What if I go and run you a nice hot bath?'

I shook my head. 'Lottie needs her bath first.'

'I'll do it.'

'No.' I smiled at him. 'I feel as though I've barely been around for the past fortnight. I *want* to do it, really I do.'

He let go of my hands and rubbed my arms before helping me to my feet. Then he pulled me towards him and wrapped his arms around me, holding me close, my head against his chest, his breath warm on my hair. I stiffened for a brief moment, resisting, and then gave in to the sensation, letting myself relax against him. *Tomorrow*, I told myself. *Tonight I need this.*

In the end we both bathed Lottie, much to her delight. She sat and splashed in a sea of bubbles, playing to her audience, until Max declared it was bed time. He laid a fat bath towel across my knees, and then lifted Lottie out and sat her on my knee, wrapping a second towel around her shoulders so that she wouldn't catch cold. And I rubbed the towel against her skin and tickled her under the arms, making her squirm and giggle. We were all trying so hard, I reflected: role-playing at Happy Families. Even Lottie seemed to be part of the conspiracy. As I got ready for bed after my own bath, hitting the hay early because I really could barely keep my eyes open, I marvelled at the human capacity for self-deceit. My last thought before sleep overcame me was, how long would we be able to keep it up?

Chapter 18

Thursday morning was a gift: high, fluffy clouds in an impossibly blue sky, the air so clear and crisp you could have breakfasted on it. Max and I had coffee and croissants together in the kitchen, while Lottie scattered Cheerios across the table and announced that she wanted Erin to come and stay overnight the following evening. I dodged the request, uncomfortable about seeing Adam after our contretemps in the hospital the previous evening, and told her, in the manner of mothers everywhere, that we would have to see.

'What will we have to see?' she had queried, refusing to be deflected.

'We'll just see, Lottie. Erin might be busy tomorrow evening.'

'No, she isn't.' Lottie fished a Cheerio out of the milk in her bowl and popped it into her mouth. 'She asked if she could come to my house.'

Max stepped into the breach. 'Don't eat your breakfast with your fingers, you revolting little savage,' he chided. 'If Mummy says we'll see, then we'll see. It's a special rule that mummies have. Now, off you go and wash your hands and face, otherwise Mrs Cramb will think you've had a bath in milk this morning.'

She skipped off, the request forgotten for the moment,

and I smiled my gratitude to Max. 'Thanks. I'm not sure how receptive Adam would be if he found out we were organising sleepovers for the girls. He wasn't exactly full of the milk of human kindness yesterday evening.'

'Well, he's not having an easy time of it, Fran. You need to cut him some slack.'

'I know. But it would be easier if he weren't such an arrogant pig.'

Max grinned at me. 'You don't take any prisoners, do you?'

'No, I don't. Why should I?'

'Life isn't black and white, Fran. There are plenty of shades of grey in between.'

I studied him for a moment. Was he dropping some kind of obscure hint? Warning me that everything in our marital garden was far from rosy? The insidious seep of infidelity that was slowly poisoning our relationship began to claw at my stomach again, and I stood up to leave before it could spoil what remained of our breakfast together. *A last supper,* I thought to myself, but never voiced the thought.

'See you later,' I said. I stood up and picked up my car keys from the dresser before heading for the front door.

'Lottie! Mummy's leaving,' Max called, and our daughter came running to the top of the stairs.

'Kiss, Mummy,' she cried, hurrying down to grab me around the legs. I caught her under the arms and swung her up in the air.

'Oof – you're getting big,' I pretended to complain. 'Pretty soon you'll be lifting me up for a kiss.'

She giggled at that, and when I'd put her down she pretended to pick me up, grunting and straining with the effort.

'Kiss, Mummy?' Max had followed me out of the kitchen and was loitering by the front door. He tilted his head to one side and looked at me imploringly.

I trod firmly on the spectre. *Later*, I promised myself, and leaned over to kiss him. A peck on the lips, light as gossamer. Lottie watched us intently.

'Daddy, did you know you're Mummy's Daisel Fly?'

'Her what?' Max never took his eyes off me.

'Her Daisel Fly. The days go by really quickly because she loves you so much.'

'Is that right?' He addressed the question to Lottie, but he was still looking at me.

'Mm-hmn. And she's going to love you till she dies. Aren't you, Mummy?'

For a moment neither of us spoke. *Now*, I thought: *tell him now and put an end to this nightmare.* And then I dropped my eyes and turned to deal with Lottie.

'Teeth,' I told her. 'You're going to be late for school.'

Chapter 19

'Ready?'

I stood up and smoothed down my skirt with trembling hands.

'Ready.' I nodded to Greg, who stood by the office door with my jacket over his arm. I took a deep breath.

'Nervous?'

I gave him a sidelong look. I had already thrown up once in the ladies' toilets shortly after arriving at work.

'Stupid question – sorry. Of course you're nervous.' He ushered me out of the door and we set off down the stairs. 'Still, at least you know it'll all be over in a couple of hours. The waiting, I mean. The not being sure.' We reached the first-floor landing, and he stopped suddenly. 'That's the worst bit, not being sure.' Then he gave a small shrug, and set off once again down the stairs. 'Of course, I never really had that with Claire. One minute she was there, the next: bam! She'd gone. Buggered off with most of our worldly goods stuffed into the back of a van. I didn't get the chance to be nervous.' At the bottom of the stairs he stopped again and stood for a moment beside the reception desk, looking thoughtful. 'I don't know what's worse, really: knowing in advance that you're heading for a fall, or just finding yourself at the bottom of the cliff with no recollection of how you came to be there. Though on second thoughts it must be worse to know in advance. Like being on a plane with a terrorist. All the time, wondering whether you're going to come out of it alive, or whether ...'

'Greg.' I stepped up close to him.

He blinked suddenly, as though he had forgotten I was there. 'Mm-hmn?'

'Shut up.'

'Oh. Right. Sorry.'

Outside the front door to the office a taxi stood idling, its driver leaning on the bonnet finishing a cigarette. As we approached he threw the butt onto the ground and extinguished it with the sole of his shoe. We had decided against driving into London, on the basis that the traffic might prove unpredictably – or even predictably – horrendous, and make me late for my appointment with Max. So we'd settled on taking the train straight in to Waterloo and picking up a cab at the other end. I asked myself more than once as the taxi rattled and bounced us to the station whether it had been a wise move: train journeys meant an awful lot of thinking time without even the distraction of other drivers to keep the brooding at bay.

And brood I did. Once on the train I slumped into a corner seat and quelled any attempts from Greg to engage me in conversation. I reproached myself over and over for not having confronted Max as soon as I'd found the photograph; for setting up this absurd date so that I could corner him and cut off any means of escape. Alison's voice kept running through my head: *Sometimes it's best not to know.* Why would she say that? It was so unlike her. If Max thought I was black and white, he should have tried

Alison. One of the things I'd always admired about her was her refusal to compromise on the things that really mattered to her. I recalled an evening we'd spent together at the home of a mutual friend. After dinner we'd played some awful game where you were given a scenario and three possible outcomes, and you had to guess the outcome a particular person would choose. What they'd do, for instance, if they found out their best friend's husband was having an affair. The group got to choose from things like: tell the friend; tackle the husband; or say nothing. I'd guessed Alison's choices time after time without hesitation. It wasn't hard: you just had to pick the one that showed the least compromise and you had her. She'd tell the friend every time. Adam had laughed and accused me of knowing his wife better than he did, and I'd had to bite my tongue not to come out with some acerbic retort. He'd been right, yesterday evening in the hospital: I'd never liked him much. But there had been a time when I'd managed to hide it better.

By the time the train pulled into Waterloo the stress was really starting to mount. A dearth of taxis on the rank outside the station had me hopping up and down with impatience, even though we still had a good twenty-five minutes to spare.

'Calm down,' Greg advised me. 'At this rate you'll have given yourself a coronary before we manage to get to the museum.'

'It's all right for you,' I chided. 'You've been here before. You're used to infidelity. I'm not. I'm used to having a husband I love and who loves me, and a daughter who knows her mummy and daddy are going to love each other until we die. I don't *do* all this sordid stuff.'

He looked at me appraisingly. 'Infidelity isn't something you get used to, Fran. Sure, you might not be so quick to trust someone second time round. Lord knows, when Cheryl came along it took me a long time before I would let myself believe that she would still be there when I came home at night. Nobody chooses to do all the *sordid stuff,* as you call it. They just find themselves in the midst of it before they realise it.' As he finished, a taxi finally pulled onto the rank, and he opened the rear door.

'Yes, but – they must have done *something*,' I protested, climbing aboard. 'I mean, why would someone in an otherwise happy relationship just decide to indulge in a bit of extra-curricular activity? Something must have gone on before then to precipitate it.'

'You tell me,' he answered, slamming the door closed. 'Natural History Museum, please, mate. And drop us on the opposite side of the road.' Then he settled back in his seat. 'You're the one whose husband we're chasing. What did *you* do, Fran?'

He gave me an injured look, and I realised I'd upset him with my stupid suggestion. I hadn't meant to be so tactless: I'd just been so wrapped up in my own misery, I'd forgotten that he'd been here before me. I reached out to touch his hand, but he pulled away and looked out of the window.

'Greg – I'm really sorry.' I leaned further and touched his arm, and this time he looked around at me, though his expression was still dark. 'I didn't mean – I wasn't talking about you and Claire. I meant—' I shook my head. 'I'm just not myself right now. I can't quite believe this is happening to me. Of course I must have done something. It's just that – I've asked myself a thousand times – what? What could have caused Max to do this? I've gone over and over everything I can think of. I know just lately I've put too much on his shoulders – I've expected him to do too much. He has a business to run, and I've just dropped everything at home – Lottie included – and left him to hold the fort so that I can keep running into the hospital to see a friend who right now doesn't want to clap eyes on me. I spend too long when I am home fretting about work – it's not easy, being the only woman on the team, you know – so that when we do get half an hour together all I do is regale him with stories about Brian bloody McKinnon and Derek's unreasonable demands on me. I can't remember the last time I cooked for him. I can't even remember the last time we went out together, just the two of us.' I ran my hands through my hair with frustration and sighed. 'But that hasn't always been the case. We *were* happy before this, I know we were. And I thought he was glad to take over at home while Alison was so ill. He always said he was. He kept saying, "It's not a problem," "Take as long as you need," stuff like that.'

'Well, what did you expect him to say? "Bugger this, Fran, where's my tea?"'

I smiled reluctantly.

He softened. 'I'm not saying you've done anything. But don't assume other people must have brought their troubles on themselves either. Shit happens. That's the bugger of it. You don't always see it coming. You don't always know what's going on in someone else's head. You can't always tell what they're thinking.'

We rode in silence for a few minutes, and then he started up again. 'Anyway. Now's your chance to find out.' He nodded towards the building opposite. 'We're here.'

We sat for a few moments while the taxi's engine idled and Greg rummaged around in his pockets for change. Across the road there was no sign of Max. The museum was just disgorging a party of about twenty schoolchildren, who milled around the entrance like bees around a hive, waiting to be gathered up by their teacher. A glance at my watch told me we were still ten minutes early. We clambered out and stood on the pavement, surveying the museum from the relative safety of the taxi's wide flank, until a businessman in a hurry pushed past us and claimed it for himself. The taxi pulled away into the afternoon traffic, leaving us naked and exposed on the pavement.

'Okay?'

I nodded. Oddly, I felt calmer now than I'd felt since the night I'd made my discovery on the internet. There was an inevitability about what was about to happen, as though I'd been working towards it for most of my adult life.

'This must be how Marie Antoinette felt when she was sent off to the guillotine,' I remarked grimly to Greg.

'Oh, I shouldn't think so. I expect they had to drag her kicking and screaming and protesting that all she'd done was offer the peasants cake,' he commented wryly. 'Joan of Arc, maybe – now there was a martyr for you.' He took my arm and made to steer me across the road, and then froze.

The party of schoolchildren had disappeared off along the street, leaving the entrance to the museum clear and revealing a solitary man loitering on the steps looking at his watch.

'That's him, isn't it?' Greg inclined his head towards the museum.

My stomach did lurch then. I felt a physical blow to the solar plexus, as though I'd been kicked by a mule.

It wasn't Max standing on the steps. Not my Max. Not my loyal, loving husband.

It was Adam.

Chapter 20

I grabbed Greg's shoulder and pulled him back into the shelter of a small tobacconist's shop.

'All right,' Greg said, turning to face me. 'Take your time. There's no hurry.'

'Let's get out of here,' I hissed, as though I feared we would be overheard.

'What? Are you sure?'

I nodded, and began walking briskly down the street. After a moment I heard Greg's footsteps hurrying to catch up with me.

'Fran!'

I ignored him and kept walking.

'Fran!'

I wheeled. 'Shut up, can't you? I don't want him seeing me.'

He ran the last few steps and caught me by the shoulder. 'But I thought the whole point of this exercise was to let him see you. To confront him. Wasn't it?'

Luck had brought us to the door of a small restaurant. I pushed it open and almost fell inside. Almost immediately a waiter materialised beside us.

'Table for two?'

I nodded. 'No – not there.' He'd been about to sit us in a dark corner beside the bar. 'Over there – in the window.'

The window afforded a reasonable view of the entrance to the museum, where Adam was leaning against the stone portico as though he hadn't a care in the world. Why should he have? According to my watch there were still a good five minutes to go before our appointment.

'What's this about, Fran?' Greg wanted to know. 'Cold feet? Dutch courage? Only, I don't think we've got time for lunch if you want to be on time for Max—'

'That's not Max, Greg.'

'It isn't?'

I shook my head. 'That's my friend Alison's husband.'

'What? The guy you bumped into the other night?'

'The very same.'

He hesitated. 'It looked like Max.'

I made a dismissive gesture. 'Yes, it did. They're very alike.'

'Ah.' He stared at me, reflecting on what I'd just told him. 'Coincidence?' he offered after a moment, without much conviction.

'I don't think so.'

'But didn't you tell me he was meeting a colleague or something?'

'That's what he said.' I thought back to the night in Babylon, and remembered the man who had waved to Adam from the other side of the restaurant. 'But, you know, I never actually saw him sit down with the guy. He could have been bluffing. It looked as though that other bloke was waving at him, but he could just have been trying to get the waiter's attention.'

Greg made to say something else, but I held up a hand

to silence him. 'I think I know what this is about,' I said eventually, my mouth dry, my heart thumping. 'It hadn't occurred to me before, but when you got out of the taxi just then and saw him and thought it was Max, I realised.' I fell silent for a moment, reflecting. 'They *are* alike, you see, Max and Adam. People are always mistaking them for brothers. Or at least they used to, in the days when we did stuff together.' It felt like another lifetime ago. 'Alison and I used to joke about it, even though we always thought the likeness superficial. You do, when you live with it. Like a mother with identical twins that only she can tell apart. To her, the difference is obvious. But to other people it's like some miracle that she knows which twin is which.' I thought back to the photograph, the two of them standing with their hands in their pockets leaning against the mantelpiece in our living-room. And then I remembered I still had it: I'd been carrying it around in my handbag for the last fortnight. I bent to pick up the bag from the floor at my feet and rummaged inside.

'What are you saying?' He waved away the waiter, who had appeared at his elbow wanting to take our order.

I looked across at the museum again. Adam had abandoned his leaning and was standing at the bottom of the steps, looking up and down the road. As I watched him from the cover of the restaurant, he made his way back up the steps and resumed his position against the portico.

'He used Max's picture.' I studied the photograph in my hand. 'Look.' I held it out to Greg. 'He knew he'd be able to get away with it: nobody turning up for a date would question it, not even if they'd brought a printout of the photo with them to help them recognise him. He could easily say it was a couple of years old or something, to clear away any doubts. But there wouldn't *be* any doubts, would there? Nobody would think to question that he was who he said he was.' I shook my head in amazement. 'He must have done it as a sort of insurance against someone seeing his picture and recognising him. After all, it's hardly the done thing to be going onto websites looking for a bit on the side when your wife's dying in hospital.' I looked across at the museum again, disgust twisting both my face and my stomach. 'God: I knew he was a sleaze. But even I never thought he would sink this low.' I suddenly recalled Max's words from breakfast time. *He's not having an easy time of it, Fran. You need to cut him some slack.* Watching him standing there on the steps to the museum, waiting to betray his wife, having already betrayed his friend and caused havoc between Max and me, I could think of something I would have enjoyed cutting. Amputating, even. And it had nothing to do with slack.

The waiter was back. 'Are you ready to order?' He tapped the top of his notepad impatiently with his pen.

'Yes,' I said decisively. 'We'd like a bottle of champagne, please.' The waiter's eyebrows shot up appreciatively. Having written us off as a couple of time-wasters, he was delighted by his sudden turn in fortune.

'Champagne?' Greg queried when he had gone.

'Absolutely.' I was overwhelmed by a feeling of euphoria. It was all I could do to stop myself from dancing on the table. 'After the hell I've lived through for the past fortnight, I'm in the mood to celebrate.'

Greg smiled. 'Well, I don't mind drinking to the fact that you've discovered your husband isn't cheating on you. But you'll be finishing off the bottle yourself. I can hardly turn up half-cut to go shopping for wedding rings with Cheryl.' He studied the photograph again. 'There really is an amazing likeness, isn't there? They could be twins.' He handed the picture back to me, and I turned it over to read the back of it to him.

'Christmas, 2006,' I said. 'We'd just finished lunch. The girls were only little – four, or thereabouts. We'd bought Lottie a Wendy house. A little wooden thing, which Max had put up in the garden on Christmas Eve. He couldn't start erecting it until after she'd gone to bed, because it had to be a surprise. He ended up finishing it by torchlight.' I smiled at the memory: Max out on the patio after dark, hampered by a bulky sweater and a head-torch, blowing on his hands periodically to thaw them out, and grinning at me conspiratorially through the French windows as I sat on the floor wrapping the rest of Lottie's presents in the warmth of the sitting-room. 'Anyway, she and Erin were out playing in it, in spite of the fact that it was freezing outside. And we were having a glass of port in the lounge, watching them through the French doors.' I turned the photograph back over and surveyed the two men. 'Alison took the picture. Adam had bought her a new digital camera, some fancy thing with extra lenses and stuff, and she was trying it out.' I looked at the writing on the back once again. 'She brought the prints round to show me. She'd done them herself, and she was really proud of them. And she'd made me copies of some of them. Mostly of Erin and Lottie, playing outside;

but she'd taken this one of the boys as well.' I hesitated, fingering the corner of the picture. 'It was just after the New Year. She'd come over with Erin for the afternoon. We had coffee in the kitchen while the girls built this ridiculous snowman in the garden.' My eyes had filled with tears. We'd never get to do anything like that again, Alison and me. It was such a small thing, that visit: one of hundreds we'd made to one another's houses. As was the nature of such everyday miracles, we'd never even realised there was anything precious about it.

The waiter appeared with the champagne, which he opened with far more ceremony than was strictly necessary. Bubbles fizzed up the neck of the bottle and spilled into the glass he was holding at the ready. He handed each of us a glass with a flourish before placing the bottle in the ice bucket he'd brought to the table and leaving us in peace.

Greg picked up his glass. 'Here's to friends,' he said, smiling at me.

'Absolutely,' I agreed, blinking away the tears and lifting my glass to touch the rim of his. 'I don't know how I'd have got through all this without you.'

'Yeah, well: you did the same for me after Claire left,' he said. 'That's what friends are for.'

I sighed suddenly, remembering Alison's hostility towards me the previous evening. 'Yeah,' I said, feeling the loss all over again. And then another thought hit me, so awful and so upsetting that I almost dropped the glass.

'Oh my God,' was all I could manage. 'Oh, shit. Shit, shit, shit.'

'What?' Greg looked at me in surprise. 'What is it, Fran?'

'She knows,' I said in a horrified whisper. 'Alison. She knows.' I thought back to the night I'd shown her the photograph, the sudden comprehension in her eyes when she recognised her own handwriting on the back and put two and two together far faster than I'd been able to, and realised that it had been her photograph, not mine, that had been used in the advert: that Adam had found her copy of it, and used it to cheat on her in the most despicable way possible.

Sometimes it's better not to know.

'Oh dear God, Greg. She's known all along.'

Chapter 21

What would you do if you found out your best friend's husband was having an affair?

Tell the friend.

Tackle the husband.

Say nothing.

Tell the friend, Alison had insisted. Tell the friend, otherwise what kind of a friend were you? If you tackled the husband and the friend found out later that you'd spoken to him instead of her, she would be justifiably furious, thinking you'd colluded with him in some way. You'd tell the friend, or she'd never trust you again. And if you said nothing you were just lily-livered, avoiding all responsibility, too scared of getting your hands dirty to do the right thing. She'd been adamant, cutting across all other arguments. You told the friend. Otherwise you were no better than the cheating husband.

'I don't know what to do now,' I said unexpectedly.

'What d'you mean?'

I looked over at the museum again. Adam was still there, looking impatiently at his watch and scanning the road outside the museum. As I watched, he pushed the door open and disappeared inside, reappearing a moment later and resuming his vigil at the door once again. It was ten past one, though it felt to me as though we'd been sitting inside the little restaurant for much longer than fifteen minutes.

'I don't know what do say to Alison.' As I spoke, Adam obviously decided he'd stood around for long enough, and made his way down the steps and across the road towards us. I shrank back from the window.

'He's heading this way.' I buried my head in the menu.

He strode briskly along the street, his eyes fixed ahead of him, though once he turned around and took a last look at the entrance to the museum, as though his date might have materialised as soon as he had left. I peered at him from behind the menu, feeling ridiculous. Just as he drew level with the window he spotted a taxi sporting an orange 'For Hire' sign, and waved it to a halt. He pulled the door open and climbed inside, and for a brief second it seemed to me that his eye caught mine as the taxi pulled away. I dived quickly back behind the menu.

'I do see a difference, close up,' Greg mused, watching the taxi disappear. 'But all the same, the likeness is remarkable. Though it's a while since I saw Max,' he added. Then he turned back to me. 'It's all right: you can come out now. He's gone.'

I emerged from behind the menu and set it back down on the table.

'What did you mean, you don't know what to say to Alison? Why do you have to say anything, if she knows already?'

I gave a sigh. 'Can you imagine how difficult it's going to be now, turning up at visiting time with this knowledge hanging around my neck, trying to pretend that I *don't* know? Things were excruciating enough when we both thought it was Max who was having the affair. But then of course Alison put two and two together and – oh!' I stopped suddenly. A niggling thought was beginning to germinate.

'What?'

'Just a minute. I need to think.'

You tell the friend. Otherwise you're no better than the cheating husband.

But Alison knew – she *knew* – that Max *hadn't* been having an affair. Surely the same rules had to apply? You told the friend. Otherwise what kind of a friend were you?

And yet she'd said nothing.

I'd gone through seven kinds of hell over the past fortnight, and my best friend – who could have put a stop to it in a heartbeat – had let me.

Sometimes it's better not to know.

And then suddenly I realised why Alison had changed rooms. It wasn't me she'd been trying to avoid. It was Adam. It wasn't me she couldn't stand to be alone with: it was him. That meaningful look she'd given me when she'd returned to the ward after her bath was nothing to do with whether I'd deleted my profile or not. It wasn't a reproach. It was an apology. And that last brief look of disgust I'd caught as I was leaving, the one that had hurt so much, wasn't meant for me.

She'd looked into my eyes, and believed herself to be unforgiven.

You'd tell the friend, or she'd never trust you again.

No: it wasn't me Alison was disgusted with.

It was herself.

Chapter 22

She was asleep when I arrived at the hospital shortly before three, having taken a taxi there straight from the station, light-headed from the champagne or the relief: it was hard to tell. Her face against the pillow had a bit more colour about it than I'd seen recently, though I'd learned not to read too much into physical signs. There was no evidence, today, of the sleeping room-mate I'd seen the previous evening: mercifully, we had the ward to ourselves.

I pulled out the visitor's chair and eased myself quietly into it, and then sat and studied her face, probing around inside my heart trying to work out what I was feeling. She looked so vulnerable, lying there with what remained of her ruined hair protruding from her scalp in tufts whilst a drip hanging above the bed pumped the latest drug into her wasted arm.

It wasn't anger, at any rate. Apprehension, perhaps? No: I felt too calm for it to be that.

You'd tell the friend, or she'd never trust you again.

Poor Alison. I remembered that dreadful dinner party game all over again. Suddenly our complacent moralising seemed farcical. How could you know what you would or wouldn't do in a given situation? Alison had judged and condemned herself based on opinions she'd formed at a time when life had seemed so much more cut and dried;

when her body wasn't infested with this infernal disease that was destroying her by degrees; when we'd both believed ourselves to be married to men who loved us; when it seemed we had everything to live for.

I recognised the feeling in a rush. It was compassion.

She must have felt my eyes upon her, because all of a sudden she woke up and looked at me.

'Fran.'

I gave her a rueful smile.

She struggled to sit up. 'I didn't think you'd come.' Her eyes glistened.

'I nearly didn't. I do have a life, you know.'

She gave a watery smile, and a tear spilled down her cheek.

'Alison—'

'I'm sorry.' It was little more than a whisper.

'Um.' I looked thoughtful. 'I suppose you're firing me.'

She looked confused for a moment, and then understanding dawned. 'It's not funny, Fran.' Another tear escaped. 'Though you're right: we can probably dispense with the matchmaking. I don't think Adam's going to be doing too much brooding, somehow.' She hesitated, plucking anxiously at the bedcover. 'How much do you hate me?'

I cupped a hand under her chin and made her look me in the eye. 'How much d'you think I hate you?'

The tears really started to flow then. 'I don't deserve you.'

'No, you don't,' I agreed, 'but then we all have our cross to bear. Now will you please stop crying? Or are you trying to get me thrown out again?'

She gave a strangulated sob that had a laugh tangled up in it somewhere. 'Oh, they won't throw you out.' She wiped the back of her hand across her eyes. 'These are good tears.' She busied herself with a tissue from the box beside the bed, blowing her nose noisily, and then used the act of looking for a bin as a smokescreen for her next question.

'When did you find out?'

'Ali—'

'No, really, Fran.' She turned to face me again. 'I need to know.'

Well, I could understand that particular sentiment. 'Not until this afternoon. He – um – he turned up for a date at lunch time.'

'I suppose after the whole Babylon episode, you could hardly write it off as a coincidence,' she said, giving a wry smile at the look of astonishment on my face. 'He told me he'd seen you there on Tuesday evening, and I put two and two together straight away. Smug bastard,' she finished with some heat.

'I didn't twig on Tuesday. He told me he was meeting a colleague. Someone called Boris. In fact, he even went over to speak to him – at least, I presumed it was him – so I figured – well, I don't know what I figured, really. It never entered my head that he might be lying.'

Alison gave a shrug. 'He's streets ahead of anyone I know when it comes to deception. Plus he knows half the regulars in there anyway – he uses the place all the time. It wouldn't be hard for him to cover his tracks.'

She seemed so resigned to Adam's duplicity: it broke my heart. When I'd thought it was Max who was playing around, my world had fallen apart. But Alison – well. Her world had already crumbled at her feet, the day she realised she probably wasn't going to be around to see her daughter grow up. Maybe, I decided, we only have room in our lives for one apocalypse at a time.

She shook her head and sighed. 'Poor old you. And poor old Max. Things okay between you two now?'

I shook my head. 'They will be. I haven't seen him yet.'

She gave me a look of dismay. 'Oh, Fran! Get out of here! Go on, now. Go and find him and straighten things out with him. I can't bear to think of what life has been like for the two of you this past couple of weeks. Oh – and Fran?'

'Mm-hmn?'

'Tell him – well, tell him—'

I nodded. 'Of course I will.' I leaned in to kiss her, and for a moment she held me close and hugged me, surprisingly hard for someone who was so ill.

'See you soon.'

'Don't go anywhere.' I grinned and took my leave.

I hummed all the way home. Now that I'd cleared the air with Alison, I couldn't wait to get back, to tell Max everything, to enjoy the first evening in what felt like weeks with nothing hanging in the air between us. As the taxi pulled up outside the house, I found I was whistling the tune from Brigadoon that Lottie liked so much.

It was still early. There was no sign of Max's car, and the house had a breathless, expectant feel to it when I pushed the front door shut behind me a little after half past four. As I made my way up the hall I spotted one of

Max's fleece jackets on the chair by the telephone, and I picked it up to take upstairs with me. Underneath it lay his rucksack.

My heart skipped a beat.

Even with the knowledge that it was Adam who was playing games and not Max, the old fear from this morning came flooding back.

My fingers trembled slightly as I tugged at the drawstring at the top of the bag. I thrust my hand inside, dreading that I might find some evidence to contradict what I'd learned this afternoon. My fingers closed around something hard, and I pulled it out.

It was a calculator.

I frowned at it in puzzlement, and opened the neck of the rucksack as wide as I could.

It was stuffed full of papers. Receipts, mostly, and copies of bills he'd issued to customers going back to the previous April.

Trust Max, I thought, relief flooding my body. Guy might have everything logged onto the computer in the workshop, but Max would have to go through the hard copies of everything, just to be sure that the books were in order for the tax return.

And I thought he'd used it for a change of clothes, so that he could go on a clandestine date with his mystery woman without anyone suspecting a thing.

I laughed out loud at my own foolishness, at the way the mind, once the subtle venom of suspicion has taken hold, can furnish the evidence to confirm the darkest fears.

The sound of a key in the door me made me turn.

'Something funny?' Max had pushed open the door and was regarding me warily.

'Nothing,' I said, smiling at him. 'Not a thing. Apart from your ridiculous, foolish wife, that is.' I wrapped my arms around his neck and kissed him full on the lips. A hard, determined kiss, full of generosity, not like the pathetic excuse for a kiss I'd allowed him that morning.

He was taken aback: that much was obvious. In fact, I couldn't swear to it, but it felt as though he recoiled from me as I leaned into him. I tightened my arms around his neck and applied myself more enthusiastically to kissing him.

And then, with great deliberation, he reached up and disengaged my arms, stepping back away from me with an unfathomable look on his face.

'Not just now, eh, Fran?' he said, and there was an edge to his voice I didn't recognise.

'What?' I had that same sensation I'd been getting for the past two weeks now, as though someone had cut away the ground from underneath me and I were falling into a bottomless chasm. There was something wrong, and I had no idea what it was. A sudden wave of panic swept through me. 'Where's Lottie?'

'At my mother's.' He pushed past me, grabbed the rucksack from the chair and headed up the stairs.

'Max?' I hurried after him. He had gone through to our bedroom and was rummaging around in one of his drawers. 'Why? What's she doing at your mother's?' I tried to rein in my muddled thoughts. Had we organised for her to stay with Max's parents? If we had, I couldn't remember. Mid-week sleepovers were usually out, because she had to be up so early for school. The rosy, not-a-care-in-the-world feeling I'd had all the way home was quickly deteriorating into the early throbbing of a headache.

'I didn't want her around,' Max said tonelessly, upending the rucksack onto the bed. Pens, calculator and a pile of papers littered the duvet.

'Why not?' I was completely bewildered now.

'Oh, come off it, Fran!' Max exploded, and I leapt away from him in alarm. He crossed back to the chest of drawers, scooping out a handful of underwear and slamming the drawer closed behind him.

'Max, what on earth is wrong?' I asked him, keeping out of his way as he stuffed the clothes into the rucksack.

He gave a bitter little laugh. 'You must have me down for a complete idiot,' he said. 'Running around after you all these months. Neglecting the business – *our* business, Fran – so that I could fetch Lottie from school and hold the fort here while you *went into hospital* to visit your sick friend.' My jaw dropped at the sarcasm in his voice. 'And to think that all the time, you were—' He crossed to his wardrobe and opened the door. 'Max the bloody mug, that's me,' he said to the clothes inside the wardrobe.

'Max, what are you talking about? I was what?'

'Jesus Christ, Fran!' Max erupted again, thumping his fist against the wardrobe door so hard that the panel in the front splintered. His anger was shocking: I found myself thinking that it was just as well he'd had the foresight to take Lottie to his parents' house.

'Max—' I began, holding my hands out in a gesture of

conciliation, but he interrupted, turning towards me, his eyes glittering.

'I *know*, Fran,' he said. 'So you can cut the crap.'

'Know what?' My head was starting to spin with confusion.

He turned away and lifted down a rugby shirt and a pair of jeans from the top shelf of the wardrobe, adding them to the other clothes in the rucksack. 'About what you've been up to.' He pulled the drawstring at the top of the rucksack angrily closed and dropped it onto the floor. 'Your little – affair.'

'My—?'

'Adam came to see me this afternoon.'

I sat down weakly on the edge of the bed. 'Did he?' I tried to think. Why would Adam go to see Max?

'Don't bother trying to deny it,' he went on. 'He saw you. Twice, now. Once this afternoon, in London. When stupid me thought you were at work. All that talk lately about how tired you've been, how hard things are in the office, how difficult it is seeing your best friend so sick. I've been jumping through hoops trying to support you, and you've been making secret assignations with your fancy man behind my back, drinking champagne, Adam said, though I didn't need him to tell me – I could taste it when you threw yourself at me just now. Infidelity doesn't suit you, Fran. You haven't got the cunning for it.'

I opened my mouth to protest, but Max swept on. 'He saw you the other night as well. Done up to the nines and practically falling out of your dress, in some fancy restaurant in the middle of London again, when you told me you were out at that work do. The one where the company was pulling out all the stops, you told me. No partners. Remember? Nobody else there, Adam said. Just you, sitting at the bar, waiting for your lover to arrive. What was it you said to me last week? People get bored, you said, and they do stupid things. And I was too dense to see what you were getting at.'

'Max, this is ludicrous. Adam's lying—'

'Is that right? Funny: Adam said you told him you were waiting for me. So who's the liar, Fran? Because I happen to know you weren't waiting for me at all. I was stuck in the workshop that night, doing the books with Guy.' He gave a sharp laugh. 'You've got some nerve, I'll give you that. What was it, Fran – just a cosy work celebration for two?'

I almost laughed out loud. 'This is all so ridiculous.'

'You know what really sickens me?' Max reached down to pick up the rucksack. 'The fact that you used your friend's illness as a cover for your disgusting little affair.'

'I never!'

'Adam says you've hardly been near the hospital these last few days. Is that true?'

'Yes, but—'

He gave a snort of disgust.

'It's not what you think!' I protested, panic making me defensive. 'Alison didn't want to see me. And Greg's just—'

'Ah. I should have known.' Max's shoulders slumped in defeat. 'Greg. You've always had a bit of a thing for him, haven't you?'

'No!'

'No wonder his wife left him. She probably just got wind of things a bit quicker than me, eh, Fran?'

'Max, this is spectacularly unfair! Greg and I – there's nothing going on between us. He's getting married in a few weeks. He was meeting his fiancée after his lunch with me to go and choose wedding rings!'

'Poor cow.' Max turned and headed for the door. 'Somebody should tip her off, before it's too late.'

'Where are you going?'

He stopped at the door and turned to look at me, and I found myself shrinking from the look of anguish on his face. 'I'm staying at Mum's tonight,' he said. 'I need some space to decide what I'm going to do.'

'Max, please – don't. We need to talk about this.'

He gave me a sad little smile. 'Like I said before, Fran – not just now, eh?' He wrinkled his nose as though he'd smelt something unpleasant. 'I need not to be around you for a bit.'

Then he closed the door behind him and was gone.

Chapter 23

How does life get to be so complicated? When we learn to lie as children, does it become so much a part of who we are that by the time we hit adulthood it's the truth that gives us all the problems? My mother had been wrong all those years ago after I'd lied to her about stealing the Jaffa Cakes: it wasn't when you lied that the ground opened up and swallowed you. It was when you were telling the truth, and somebody that mattered didn't believe you.

I tried to stop Max. I ran down the stairs after him and clung to his arm. He extricated himself just as deliberately as he'd disentangled himself from my earlier kiss. I pleaded, cajoled, protested my innocence. He was immovable. It was as though he had already made up his mind about my guilt, and wasn't going to brook any argument. I tried telling him again that it was Adam who had been playing about, Adam who had been on the secret assignations. 'Save it, Fran,' he'd said in answer. 'Save it for the birds.' And he'd climbed into his car and driven off, and I had stood on the doorstep and watched until he'd disappeared around the corner.

Then I went inside and fell apart.

I threw myself down onto the sofa and cried for what felt like hours. I let myself fall into a deep pit of self-pity, and wept at the injustice of what had just happened. I cried for the hurt I'd inadvertently caused Max; I cried out of grief for our relationship, and out of fear for what the future might hold. I cried angry tears at myself for agreeing to Alison's ridiculous scheme in the first place, berating myself for not having told her it was a disaster waiting to happen. I shed hot bitter tears at the devastation that I knew was still to come. I raged at the gods for allowing shit like cancer to destroy someone who had never done a mean thing to anybody in all the time I'd known her.

Finally, when I'd cried myself dry, I got mad. And that was when I called Adam.

'You low-down, deceiving little shit,' I said by way of a greeting.

'Francesca!' His voice was warm, laden with laughter. 'You just can't seem to get enough of me these days, can you?'

'How could you?'

'How could *I*? Oh no, Francesca: how could *you*? Poor Max is quite broken-hearted.'

'You bastard.' A great surge of anger swelled inside me. 'He's left me. Do you hear me? Because of your – *disgusting* lies.'

Adam gave an indignant laugh. 'I didn't want to tell him. But, after all, what kind of a friend would I be if I hadn't? That's what you think, isn't it, you and Alison? No holds barred, tell it like it is?'

'There isn't anything to tell!' I protested, and then kicked myself for sounding defensive with a man I loathed so completely.

'Really?' His tone was mocking. 'Well, that is very

strange. Because when you and I bumped into each other the other night in Babylon, I could have sworn you said you were meeting your husband. I thought to myself at the time, it isn't really Max's kind of place – I believe I may have even said something to you on that very subject – and it turns out I was right, because he claimed to know nothing at all about it. And if it wasn't Max you were meeting, Francesca, just who was the lucky beneficiary of that delectable silk number you were wearing? Hmmn?'

I didn't answer.

'Gone all bashful all of a sudden, have we? Well, I'm presuming it must have been the same person who was lusting over you at lunch time today. Unless you have more than one lover? No? Just the one, then. Lucky chap. Of course you knew I'd seen you, hiding away in that ridiculous manner behind the menu. Really, Fran, I never knew you had it in you: you've always struck me as a bit of a prig when it comes to affairs of the heart.'

'Go to hell, Adam.'

'Oh, now, don't be like that! This could be the beginning of a beautiful relationship. After all, it looks very much as though you and Max are headed for the rocks. And, as you know, the prognosis for my own marriage doesn't look much better, though for different reasons. Who knows what the future might hold?'

'You disgust me,' I said, and he allowed the laughter in his voice to spill over into the receiver.

'I can handle disgust,' he said. 'If you'd been indifferent – well, that would have been much harder to work with.

But disgust – now, that's got a bit of passion about it. And to think I once thought you a prude.'

I drew in my breath sharply. 'That's what this is about, isn't it? You're trashing my marriage because I wouldn't have some cheap little fling with you.'

'Oh, don't be ridiculous. That was years ago.' I could tell from his tone that I'd hit on something.

'You can deny it all you like. I can't believe you would hold a grudge for all this time.'

'What – you mean like the grudge you've held against me ever since that night?' His tone became bitter all of a sudden. 'You think I don't see the loathing in your eyes when you look at me? You're nothing but a hypocrite, Fran, and Max deserves better.'

'I'm hanging up.'

'Really? What a shame. Well, thank you so much for calling. I have enjoyed our chat. I'll look forward to telling Alison all about it when I see her this evening. I shan't pass on your regards – I got the distinct impression yesterday that she doesn't have a great deal of time for you these days.'

With that he replaced the receiver before I had recovered sufficient wit to beat him to it.

I actually screamed aloud after he'd hung up. I called him every name I could lay my tongue to. I threw the handset down so hard that the back came off and the battery went skittering under the chair. I kicked the bottom stair, and a bone in my toe cracked in protest. I screamed again, though without so much heat the second time. And finally, I retrieved the battery, reassembled the handset, and dialled Max's mobile.

There was no answer. Of course there wasn't. He would see the number and know it was me trying to reach him, and he would ignore it. The phone finally switched over to voicemail, and I left a short message saying that he was being ridiculous, and that we wouldn't solve anything if he ran away when I was trying to talk to him.

I regretted it the moment I had hung up. I'd sounded terse, I decided: even though I felt like the injured party, some small voice inside my head told me that Max hadn't been without justification for feeling the way he did, particularly after the malicious stunt Adam had pulled. I rang back and left a second message, more conciliatory this time, telling him I loved him and I wanted to see him, and imploring him to come back so that we could talk.

The tone of my second message brought on a fresh bout of tears, and I was still snivelling when my mobile started to shrill from the bedroom. I raced up the stairs to pick it up.

'Max?'

'Greg. Sorry.'

'Oh. Right.' I blinked back disappointment.

'I was just calling to see whether you wanted a lift in the morning.'

'What?'

'A lift. In my car.'

I tried to focus, though my head was reeling. Coming so hard on the heels of the accusations Max had just levelled at me, I thought for a moment that Greg was about to give truth to Adam's outrageous stories and suggest we run away together. 'Why? Are we going somewhere?'

'It's Friday, Fran. We're going to work. That's what we do on Fridays. And you left your car in the car park this morning when we went into London, remember? Look, if you're already sorted then it's no problem. I just thought I'd offer.'

'Oh! No – I mean, yes. A lift would be good. Thanks.'

'Are you all right? You sound a bit – odd.'

I gave myself a shake. *Get a grip, Fran.* 'Fine. I'm fine. Sorry. It's just – it's just the stress of it all. I'm knackered. Shouldn't drink at lunch time.' I needed to get off the line. 'I'll see you tomorrow, yeah?'

'Right. I have to be in smartish, so I'll be round about a quarter to eight. Is that okay?'

'Sure. Thanks, Greg.'

'Okay – well, bye, Fran. See you bright and early in the morning.'

I swallowed hard. 'See you, Greg.'

I cut the connection and took a deep breath, looking around the bedroom, inspecting the mess that Max had left behind when he'd stormed out. I made a half-hearted attempt to gather up the papers from the bed, and stacked them raggedly on the dressing-table. Then I went across and opened the drawer he'd ransacked earlier for underwear, and began tidying up what he'd left behind, as though straightening up the disorder might restore some sense of normality to what had quickly descended into a nightmare of an evening. After I'd finished with the drawer, I moved over to his wardrobe and opened it, running my finger along the splintered wood in the door and shuddering as I remembered the rage that had produced it. There was nothing to tidy inside the wardrobe, so I just stood and surveyed the clothes that were hanging inside. His ancient blue jumper was stuffed onto one of the shelves, and I took it out and buried my nose in it, inhaling deeply. What if we couldn't sort this out? What if this was more than an overnight sulk? Supposing he'd gone for good? Would this be all I had left of him: the lingering traces of his smell on a jumper?

I pulled the sweater over my head and pushed my arms into the sleeves. They were too long: they dangled a good few inches over the ends of my fingers. I wrapped my arms around my chest and hugged myself for a moment. If I closed my eyes and inhaled through the jumper, I could almost pretend that Max was hugging me. Then I sat down on the edge of the bed and leaned back into the pillows, turning onto my side and curling my legs up to my chest, my arms still wrapped tightly around my body, and I began to cry again: hot, silent tears that ran down the side of my cheeks and soaked away into the pillow, and blurred the numbers on the clock beside the bed as they worked their inexorable way into the night.

Chapter 24

I slept, eventually, though not before I'd watched the clock labouring through into the early hours of Friday morning. The night was interminable, long dark hours laden with despair, through which I tried a thousand means of figuring my way out of the mess I was in. When I did eventually slip into sleep I was cursed with a couple of hours of dreamless oblivion, so that when the beeping of the alarm penetrated my unconsciousness at seven o'clock the following morning I was forced to remember the whole nightmare afresh.

I fell reluctantly from the bed and stumbled into the shower, allowing the steaming water to wash over me for a good ten minutes before I lifted a hand for shampoo or soap. The whole situation had taken on an unreal quality: not so much as though it were happening to someone else, but more as though *I* had become someone else, masquerading as me. By the time I switched off the shower and wrapped myself in a towelling robe I half-expected to find my morning mug of tea from Max waiting on the bedside table when I came back through to the bedroom.

Its absence only served to emphasise my isolation. I lay down on the bed again, robe-clad and damp, and stared blankly at the ceiling, wondering what I was going to do with myself. Without Max and Lottie around, I felt as though I were spinning through a vortex with nothing solid to hold on to. The house was eerily quiet, with none of the usual weekday morning sounds to define it as our home. I closed my eyes and breathed deeply, in a vain attempt to settle the churning of my stomach.

I must have nodded off again, because when I opened my eyes for the second time that morning the clock was reading 7.45, and somewhere in the dark recesses of my mind I could hear a shrill, persistent ringing. It took me a moment to realise that it wasn't the alarm: that had already done its work forty-five minutes earlier. And then it hit me: it was the sound of somebody leaning relentlessly on the doorbell.

Greg. Shit. I shot off the bed and down the stairs, pulling the belt of the robe tightly around my waist in some attempt at respectability before opening the door, breathless and dishevelled, and far from ready for work.

'Sorry – God, sorry, Greg,' I apologised as he stepped into the hall with a wry look at my state of undress. 'I fell asleep after my shower.'

He regarded me quizzically. 'Rough night?'

I gave him a resigned look.

'Tell me it's the result of your grand reconciliation with Max.'

'Um. I suppose you could say that.' I ushered him through to the kitchen. 'Coffee?' I picked up the kettle and filled it.

He gave his watch a surreptitious look, and suddenly I remembered what he'd said about needing to be in early. 'Oh – crap. God, Greg, I'm sorry. I forgot. You have to get to the office early, don't you?'

He pulled a face. 'That was the general idea.' He shrugged himself resignedly out of the leather jacket he was wearing and hung it on the back of one of the kitchen chairs.

I hadn't thought it possible to feel worse than I'd felt on waking up a little under an hour ago, but it was. Now I had the added guilt of having let down a friend who'd been trying to do me a favour.

'I'm sorry. Look: you go. I'll get the bus in.' Absurdly, I felt tears threatening again, and I turned away from him and busied myself spooning coffee into the cafetière so that he wouldn't see my distress.

'Can't you get Max to drop you off?'

I froze, the spoon poised over the rim of the bag of coffee, and in the small hiatus that followed neither of us said a thing.

'He isn't here, is he?'

You could have shattered the silence with a whisper.

I felt rather than heard him come up behind me, and then a hand on my shoulder turned me around. The other hand cupped my chin and lifted it so that I was forced to look him in the eye. Then, without a word, he wrapped two strong shirt-clad arms around me, enveloping me in a tight hug, and I fell into him and began to weep all over again.

We must have stood like that for five minutes or more, while I did nothing but cry, his shirt soaking up my tears the way the pillow had soaked them up the previous night. Throughout it all he never spoke: he just held me and stroked my hair and let me cry, using his thumb to wipe the tears from the side of the cheek that wasn't pressed to his shirt. I wanted so much for it to be Max who was holding me, and the fact that it wasn't only made me weep all the harder.

Eventually the crying gave way to a few hiccupping sobs, and I drew back a little from Greg, feeling suddenly embarrassed at my lack of clothing. The front of his shirt was a mess. I drew a deep, shuddering sigh.

'I seem to do nothing but cry on you lately,' I said ruefully.

He gave me an inscrutable look, still holding me loosely in his arms. 'That's what friends are for,' he answered eventually.

'I'd better—' I gestured towards the door with my head.

'Fran—' he began, and I froze.

He looked as though he were about to say something, and then collected himself.

'Nothing. I'll make some coffee, shall I?'

I ran a hand across the front of his shirt. 'I've soaked you. I'm sorry.'

He made a dismissive motion with his head. 'Doesn't matter. I'll stick it on the radiator while the coffee brews.' He still hadn't let go of my arms.

'Right: well, I'll—' I pulled against his hands slightly, and he released me, running his fingers through his hair awkwardly before folding his hands behind his head as if to keep them from doing anything untoward. I could feel his eyes upon me still as I left the kitchen and went upstairs to get dressed.

By the time I came down some ten minutes later I was feeling slightly more in control of myself. Greg had his back to me as I came into the kitchen and was staring out of the window, a mug of coffee cradled in his hands. His shirt was draped over the kitchen radiator; his tie hung over the back of the chair on top of the jacket; and the pale blue T-shirt he was down to had a feeling of incongruity about it, as though the person wearing it were a stand-in for the man who normally hung around the kitchen in the mornings, brewing coffee and sharing inconsequential talk with me before we both went off to work. He turned as he heard me behind him and, putting the mug down on the worktop, wrapped me in another bear hug.

'Better?'

I nodded, my cheek against the T-shirt. Through the thin fabric I could feel the soft beating of his heart. 'No crying, now,' he said, mock-sternly, nuzzling the top of my head with his chin. 'I'll have nothing left to wear for work.'

I smiled against his chest and didn't answer, stamping down firmly on the little worm of unease that was squirming around somewhere in my stomach, reminding me that this man had once kissed me and that, under different circumstances, I might have enjoyed the fact that he had. Might even enjoy it now, in fact, I was feeling so shit about myself. All I'd have to do would be to lift my head up off his chest and look him in the eye.

I sighed and kept my head where it was, contenting myself with the comforting warmth of another human being. We were still standing with our arms around each other when a movement in the doorway made me look up.

'Max!' I straightened up, feeling wrong-footed once again.

His gaze swept the kitchen, taking in the coffee, the jacket and tie on the chair, the shirt hanging on the radiator, before coming to rest on Greg and me.

'You don't waste much time, I'll give you that,' he said, turning towards the front door.

'Max – stop! It's not like that!' I protested. I hurried after him into the hall.

'I got your message,' he said stonily. 'I didn't pick it up until this morning: I'd left my phone in the car. I said to myself, "She's right, Max. You're being ridiculous. And we won't sort anything out if you don't go home and talk to her properly." So I came home. I thought I'd catch you before you went to work.' He gestured towards the kitchen. 'Nice homecoming.'

'Max, please. Listen to me.'

'Why? So that you can think up a pack of lies to try to cover up whatever sordid little mess you've got yourself into? Leave it, Fran,' he said, holding a hand up as though to ward me off. 'Just – leave it.'

'Max.' Greg had followed us through to the hall. 'I really think you should listen to what Fran has to say.'

Max pushed past me and squared up in front of Greg, holding a finger threateningly under his nose. 'Don't you dare tell me what to do,' he spat. 'Who the hell d'you think you are, coming into my home and laying down the law? Not to mention helping yourself to my wife.'

'Max – he hasn't!' I protested.

'Not much, he hasn't.' Max shoved Greg's shoulders with the palms of his hands. 'Think I'm blind, do you? Eight o'clock in the bloody morning and you're cosying up together in my kitchen. I suppose you spent the night,' he added bitterly. He shoved again. Greg remained impassive, keeping both hands resolutely by his sides.

'Stop it, Max!' I protested, stepping between the two of them. 'Of course Greg didn't spend the night. He came to give me a lift to work.'

'You know what?' Max held both hands up suddenly in a gesture of surrender and stepped back to regard us both in disgust. 'You're not worth it, either of you.' He turned and made his way towards the front door again. 'You're welcome to her, Greg. In fact, you deserve each other.'

He was almost out of the door when Greg spoke.

'She certainly doesn't deserve a prat like you for a husband.'

This time Max didn't hesitate. In one swift move he crossed the hall, so quickly I had barely enough time to lift a hand in protest, and drove his fist into Greg's face. Greg crumpled, clutching his nose, but still made no attempt to retaliate. I stood watching in horror, not knowing which of them to go to first. And then Max took the decision away from me by turning on his heel and leaving without so much as a glance in my direction.

Chapter 25

Only after the door had closed on Max did Greg allow his control to slip. 'Jesus Christ,' were his first words from the floor, followed by, 'I think he broke my nose.'

I stood frozen for a moment, staring at the door, and a wave of nausea swept over me. Max's departure had ripped a jagged hole somewhere deep inside me. I'd never, in ten years of marriage, seen such anger – hadn't known that he was capable of it. I slid down the wall and joined Greg on the carpet, wrapping my arms around my shoulders, numb with despair.

'Fran?'

'Mmn?' I realised I'd been staring at the skirting board opposite. 'Oh God, Greg – I'm so sorry!'

He was bleeding copiously over his T-shirt. I jumped up and helped him to his feet, ushering him solicitously back through to the kitchen and settling him in a chair before soaking a cloth in cold water and passing it to him. While he cleaned up the worst of the mess, I wrapped a bag of peas from the freezer in a tea towel and brought them across to him, instructing him to tilt his head back. He swore quietly as I placed the pack as gently as I could over the bridge of his ravaged nose.

'That's some right hook your husband's got.'

'Mmn,' I said again, dropping into a chair, a blank

numbness settling back onto my shoulders. There had been something final about the way Max had left: a bruised look in his eyes as he'd shouldered past me that made me realise just how unreachable he'd become. I wanted to go to him and put my hand into his heart and take the pain away. And I wanted to kill Adam for putting it there in the first place.

'Fran.' Greg had put the improvised ice pack down and was regarding me through smarting eyes. 'You have got to get a grip.'

I looked at him bleakly. 'He's gone, Greg. I've lost him.' I replaced the ice pack distractedly. 'Keep that on. It will help the swelling.'

'Of course he hasn't gone,' Greg countered, lowering the ice pack once again. 'He just over-reacted to finding me in his kitchen straight after whatever happened between the two of you last night. And by the way, what did happen? I'd have thought you'd have spent the night celebrating.' He winced suddenly and put the ice pack back.

I gave a bitter laugh, and immediately sobered. 'Adam got to him before me. I stopped in at the hospital on my way home, and while I was there Adam went round to the workshop and collared Max. He told him I was having an affair: said he'd bumped into me twice now. Max went and picked up Lottie from school and took her round to his parents, and then he came home to confront me.'

'But why didn't you just tell him what's been going on?'

'I tried!' My voice rose on a wail. 'But he wouldn't listen. He'd twisted everything around – or at least Adam had – and made the whole thing look very damning. He accused me of using Alison's illness to cover up my sordid little affair, as he called it.'

'All the same. There's a bit of a leap between thinking your wife's playing away and decking the next bloke you see her with.'

'Well, you did call him a prat, remember. It wasn't an unreasonable assumption to make. Particularly when—' I broke off.

Greg lifted the ice pack from his eyes. If he could have narrowed them at me, he would have. 'Particularly when what?'

'Well, you were standing in his kitchen with your arms around me and half your clothes hanging off the furniture.'

Greg tutted. 'Knock it off, Fran. That wasn't what you meant. Particularly when what?'

'Nothing.' I studied a fingernail. Greg continued to regard me quizzically.

'Oh—' I gave an exasperated sigh. 'The thing is, he knew it was you I was with in London yesterday.'

Greg's brow furrowed. 'How did he know that?'

'Well – I told him,' I said sheepishly.

He gave a sigh. 'Fran, are you *trying* to get me killed?'

'Of course I'm not.' I shrugged impatiently. 'Look, it's not as if we had anything to hide. Why shouldn't I have told him? In the context of, "Greg came to London with me to help me find out why you were having an affair", it's not such a ridiculous thing to have done.'

'No, it's not. What I want to know, though, is how we got from the Greg-supporting-a-friend-in-need scenario to the point where Max decks Greg and Greg ends up with a broken nose.'

'Well, I never got around to telling him I'd thought he was having an affair. The moment I mentioned your name he just—' I stopped again, embarrassment making me squirm. 'He jumped to the wrong conclusion.'

'No: really?' Greg grimaced in pain. 'That much was obvious. But why on earth would he think you and I were – you know? I mean, this was yesterday, right? Before the whole clothes-hanging-off-the radiator moment.'

I swallowed. 'He—' I was cringing inside.

'He what? Come on, Fran: I just took a bullet for you. Stop holding out on me.'

'He said I've always had a bit of a thing for you …' I trailed off, feeling mortified.

There was a small hiatus. Then Greg spoke.

'Ah.'

He placed the ice pack very carefully on the table, and I made no move this time to put it back. Then he cleared his throat.

'And have you?' He regarded me through smarting eyes without moving.

I knew he was thinking about the time he'd kissed me, because I was too. You could have cut the air with a knife.

'Greg—' I stopped. Whatever I said now, it seemed, would only make things worse.

'Have you, Fran?' he asked, more quietly this time.

A tear began to trickle down my cheek. *Yes*, a part of me wanted to say, and another tear followed the first, because I realised that Max hadn't been entirely wrong in his suspicions, and no matter what lies had been told yesterday, it wasn't Adam who had brought about that empty, defeated look in his eyes. It was me.

'Because if we're going to be completely honest with each other, *I* have, you see. I definitely have a bit of a thing for you.'

In the silence that followed my heart started to thump so loudly I was surprised he couldn't hear it. I looked at him in dismay. 'You don't mean that.'

He reached out and covered my hands with his own. 'If there were no Max in the world, I wouldn't let another man within fifty yards of you if I could help it.'

If there were no Max in the world. My heart continued to hammer in my chest. I had never felt more alone in my life.

I sat for a few moments staring at our clasped hands, trying to digest what Greg had just said. His hands were smoother than Max's, which had roughened over the years from too much exposure to dodgy car engines in an under-heated garage. I could see them now in my mind, the backs of them creased like a well-used map, the nails outlined more often than not with a trace of engine oil that nothing other than a long soak in a hot bath would shift. 'I love Max, Greg,' I said to the table. Then I lifted my head and looked him in the eyes. 'I love Max.'

For a moment it seemed that something sparkled beyond his smarting eyes. And then a shutter came down over whatever it was I'd seen and he straightened up, lifting the ice pack back into position.

The fragile, ragged feeling that hung in the air between us was suddenly rent apart by the clamorous ringing of the telephone. I let my eyes linger on Greg's face for a moment before pushing back my chair and crossing through to the hall to answer it.

'Mrs Howie?' The tone was brisk, businesslike.

I swallowed, trying to clear my head of what had just happened. 'Speaking.'

'This is Sister Harrington from the Infirmary. I'm calling you because Mrs Beckett named you on her admission sheet as a next of kin.'

No. My mouth went dry. I felt as though I had swallowed a large piece of lead.

There was a silence from the other end of the line, and I knew without a shadow of a doubt that the nurse was weighing up how to tell me that my friend had died and I hadn't been there for her.

'Something's happened, hasn't it?'

'I'm afraid so.' The nurse's tone was clipped. 'I've tried to reach her husband, but I haven't been able to get hold of him.'

'When?' The question came out automatically: I didn't want to know. If she didn't tell me, it might not be real, might it? I took a deep breath. 'When did it happen?'

'About half an hour ago.' That same brisk tone. She even sounded a bit pissed off. 'We aren't very happy about it, Mrs Howie, but there was nothing we could do.'

'No – I'm sure you did all you could.' I was speaking automatically now, not really focusing on what I was saying. 'Did she – was she in any pain?' I reached out a hand to the wall to steady myself.

'Not that she would admit to.'

Did she have to sound so matter-of-fact? I bit my lip, feeling the now-familiar tears starting to spill down my cheeks again. At this rate my eyes would be as red and swollen as Greg's. 'Was there somebody with her? I mean, she wasn't alone, was she?'

'Of course she wasn't alone,' came the tart rejoinder. 'I was with her myself. As a matter of fact, I spent a good half-hour trying to persuade her not to leave us, but she had obviously made up her mind.' She gave a disgruntled sniff. 'We were hoping that you might have some idea where she may have gone.'

I stiffened, confused. 'I beg your pardon?'

'I tried her home number, but nobody is answering. And as I said, I haven't been able to reach her husband. We're all very concerned for her health.'

'I – what?' My voice rose a notch. 'Her health? I thought you said she was dead.'

There was a spluttering sound from the other end of the line. 'Dead? Where on earth did you get that impression?'

'But you just said—'

'Mrs Beckett discharged herself, Mrs Howie. About half an hour ago, as I said. Against the advice of every medical professional on this ward, I might add.'

'*What?*' I collapsed against the wall, relief flooding my body. 'I thought – oh, thank God!'

The nurse made a disapproving noise in her throat. 'Mrs Howie, your friend is very sick. If you should see her, I do urge you to try to get her to reconsider her decision. She needs specialised care.'

'Yes. Yes, of course I will.'

I hung up, my mind in a spin. So Alison had discharged herself. How? When I'd seen her yesterday she'd been hooked up to a drip and looked barely capable of standing. And where would she have gone? Not home, I wouldn't have thought – not with what she'd discovered about Adam. To her parents' house, maybe? They'd had Erin staying with them since Alison had been admitted to hospital. I thought about calling them to check; I actually reached out and picked up the receiver to dial the number.

Then suddenly I knew, beyond a shadow of a doubt, where she'd have gone.

I replaced the receiver in its cradle and went and opened the front door.

She was still far too pale. And far too thin. But she'd procured a beanie hat from somewhere and had pulled it down to cover her hair. She was dressed for the first time in weeks. The drip was gone. And she was there, standing on my doorstep, and she smiled at me as I swung open the door.

'Can you lend me twenty quid for the taxi?' she asked, before collapsing into my arms.

Chapter 26

'You look amazing.'

'Liar. I look like shit.'

We'd been here before, I remembered, and so did she, and it made us both smile. I was sitting in an armchair opposite the sofa, where Greg had lain her down after carrying her into the house. He had paid the taxi, too, and called the office to tell them neither of us would be in, doubtless sparking off a whole raft of speculation, before coming back through to the sitting-room.

'I'm going to make a brew,' he informed me.

'No, Greg – you're hurt. I'll do it.'

'I can manage.' He waved an arm towards Alison. 'You stay with your friend.'

Alison gave me an enquiring look as he left the room. 'Is there a reason you have a bloodstained demi-god in your house?'

'Yes,' I answered shortly. 'But before we get into that, is there a reason I have a sick friend who's supposed to be in hospital in my house? I've just had them on the phone, Ali. They want you back.'

She grinned at me mischievously. 'God, Fran, you should have seen their faces. They were so annoyed with me.'

'They're worried about you, hon.' I took one of her hands in mine. 'So am I. You should be in bed.'

She gave a short laugh. 'I would have thought Adam was doing enough of that for both of us.' Then she smiled tiredly. 'Kidding. Though he's the real reason I'm here.'

I frowned at her. 'I don't follow.'

'Sure you do.' She leaned her head against the back of the sofa and closed her eyes briefly. 'I had to come, Fran. I had no choice. I had to come for Erin. You don't really think I'm going to lie around in a hospital bed anchored by drips and God-knows-what and leave her with that bastard, do you? I mean, I actually thought he'd turned over a leaf, you know? I thought the cancer had done at least that.'

'Alison, I don't understand.'

She lifted her head to look at me. 'He's been playing around for years, Frannie. There've been at least four indiscretions that I know of. I don't like to think how many there are that I don't. But I never, ever, thought he'd stoop this low. I mean, I haven't even died yet. Has he no decency?' She smiled resignedly at the look of shock on my face. 'That was a rhetorical question, by the way.'

'You never told me.' *Why* had she never told me? I began to feel irrationally angry with her. 'What does that say about our friendship?'

She leaned towards me and squeezed my hand. 'It says that I love you enough not to want to dump all my crap on you. Not to let Adam and his infidelities define our relationship – yours and mine. It wasn't some secret I knew about Max that I was keeping from you.' She wrinkled her nose. 'This was something that I knew about Adam: something that I didn't really want to admit to myself.' She sighed, and then gave a weary shrug. 'Anyway, it's a bit late for all that now.'

I thought about what she'd said. Maybe she had a point. Maybe lying to yourself is different from lying to a friend. Maybe it's easier for the friend to forgive.

I looked at her ruefully. 'So when I came blundering in with that picture, convinced that Max was up to something—'

'I knew the game was up,' Alison cut in. 'And yes, I was mad. I was mad with myself for ever dreaming up that stupid plot to find Adam a wife. I knew in my heart he probably wouldn't be on his own for long anyway. I suppose I thought that if I got you on side, you might make sure he picked someone suitable. Someone who would be nice to Erin, at any rate. And then when it all went awry, I was mad at you, because I *knew* you wouldn't be able to leave it alone.' The soft smile she gave me took the sting out of her words. 'But then I went back to being mad with myself again. Especially for what I let you and Max go through. I don't think I'll ever forgive myself for that.' She narrowed her eyes at me. 'Which brings me back to my question.' She gestured towards the door with her head. 'Who's the hunk?'

I wondered how to break it to her gently. 'He's a colleague. He came to give me a lift to work.'

'Don't be so annoying: you know what I mean. Why is his face in such a mess?'

'Oh – that.' *Keep it light, Fran,* I told myself. 'Max hit him,' I said airily.

Alison looked at me sceptically. 'Cut it out, Fran. Really: why's he here?'

'I'm serious. Max thinks I'm having an affair with him. And so he hit him. Just before he walked out on me.'

I wouldn't have thought it possible, but Alison paled. 'So it's true,' she said, confusing me. Her shoulders slumped. 'And tell me, Fran – just so that I can be absolutely clear – why on earth would Max think you were doing something like that?'

I hesitated for a moment before driving the final nail into the coffin of her marriage. 'Because Adam told him I was.'

Chapter 27

Before Alison could comment on my bombshell, Greg came back through from the kitchen with a tray. His nose had stopped bleeding, though his eyes still looked a little swollen. Alison leaned across to squint at his face as he eased himself into the other armchair, and sucked in her breath.

'Sore. Is it broken? Sorry for barging in, by the way.'

He waved an arm dismissively. 'Hey, I carried you over the doorstep. We're practically married.'

'I'm Fran's friend, Alison.'

'I kind of guessed.' He held out a hand. 'I'm Greg.'

'Greg!' Alison's face split into a beam. 'Greg who met his fiancée on the web. You know, we're all in the most terrible mess because of you.' She grinned at him. She seemed so buoyed up: it was hard to equate with the girl I'd been visiting in hospital for the past few months, not to mention the one who had collapsed on my front doorstep not half an hour before.

'Yeah – I think I figured that one out, too.' Greg touched his nose tentatively. 'How do I tell if it's broken?'

Alison took his chin in her hand and tilted his head forwards. 'Doesn't look too wonky. That's a good sign. Can I?' She reached out her other hand and touched his nose gently, feeling along each side before pinching it tentatively between thumb and forefinger, making his eyes water again. 'Does that feel like it's grating to you?'

'Ouch – no. I don't think so.'

She leaned back into the sofa. 'You won't really be able to tell properly for a few days, until the swelling goes down. But initial diagnosis – no. I don't think it's broken. You're going to have a couple of shiners tomorrow, though. Take some Panadol for the pain. Not ibuprofen.' She smiled at the look of surprise on Greg's face. 'I used to be a nurse before I had Erin.'

'Speaking of which,' I interrupted, 'shouldn't you think about getting back to the hospital, Ali? Seriously. Whatever it is you want to do, we can plan it from there.'

'Like we planned our last campaign, you mean?' She shook her head determinedly. 'I'm not going back, Fran. I can't think straight when I'm strapped to a hospital bed by a drip.'

'Yes, but that drip was important!'

She shook her head again. 'I don't need it.'

'But – the drugs—'

'I'm taking them orally – at least, I will be. I saw the oncologist yesterday, after you left.' Her eyes shone. 'He didn't want to say anything before he was sure, but he's been running tests for weeks now.' She paused dramatically. 'Yesterday he told me I was N.E.D.' She beamed at us. 'He's American,' she added, as if that explained everything.

I looked at her blankly. 'N.E.D.?'

'It stands for no evidence of disease,' she clarified.

I still didn't get it. 'What does that mean?'

She leaned towards me, her hands clasped in front of her

knees. 'It means there's no evidence of disease.' Her eyes sparkled. 'It's gone, Fran. That awful thing that's been growing inside me. It's gone. There might still be some microscopic tumour in there somewhere, but everything they've been blasting for so long now has gone. I'm in complete remission.'

'What?' I looked at her in confusion. 'But – you can't be.'

She gave a laugh. 'Why can't I? It happens, you know. There was that woman, remember, who sued the NHS because they wouldn't give her the drugs she needed, and then she went into remission.'

'What woman?'

'I can't remember her name. What does it matter, anyway? I'm just saying. It happened to her. And it's happened to me.' She leaned forwards and punched me lightly on the arm. 'Don't tell me you're not pleased.'

I stared at her, wanting to believe her, looking hard into her eyes. And then it seemed that the room in which we were sitting somehow shrank into a tight ball around my heart and exploded and I burst into tears.

A pair of slender arms wrapped themselves around my neck. She was crying, too: I could feel the hot tears on my cheek, merging with my own tears and spilling down our necks together like a balm. I kept her like that for a long time, hugging her tightly to my chest while my body rid itself of its own cancer of grief, the one I'd been carrying around inside me ever since she'd first been diagnosed. It poured out of me and spilled onto the floor and ran away, until finally I was emptied and exhausted and able to draw back a little, still hanging on to her hands.

'I'm not cured,' Alison warned me, easing us back onto the sofa. 'But I'm better than I was. Of course, they wanted to do a whole barrage of tests to be sure, but there wasn't time. That's why they were all so mad when I said I was leaving.' She grinned at me. 'I've even got a bit of hair: look. She pulled the beanie from her head and ran her hand over her scalp.

'But – how?' I leaned over and examined her scalp, but couldn't see anything in the way of new growth, and hoped the whole business wasn't wishful thinking on Alison's part. 'Don't tell me they found that miracle drug after all.'

'I found it myself.' She set her mouth in a firm line. 'I knew Adam was a bit of a shit, but even I never thought he would stoop so low as to pull a stunt like this while I was wasting away in hospital. I have to put it right, don't you see? Particularly since the whole mess is my fault in the first place.'

She leaned back against the cushions and closed her eyes, tired all of a sudden.

'You should rest,' I said. 'You're all in.' I looked around suddenly. 'Where's Greg?'

I found him out in the kitchen, his hands holding on to the front of the sink, staring out of the window. He turned when he heard me behind him and gave me a lopsided smile.

'It's great news.'

'Yes.' I drew a deep, shuddering sigh. 'Yes, it is.'

'I thought I'd—' He gestured. 'You know. Give you both a bit of privacy.'

'Thanks.'

We regarded one another for a moment in silence. 'Did you find the Panadol?' I asked eventually.

He never took his eyes off me. 'No. I haven't looked.'

I crossed to the cupboard where we kept a rudimentary first aid kit and lifted out a small bottle. 'Here.' I held it out to him.

'Fran—' He took hold of the hand that was proffering the painkillers, and then immediately dropped it. 'Look – I should go. You two have a lot of talking to do.' He ducked his head away from me abruptly.

'Hey.' I caught hold of his arm and leaned around so that I could see his face, which he tried to keep averted from me. 'Hey.' And then I realised that he was fighting to keep control of himself.

'Greg, what is it?'

His mouth twisted. 'She's lucky, your friend Alison.'

'I know. I can't believe the cancer's just disappeared like that.'

He squeezed his eyes closed and shook his head. 'That's not what I meant.' He looked back down at me.

He looked so woebegone, his eyes full of anguish that had nothing to do with the wallop he'd had from Max earlier. Before I could stop myself I put my arms around him the way he'd done with me earlier that morning, and let him lean on me while he dealt with his own pain.

Never mind that he was getting married in a few weeks, and that this was just complicating the whole mess even further. Never mind that I had a friend through in the sitting-room who had absconded from hospital that very morning, and a husband who had walked out on me a couple of hours earlier. Never mind that my life was a quagmire of crises and that I didn't know where to start to sort them all out. Sometimes you just needed to find someone to lean on until you found the strength to stand on your own again. And frankly, right now in the kitchen, I wasn't sure who was doing the most leaning.

Eventually he straightened up in my arms. I could feel him pulling himself together. 'Right,' he said, inhaling deeply. 'Come on.'

'Where are we going?'

'I'm not leaving you to straighten out this mess on your own. God knows where we'll all end up. First things first, though, eh?' He gave me another wobbly smile. 'One way or another, we have to work out how we're going to get you your husband back.'

Chapter 28

'We need proof,' Alison said decisively, tutting at the look of scepticism on my face. 'Trust me, Fran: it's the only thing that will work. We need hard and fast evidence of what Adam's been up to.'

It was lunch time, and we were still ensconced in the living-room, which had taken on the appearance of a campaign party headquarters. There were papers scattered around us: printouts of Max's advert from the dating site, along with my own advert; copies of the emails Adam and I had exchanged; credit card statements dating back to the month when the account was set up, which I had insisted upon checking just to eliminate any last possibility that we might have got everything horribly wrong (or horribly right, depending on how you looked at the thing) and that Max really had put the advert on the site himself. Amongst all the papers were scattered crumb-covered plates and empty coffee mugs, the detritus from a long morning's debate followed by a piecemeal lunch.

I started to stack the plates tiredly. After the drama of the morning, the day already felt as though it had lasted longer than a week, and I was exhausted. 'What difference will having proof make? Max won't even hang around long enough to give me a chance to explain.' I had repeatedly tried calling Max's mobile with no success. I'd rung the garage, too, and Guy had answered, sounding surprised when I asked for Max, and saying that he had called to say he wouldn't be in today. I wouldn't have thought it possible to feel any more humiliated, but finally I called his mother's house and found myself almost immediately wrong-footed when she told me that Max had taken Lottie out of school for the day and the two of them were on their way up to his brother's house in Penrith for the weekend. Her manner towards me had been wary though solicitous: obviously she knew there'd been a fight, but Max couldn't have voiced the worst of his suspicions to her. I balked at the prospect of phoning his brother: aside from anything else, they wouldn't be arriving much before tea time, and I didn't relish the prospect of having to try to explain the whole sorry mess to anyone else.

Alison's tone was conciliatory. 'Look. Max is upset—'

'So am I!' I wailed.

'I know you are, sweetie, but this isn't about you. It's Max we're trying to sort out. I mean, one minute there he was, being a devoted husband and father and running around after you while you ran yourself ragged between work and visiting me and everything, and the next he's watching you dress yourself up and disappear off for the night, leaving him with some cock-and-bull story about a company bash. And then along comes Adam, who tells him he's seen you cavorting all over London with another man. It's no wonder he thinks the worst. But once we discredit Adam then the whole charade will crumble and Max will come home.'

'Max will come home anyway,' I said, sounding more

confident than I felt. 'Just as soon as I manage to speak to him. I'll make him listen. I will. And he'll believe me: he won't need evidence.'

Alison gave me a sympathetic look. 'I'm sure you're right,' she said, 'but it won't do any harm to have some insurance.'

I pursed my lips sceptically. 'Why can't we just call Adam and tell him we know what he's done?'

'Because we can't prove a thing.' Alison added a mug to the pile of plates. 'That's my point. If we did that, he would just deny having the first clue what we were talking about, and we'd be no further on than we are now. Face it: he probably doesn't even know you're "Sassy". He's so wrapped up in himself, it won't have occurred to him that you've been out to trap him. I know it's no consolation at all, but he probably genuinely believes you two are up to something.' She raised what was left of her eyebrows at Greg and me, and I felt myself flush. 'But if we get proof, he can't deny it and Max will see what a low life he really is. And Adam will have to give me a divorce.'

'I think Alison has a point,' Greg chipped in. 'You need something tangible to show Max, to make him stop and pay attention instead of going off the deep end. Preferably something we can post,' he added feelingly.

'I don't!' I was still unconvinced. 'I just need to speak to Max. Anyway, it's not as if we can call in the maître 'd from Babylon as a witness.'

Alison wrinkled her nose. 'Wouldn't work anyway. It's still all hearsay. We need to catch him *in flagrante*, as it were, and get pictures.'

'Well, I don't see how we're going to manage that.' I sighed. 'It's not as if we know his every sordid little move.'

'We could have him followed,' Alison suggested. 'Hire a private detective or something.'

'Oh, Alison!' I protested. 'Don't be ridiculous.'

'Just a minute.' Greg was looking thoughtful. 'I think I've got an idea.' He pursed his lips at Alison. 'You reckon he doesn't know that Fran's "Sassy", right? That he really hasn't connected the dating site with Fran and me.'

Alison nodded. 'I'm almost sure of it. If he had, he wouldn't have been able to resist crowing when she rang him up. I know he wouldn't.'

'In which case—' He stroked his chin thoughtfully. 'We could use the account to set him up.'

'How?'

'Easy.' He grinned at us both lasciviously. 'We bait the trap. We'll put a picture up of a beautiful girl – someone he just won't be able to resist – and then we'll email him with some cock-and-bull story about how we managed to miss each other yesterday.' He was warming to his theme. 'We'll say we only got there at one-fifteen, and sound a bit hurt that he hadn't waited for us – put him on the defensive. That should convince him that *somebody* turned up, at any rate. And then once we've got the dialogue going, we send our beautiful girl on a proper date with him, and you and I, Fran, will follow them and take pictures.'

I looked at him as though he were insane. 'That blow to the face must have knocked your brain clean out of your ears.' I shook my head at him. 'Even supposing you and I managed to pull off this whole Starsky and Hutch act –

which, if you ask me, is the tiniest bit optimistic – where on earth are we going to find a beautiful girl? And not just any old beautiful girl: one who's prepared to kiss the bastard?'

'No problem.' Greg was unabashed. 'I'll ask Cheryl.'

I almost dropped the plates. 'Greg, you can't!'

'Of course I can.'

'You can't! You can't do that to her.'

'Do what to her? It's just an acting job. She spent three years at drama school before she got into modelling. She'll be well up for it. Particularly when I tell her I'll probably have a couple of shiners for the wedding. *Hello!* were going to run a feature on it. She was chuffed to bits.' He grinned at me through his swollen eyes. 'Personally, I can think of nothing worse. I should probably thank Max.'

'She must be quite something, your fiancée,' Alison commented.

'Yeah, she is.' Greg looked momentarily discomforted, and his eyes flicked onto me and then away again. 'She's pretty special.'

I saw Alison catch that brief glance; took in the flash of understanding on her face, and felt myself colouring up again. Then she moved tactfully on. 'Well, I think that sounds like the perfect plan,' she announced.

'I think it's a disaster waiting to happen,' I cut in.

'And I think it's the best shot we've got,' Greg said firmly. 'So that's two against one, Fran.' He stood up and took the plates from my hands. 'I'll go and stick the kettle back on,' he announced. 'And then I'll give Cheryl a ring and see what she says.'

In the silence that followed his departure Alison gave me a speculative look. 'I can see why Max hit him,' she said evenly.

'Alison—'

'What? You're not going to deny that he's in love with you?'

'He's not in love with me,' I said, once again sounding more assertive than I felt. 'He's just – we're – well, we just get along well. As colleagues,' I added lamely.

Alison shook her head at me sadly. 'That's the trouble with you, Fran. You can't lie to save yourself. Not even when it's yourself you're lying to.'

Chapter 29

Greg disappeared off after speaking to Cheryl, saying he would be back later in the afternoon. After he'd left I persuaded Alison to bed for a rest, and she was still asleep when he returned shortly after four, clutching a bag of Danish pastries and a CD. He'd changed while he was away: the bloodied T-shirt and work clothes had been replaced by jeans and a jumper. He looked younger, somehow, without the suit: younger and more vulnerable.

'Cheryl's portfolio,' he said shortly, dropping the CD onto the kitchen table. 'She says we can use whatever we like from it.'

'How's the nose?'

'Unbroken, no thanks to that Neanderthal you married. But I suspect Alison was right about the black eyes.'

'Oh dear. And *Hello!*?'

'Looks like it's going to be less Hello, more Goodbye.'

I winced. 'Cheryl must be disappointed.'

'Yeah, well: it's the publicity. She was flattered to be asked. I couldn't give a flying fuck myself.'

I fingered the CD case thoughtfully. 'She's really up for it, then?'

'Are you kidding?' Greg crossed to the sink and filled the kettle. 'When she saw the state of my face, she went into orbit.' He stood the kettle on its base plate and flicked it on.

'And will she be able to carry it off, do you think?'

'Of course she will.' He rinsed two of the mugs we had used earlier and wiped them dry with a tea towel. Then he reached into the cupboard alongside the cooker and fished out the teabags. It struck me irrelevantly that he'd become quite at home in my kitchen over the course of the day. It was just as well Max wasn't around to see him. 'She's a great actress. If she hadn't gone into modelling, she'd probably be a household name by now.'

'So why'd she choose modelling, then?'

'More money.' Greg dropped the teabags into the mugs and carried them over to the kettle. 'More money, and more regular work. Acting can be a bit precarious until you've made a name for yourself. Though she'd still love to give it a shot one day.'

I smiled. 'It all sounds very – glamorous.'

'You mean, what's she doing with a boring old fart like me?'

'No! I never—'

'Ach.' He filled the two mugs with boiling water. 'A few of her previous boyfriends have been in the same line of business as her. And she's the first to admit that they're an empty-headed lot, by and large. That's why she used the dating agency. When your whole life revolves around the way you look, it can be hard finding someone with their feet on the ground. That's where I come in. Mister Reliability. Safe. Dependable. Boring,' he finished with an ironic smile. 'She'll probably end up running off with some film producer in a couple of years.'

'Then why are you marrying her?' The words were out before I could stop myself.

He placed a steaming mug and a Danish in front of me. 'Because she'll have me,' he answered briefly, picking up the CD from the table. 'Come on: let's get busy.'

In the study, he slipped the CD into the drive on my machine so that we could browse through the photographs. I brought a chair from the kitchen and watched as he logged onto the profile I'd set up as 'Sassy' and selected the option to add a picture. Then he opened up the folder containing Cheryl's photographs and clicked on one to view it.

She was a real stunner. Shining blonde hair fell in a cascade to her shoulders, and white teeth gleamed immaculately in a wide smile. The eyes sparkled; the skin was flawless. I felt tired and grimy all of a sudden.

'She's a knockout, Greg,' I said, and he grunted noncommittally, bringing up another dozen or so photographs. 'You know, any one of these ought to do the job. Adam won't be able to resist her.'

I pointed at a particularly striking picture in which Cheryl was leaning smoulderingly towards the camera, her hair blown back away from her face, her lips parted slightly as though she were preparing to be kissed. Greg imported the file onto my PC, then added it to Sassy's profile, saving the changes before going to the profile Adam had set up using Max's photograph and selecting the 'Email this member?' button.

'Go for it,' he said, pushing the keyboard towards me.

'You know I'm only agreeing to this to help Alison,' I

said. 'Max and I – we'll be fine. Just as soon as I get to speak to him.'

'Sure you will.' Greg didn't look at me.

I hesitated. 'Greg, why are you doing this?'

'Doing what?'

'Helping me.' I swallowed. 'Helping me get Max back.'

He kept his eyes fixed on the screen. 'Because that's what you want.' Then he turned to look at me. 'Isn't it?'

I held his gaze. 'Yes,' I said after a moment. Then I reached out for the keyboard and started to type.

I kept the tone of the email light, apologising for having missed him outside the museum, claiming that there had been a breakdown on the Tube that had held me up. If he still wanted to get together, I wrote, I was free over the weekend.

Alison appeared behind us just as I was about to hit 'Send'. 'Change that,' she said, after reading what I'd written. 'Tell him you can meet him tonight, but you're going to be away all weekend. We need to hook him before he finds out I've discharged myself.'

I did as she had instructed, and sent the mail. 'What if he finds out anyway, before this evening?' I queried. 'What if he already knows, for that matter?'

She thought for a moment, then shook her head. 'If he knew already, he'd be round here like a flash. He knows where I'd head for if I hadn't gone home. And as long as the hospital don't get hold of him, we're safe enough for this evening. I told him yesterday not to bother coming in tonight. I said I was having another radiation session and would be too out of it afterwards.'

I looked at her appraisingly. 'You had this all planned, didn't you? Discharging yourself, I mean.'

She gave me an enigmatic smile. 'Course I did. After Adam's visit last night—' She broke off suddenly and smiled again. 'Well, let's just say I figured the time was ripe.'

I bit my lip anxiously. 'But supposing the hospital do manage to get hold of Adam? Won't that put him on his guard?'

She thought for a moment. 'Tell you what, I'll ring them. I'll let them know I'm home safe and sound and I'll be back on Monday to collect my medication. That should put them off calling anybody else.'

We left her to it and wandered back through to the kitchen to top up our tea. There was still an awkwardness between us: it was as if, by admitting to his feelings earlier in the day, Greg had forced us both to face up to some inconvenient truth that we'd hitherto managed to avoid. I wondered whether we'd ever get back to the comfortable camaraderie we'd always enjoyed up until now.

A few minutes later Alison joined us. 'That's the hospital told,' she began. 'And I called my parents too. I didn't give them too many details over the phone: I just said I was being allowed out for the weekend and I'd be round later – I can't wait to see Erin – but not to say anything if Adam called them. I told them I wanted to surprise him.'

I nodded. 'That's no problem. Greg and I can drop you off.'

She nodded towards the clock on the stove. 'We'll

have to get a shift on, then. While I was on the phone to Dad, you got a reply on your computer. You're meeting Adam – or rather Cheryl is – at seven-thirty outside the Pizza Hut by King's Cross.' She nodded towards the clock on the cooker: it was almost four-thirty. 'If you and Greg are going on a stake-out, you'll need to get your acts together.'

'Pizza Hut?' Greg frowned. 'Is that it? What else does he say?'

'That's all there is, Greg. Pizza Hut, King's Cross, seven-thirty p.m.'

'Shit. Nothing about the photo?'

'Not a word.'

'Cheryl can't go to a Pizza Hut. She's more your Ritz kind of girl.' He hesitated. 'Look, Alison: I'm not happy about this. I mean, Pizza Hut? After Babylon? It sounds as though he's playing silly buggers with us. There's no way he can have sussed us, is there?'

'I don't think so, Greg. As far as he's concerned, he's already been stood up twice. I expect he's just playing it cool.'

He gave a sigh. 'Okay, I guess you know the creep better than the rest of us.' Then he looked sheepish. 'Sorry, I shouldn't have called him that.'

'Oh, no apology necessary,' Alison said cheerily. 'You can call him what you like.' She looked from one of us to the other. 'The pair of you look wrung out.' She held out her arms and pulled us both in close for a hug. 'Things *will* be okay, you know. Eventually. One of these days we'll look back on all of this and laugh.'

I was about to make some sort of caustic retort when the telephone began its strident ringing from the hall. I pulled away from our group hug and went through to pick it up.

'Fran.'

It was Max.

That was it. Just one word. I winced at the flatness of his tone. I opened my mouth to say something, but found I couldn't form any words.

'Are you there?'

'Yes.' It came out in a croak.

'Mum said you'd called.'

'Yes.' I cleared my throat. 'She said you'd gone up to your brother's for the weekend.'

'I'm moving out, Fran.'

'I – *what*?'

'I'm going to be staying with my parents for a bit after I get back. While I get my head straight.'

'But – I don't understand. I thought you just wanted some space last night. I don't – *why*?'

'I just – it's something I need to do. I can't be around you at the moment.'

Panic swept through me. 'Is this because of this morning? Because if it is, Max, I know how it looked. But you have to believe me: there is nothing going on between Greg and me. Nothing.' My voice rose. 'Please don't do this, Max. Don't do it to us. Whatever's wrong, we can sort it out.'

There was a silence from the other end of the phone.

'Max?'

'I—' He paused. 'Look, Fran: I have to go. I can't talk about this just now. Janet and Alastair are just next door—'

'Sod Janet and Alastair!' Terror pushed my voice up another couple of decibels, and Greg and Alison looked over from the kitchen in alarm. 'Max,' I continued in an undertone. 'You can't just tell me over the phone that you're leaving me. That's not how it works.' I was growing angry as I spoke, and I struggled to stay on top of the fear that was coursing through my blood. 'We've had – that is, *something* has happened between us – and we need to sort it out somehow. But running away isn't going to do that. It's just – well, it's the coward's way out, isn't it?'

He gave a hollow-sounding laugh. 'I doubt your lover thinks I'm a coward.'

'What? You think he didn't retaliate because he's *scared* of you, Max? Is that it?' I realised as soon as I'd said it that I'd forgotten to deny that Greg was my lover.

'Look, I'm sorry, Fran. I don't want to discuss this at the moment. I'll drop by the house on Monday to pick up a few things, and I'll be gone before you get back from work.'

'And what about Lottie?' Fear clutched at my stomach. 'Where does she fit into all this?'

He didn't answer me straight away. Then I heard him draw a deep breath.

'I'm keeping Lottie with me for the moment. I think that's best. She was going to be spending Easter with Mum and Dad anyway.'

'Max, you don't just get to decide like that! We need to talk about this properly. She's my daughter!'

'Yeah, well.' The flatness was back in his tone. 'You're never there for her anyway these days.'

I felt the injustice of that remark like a knife to my stomach. 'What have you told her?'

'Nothing. No point in upsetting her unnecessarily. I need some space, Fran. I need to get my head around it all. Just – don't call me, okay? I'll ring you when I can think straight.'

The silence between us crackled down the line. My thoughts were in turmoil and I fought to make sense of them. If he hadn't told Lottie, did that mean he wasn't leaving me? That he really did just need a bit of space? After a moment I gave a sigh of defeat.

'All right. If this is what you want, Max. But just remember: this was your decision. You've made your mind up about this without giving me a fair hearing. And I think that stinks.'

It took me a moment of listening to the absence of static on the line to realise that he'd hung up on me. I replaced the receiver in its cradle and then turned to where Greg and Alison were standing in the kitchen doorway trying to gauge my mood.

So much for my conviction that things would be fine between us once we'd managed to talk. I grabbed my coat from the banister.

'Seven-thirty outside Pizza Hut, wasn't it?' I said to Alison.

She nodded and stretched out a hand towards me. 'Hon—'

'And we still have to get our hands on a camera, right?' I looked to Greg for confirmation.

'Yeah, but—'

'Then what are we waiting for?' I shrugged myself into my coat. 'Let's get out there and nail the bastard.'

Chapter 30

'Have you got the camera?'

'Check.'

'And your mobile?'

'Check.'

'God, I feel like a really bad actor in a ham movie.'

'Check.'

I thumped him on the arm. 'Stop it. I can't believe I'm doing this, hanging around street corners waiting to catch my friend's husband making whoopee with your fiancée just so that I can get my husband back.'

Greg gave a wry smile. 'Put like that, it does seem a bit insane.'

'Greg?'

'Hmn?'

I hesitated. 'Thanks.'

'That's okay.' He gave me one of his searching looks, and then smiled. 'I've told you before: it's what friends are for.'

I looked at him, and felt a wave of affection for him wash over me. Maybe Alison was right: maybe we would look back on this some day and laugh.

Then suddenly he clutched my arm and nodded towards the Pizza Hut opposite. 'There he is.'

A black cab was just disgorging a tall figure onto the

pavement. He straightened up and looked around him, and Greg and I shrank back behind the SUV we'd been using for cover.

'What time is it?'

I checked my watch. 'Almost half-past.'

Greg clicked his tongue. 'I hope she's not late. I don't want him smelling a rat.'

We hadn't been able to meet up with Cheryl prior to the date. After she and Greg had finished their pow-wow earlier she'd been tied up for the rest of the afternoon on the same shoot she'd been doing the previous day, modelling swimwear for one of the glossy magazines, and when she'd rushed home afterwards to shower and change we'd been out trying to lay our hands on a digital camera, eventually paying a small fortune to a gloating assistant in Currys for something that he assured us that even an idiot couldn't fail to operate. So we had no idea what to expect when she finally did turn up, but if we'd been hoping that she'd pull out the stops to put Adam off the scent, I had to admit she'd done us proud.

I'd swear she was walking in slow motion. She had a grace about her that set her apart from us lesser mortals. Her hair, which she was wearing loose, tumbled shimmering down her back in the evening light. Between that and the deceptively simple little black number she was wearing, which clung to every perfectly honed curve before stopping unapologetically somewhere midway up her thigh, she actually took my breath away. She turned heads as she strode confidently along the pavement and stopped right outside the entrance to Pizza Hut, checking her watch and then looking around her as though she were expecting someone.

'Oh my God, Greg.' My jaw dropped open.

I wasn't the only one who was impressed. Across the road from us, Adam looked pretty blown away too. I watched him hesitate before going over to her, as though he couldn't believe his luck. And then he moved across and said something to her, and she laughed and nodded. He gestured with his head towards the Pizza Hut, and this time they both laughed and she placed the palm of her hand against his chest. He leaned in close to her and said something else, before sliding a hand around her waist and steering her towards the edge of the pavement, where he lifted his other hand to flag down a passing cab. Then he opened the door and ushered her inside, taking a last look around him before ducking in after her. Before we had time to gather ourselves the taxi indicated and pulled away into the evening traffic.

'Shit!' I looked at Greg in dismay. 'What do we do now?'

'We wait.' Greg looked unperturbed. 'She promised she'd text me if they went off anywhere. No point hanging around on the street though – I'm starving.' He nodded across the road. 'Fancy some pizza?'

We were midway through our food when his mobile beeped. He wiped his mouth with a napkin and read the text to me. 'He's taken her to the Oyster Bar at a place called Bentley's in Swallow Street,' he said. He threw his napkin down on the table. 'Come on.'

We made a hasty departure back onto the street, where it took fifteen frustrating minutes to find a vacant cab.

'Calm down,' Greg said to me as I hopped up and down with impatience on the pavement. 'They won't be going anywhere for a bit. And even if they do, Cheryl will keep us posted.

He whistled when we pulled up outside the restaurant, all the same. 'Bit more upmarket than pizza, eh?' he said as we tumbled inelegantly from the taxi.

'What do we do now?' I asked. 'I mean, we can hardly go striding in there, can we? If Adam spots me, the game will be well and truly up.'

Greg thought for a moment. 'You hang on here. I'll go and take a quick gander: he doesn't know me. I'll be right back.' He disappeared through the glass doors before I could open my mouth to protest.

I paced the pavement while he was gone, partly because there was a bit of a chill in the air, but mostly to stop my thoughts, none of which were particularly helpful, from running away with me. I kept hearing Max's voice in my head, telling me he needed not to be around me. How could this have happened to us? To *us.* We'd always been rock-solid. Now he was keeping my daughter away from me because he thought I wasn't fit to look after her. This just wasn't my life any more. This kind of nightmare was what happened to other people. People who didn't love each other the way Max and I did. Had. Would again. I drew a deep breath and paced some more.

After a few moments the door to the restaurant swung open, and Greg beckoned me over. 'I've got us a couple of drinks,' he said. 'There's a good crowd in: I don't think he'll spot you.' He pulled me inside. 'I went right up and stood behind them and ordered. I actually had to lean across them to take the glasses from the barman.' He grinned at me. 'Cheryl was amazing. She never batted an eyelid.'

He positioned us close to the door, where a pair of full-length curtains hanging either side of the lobby offered some cover if Adam happened to look our way. Fortunately he was sitting with his back to me, though I had a pretty clear view of Cheryl's profile. He was fawning – that was the only word for it – all over her, and kept topping her glass from a bottle of champagne into which they'd already made heavy inroads that was sitting in a bucket on the bar in front of them. I took a sip from my own glass: it was sparkling water.

'Sorry,' Greg murmured apologetically. 'But we need to keep our heads clear.'

I took another sip from the glass and surveyed the room. 'You know,' I said after a few more moments had passed, 'I don't see how we're going to get any photos in here. If you start popping off shots we'll be thrown out onto the street.'

'You're right,' Greg said glumly. 'We'll just have to stake them out for a bit and then wait back outside for them.'

We hung around for another fifteen minutes or so, watching Adam and Cheryl talk and laugh and generally have a good time, and I sipped at my sparkling water and tried to resist the urge to go over to the bar and smash the glass over the top of Adam's head. Cheryl was good, I had to admit: to all intents and purposes she looked to be having the time of her life. Easy to do, though, I reflected a trifle sourly, when you looked like she did and were guzzling champagne instead of sparkling water and had the attention of most of the men in the place, even those who were there with their own dates.

Over at the bar a platter of oysters had just been set down between Adam and Cheryl. He was leaning into her, pointing, and after a moment he lifted one of the shells and held it to his lips, demonstrating. Then he reached over and selected another oyster, holding the shell to Cheryl's lips this time, and laughing as some of the juice ran down her chin. She laughed as well and wiped at her chin with her finger, and he caught hold of the finger in his fist and licked it.

It was a horrible, fascinating, intimate gesture that it felt wrong to be witnessing. I glanced at Greg beside me, but he wasn't looking across in their direction. Suddenly I remembered what he'd said earlier, about Cheryl running off with a film producer, and I didn't want him seeing a repeat of what I'd just seen. I put what remained of my drink down abruptly on a table to the side of us.

'Let's wait outside, eh? The heat in here's making me feel light-headed.'

I pushed my way back outside and crossed onto the opposite side of the street, and he followed a moment later. 'Fran? You okay?' He caught up with me as I took refuge behind a parked car.

'Fine.' I looked at his face, his nice, open, honest face, which was now wreathed in concern for my wellbeing. Safe, dependable Greg, who had a bit of a thing for me and who I loved just a little bit myself, if I were really honest, but who knew he couldn't have me and was marrying someone who just seemed all wrong for him somehow and would probably leave him anyway. He deserved better.

And then suddenly the door to the restaurant opened again, and all at once they were tumbling out of the door and laughing on the other side of the street from us.

'Showtime,' Greg murmured, reaching for the camera.

It was Cheryl who made the first move. I watched with something approaching admiration as she hesitated at the door and took hold of Adam's arm. She lowered her head and said something, so that he had to duck low to hear her. And then she lifted her chin so that she was gazing straight into his eyes, and he kissed her, just as she'd intended him to, softly at first, and then with growing intensity. The admiration I'd felt initially gave way to something closer to revulsion as he pushed her against the wall of the restaurant and slid his hand down the front of her dress, lunging at her neck, and she threw her head back and gasped. I half expected them to lie down and make love right there on the pavement. Beside me, Greg clicked away, his face a study in impassivity. Then after a few more heavy gropes from Adam and gasps from Cheryl, a taxi pulled up and the two of them fell inside.

'God, she's good.' Greg caught the look of shock on my face. 'Don't take it so seriously, Fran. She's acting, remember?'

She was some actor. 'Where are they going now?' I asked numbly.

'Dunno, but Cheryl will slip us another text when she gets a chance. Come on: let's go back inside and have another drink and see what we've got.'

What we'd got was plenty – if it had been Cheryl we'd been trying to set up. If you zoomed in on the tiny viewing screen, you could make out quite clearly her parted lips and sparkling teeth – could almost hear her cry out – as Adam thrust himself against her and pushed his hand further down the front of her dress. All we had of Adam, though, was a rear view of his head and shoulders, his hair dark against her pale neck, the back of his hand crushing her left breast through the fabric of her dress. He could have been any tall, dark-haired lust-filled slimeball.

We sat and studied the shots in silence for a few moments. 'What do we do now?' I asked eventually, after we had finished viewing the sordid collection.

Greg didn't answer immediately, and then he licked his lips and seemed to collect himself. 'I suppose I'd better get on to Cheryl and let her know we need more.'

He didn't look thrilled at the prospect.

'Look,' I said after a moment. 'We could just abandon the idea and go home. Cheryl's done her best. She can't be exactly enjoying this.' I hesitated after saying that: from the expression on her face in some of the pictures it seemed she was enjoying it far more than any of us could have foreseen.

Greg shook his head. 'No. We've started this: let's finish it. I'll see if I can get her to set something up so that we can see his face next time.'

He sent off a brief text, and then we got another couple of mineral waters and waited for her to get back to us. After three-quarters of a nail-biting hour I went to the bar and bought us a couple of proper drinks: a whisky for Greg and a Drambuie on the rocks for myself. We managed to nurse them through another hour, and still there was nothing from Cheryl. Greg's control was starting to crack: his face was looking increasingly drawn and at one point he banged his glass down on the table and swore. Then, just as I was starting to believe we wouldn't be hearing anything more from Cheryl this evening, his mobile beeped again. I watched him read the message, saw his face fall as he handed me the phone.

'"Sorry, babe. No can do."' I looked across at Greg, whose expression was unreadable. 'She's probably just got cold feet,' I hazarded, though even I knew I was clutching at straws.

He shrugged, though I could see that the text had troubled him. 'Might as well get back,' he said eventually. 'Get this lot downloaded and have a proper look at it. You never know – we might have missed something.'

We walked back to the station, each of us wrapped up in our own thoughts, and caught a late train back to Bracknell, where we'd parked up earlier before taking the train into London. During the journey Greg stared out of the window into the blackness of the night without speaking. Once we arrived at the station he drove us back home stopping off at the office en route so that I could collect my car. There was a message from Alison on my answerphone saying she was staying the night with her parents and Erin, and she would call me in the morning.

So by the end of the night it was just Greg and me, hunched over my computer and printing out the details of Adam's lust as captured by our new digital camera, which had been as horribly effective as the salesman had promised, if only it had been Adam's face we'd captured and not Cheryl's. And eventually, when the time came for Greg to leave, and neither of us could face spending the night alone, we ended up going through to the sitting-room and watching a late-night film, though I couldn't recall the next morning what it was as I woke up and discovered that we'd spent the night together right there on the sofa, my head in Greg's lap and his arm across my chest. From the look of him when I crawled back to consciousness around six o'clock, though, I don't think he'd closed his eyes at all.

Chapter 31

Saturday morning passed in a fug of confused thoughts and heart-searching. Greg left around seven, after a fragile hour in which we moved around one another cautiously, saying little, like the bewildered victims of a car accident waiting for someone from the emergency services to come along and tell them what to do. Just before he left I found him in the study, poring over one of the photographs we'd printed out the previous evening, in which Cheryl's head was flung backwards and Adam's face was buried in her neck. The camera had captured a raw hunger in her expression that caused me to think that if this were acting, she really ought to give up modelling and head for Hollywood.

'Can I take this with me?' Greg turned when he heard me behind him. His expression was inscrutable.

I looked at him, trying to work out what was the real question he was asking me. 'Sure.'

'I'll call you later. After Cheryl gets back. Let you know how things panned out.'

I nodded. ''Kay.'

We hugged briefly in the hall, and then we pulled awkwardly apart and he swung open the front door and left, folding himself into his car and driving away with a brief wave. I watched until he disappeared around the corner at the end of the road, and went back inside the house, shutting myself inside with the emptiness and wondering what I was going to do with myself for the rest of the day. In the living-room I sat back down on the sofa where we'd lain all night, and wrapped my arms around my shoulders like I'd done just after Max had gone storming out, and speculated about what kind of betrayal Greg's staying had constituted. I could hear Max's voice in my head, the bitterness in his tone as he'd accused us of having spent the night together, and reflected wryly that if he were to level the same accusation at me now, I wouldn't be able to deny it. Was he awake yet, I wondered? Had he, in fact, slept? Closed his eyes on all the problems he'd run away from and managed a few hours of oblivion? If he had it wouldn't help: I knew from experience just how hard reality kicked in once you woke up.

It was a little after seven-thirty: still too early to start making phone calls and trying to regroup after yesterday's campaigning. I began mechanically tidying up all the papers we'd gathered yesterday, stacking them into a pile on the coffee table and adding the printouts from the photographs we'd taken yesterday evening to the pile. I managed to spin out the tidying for over an hour by re-reading all the emails and scrutinising the photos again for some clue about what was going through Cheryl's mind. One thing was certain: there was nothing here that Alison could use to bring Adam into line. Unless Cheryl were prepared to make some kind of kiss-and-tell statement, it looked as though yesterday's activity had been a complete waste of time.

The morning crawled inexorably by. At nine I tried Max's mobile, only to be told for the umpteenth time in twenty-four hours that the person I was calling was not available. I could picture him in my head, picking up the ringing handset and then shaking his head as he read the caller ID before hitting the cancel button. In a fit of masochism I went through to the study and did a Google search on grounds for divorce, to try to establish whether I had anything at all resembling a leg to stand on if Max decided to go down that path. I found a site that offered a complete divorce solution for £69. They made the process sound straightforward and painless, avowing that it was possible to initiate a divorce in less than three minutes. It didn't seem right, somehow, that something Max and I had been building for years could be destroyed so precipitously. Another site I checked out listed unreasonable behaviour as the most common reason cited for divorce. Had I behaved unreasonably? I scoured the paragraph, and my heart plunged when I came to the part that said relatively mild allegations may suffice a court, such as having no common interests (we had Lottie, I thought desperately), pursuing a separate social life (I wondered whether the night I'd spent in Babylon and the lunch with Greg would count against me), or devoting too much time to a career.

No: on the whole, I realised, I probably didn't have a leg to stand on.

Around eleven-thirty Alison's mother called. Alison was fine, she told me in response to my enquiry, but a little tired after all the excitement of yesterday. No wonder, I thought to myself, remembering how she'd collapsed in my arms when the taxi had dropped her off. She was, however, desperate to see me, which was why her mother was calling. Could I come over there, she wanted to know? Goodness knew, Alison wouldn't rest otherwise.

Of course I could. I would come straight over, I promised her. And wasn't she thrilled with Alison's progress, I wanted to know.

She went quiet. 'We're happy to have her here, of course,' she said after a moment. 'But we're not forgetting how sick she is.'

Alison was lying on the sofa with a rug over her and looking pretty wiped out when I arrived fifteen minutes later, though her eyes were bright enough. 'Hey, hon,' I said by way of a greeting. 'How are you feeling?'

'Never better.' She laughed at the look of scepticism on my face. 'No, seriously. Ignore the rug. It's just Mum: she likes to fuss. I feel fine, really I do. Just a bit knackered. I'd forgotten how exhausting this being out of bed lark can be.'

Alison's mother appeared at the door to the living-room. 'Some tea, Fran?' she offered. Then to Alison, 'Dad's taken Erin down to the shops for ice cream – give you a bit of peace. She's so excited to have Mummy here,' she said, addressing me again. 'But Alison does need to rest.'

'Don't worry,' I assured her. 'I won't stay long, I promise. And no to the tea, thanks: I've drunk about six cups of coffee already this morning.'

'Don't mind Mum: she's in over-protective mode,' Alison said when her mother had withdrawn. Then she pursed her lips at me. 'You know, you don't look so hot yourself this morning.'

I ignored her. 'You haven't told them, have you?'

'About the remission? No, not yet.'

'But – why on earth not? If you're sure, that is. Surely they'd want to know. They've been so worried about you.'

'I will, I promise. It's just – well, I'm still coming to terms with it myself. I couldn't cope with the inevitable excitement, all the decision-making that'll have to happen.' She wrinkled her nose at me. 'Just give me a couple of days, okay?'

She pushed herself into a sitting position and patted the sofa at her feet. 'Come on: dish the dirt. What happened on your stake-out last night?'

I sat down in the space she'd made and gave her a brief recap on the previous evening's activity, skipping the bit where Greg and I spent the night together. Not that we had anything to hide, I reasoned to myself – I just didn't feel up to trying to justify what we'd done. Or not done. I'd brought the printouts we'd made of Cheryl and Adam in action, and she spent some time looking over them, shaking her head and tutting at the raw lust we'd captured in the shots. If she were shocked at such concrete evidence of her husband's infidelity, she was careful not to let it show. 'Poor Greg,' she commented eventually when she'd gone through them all. 'This must have been hard for him to watch, even if she was only acting.'

'Mmn,' I murmured noncommittally. 'He wasn't giving anything away when he left—' I bit my tongue: I'd almost added *this morning*.

Tired as she was, it was a relief being around Alison. She set the pictures to one side and began telling me about her evening. Erin had been thrilled to see her out of hospital. 'I can't tell you how good it felt to give her a hug without a load of tubes attached to me.' She stretched out her drip-free arms to demonstrate.

'So – if you haven't told them about the remission, what exactly *have* you told them?'

'That I've been let out of hospital for the weekend for good behaviour. I've got to go back in on Monday anyway, to sort out a drugs regime with the oncologist.'

'And then?'

She wrinkled her nose at me. 'I haven't quite worked out the next step yet. Mum and Dad would put me up, of course, but to be honest I think it'd be too much for them. They're already knackered from looking after Erin all these weeks.' She gave me a beseeching look and I tutted.

'You know you don't have to ask.'

She broke into a beam. 'Are you sure? You've got a lot on your plate yourself just now.'

I shrugged. 'It's not as if the house is bursting at the seams, is it?' I thought with a pang of the horrible empty feeling that had overwhelmed me after Greg had left earlier. 'It'll be a relief to have some company, even someone who's bald and sleeps all the time.'

'Oh, Fran, you're a star.' She hugged her knees excitedly. 'It won't be for long, I promise.'

'Well, not that I'm trying to hurry you or anything,' I told her, 'but you can initiate a divorce in three minutes.'

'What? Where on earth did you find out something like that?'

'I checked on the internet.' I told her about my earlier

masochistic ferreting, and she leaned forwards and wrapped her arms around me. 'Oh, Fran. You and Max aren't going to get divorced. Like you said yesterday, the two of you just need to sit down and talk properly, sort out all the misunderstandings.' She narrowed her eyes thoughtfully. Sixty-nine quid, eh?' She grinned lasciviously. 'Bit ironic, don't you think? D'you reckon that's a special price for adulterers, or can anyone get it?'

'Alison, what are we going to do?' I stood up and crossed to the window. 'Greg and I wasted a whole evening trying to get evidence, and what we got isn't the slightest bit of use – to you or to me.'

She thought for a moment. 'Well, we could do with some feedback from Cheryl. Could be, she's quite happy to tell all, even if the pictures haven't been as much use as we were hoping. I wonder if Greg's heard from her yet?' I shrugged. 'Maybe you should call him.'

And as if on cue, my mobile began to ring in my pocket. I grabbed it and hit the 'Accept' button.

'Very clever, Fran.'

I almost dropped the phone. Adam's voice was rich with irony.

'I just wanted to thank you,' he went on. 'There I was, thinking you were mad with me. And then you went and sent me such a beautiful gift.' In the background I heard somebody say something. 'Look, I'm afraid I'm going to have to renege on the invitation I made you the other day. You remember? You do remember, don't you, Fran?'

'Look, Adam—' I started to say, and he laughed.

'I can understand that you're disappointed,' he went on.

'We'd have made such a beautiful couple, you and me.' I clenched the handset and resisted the urge to hang up. 'But I don't think Cheryl is the sort who would share. Are you, pumpkin?'

'You're still with her.' I couldn't believe what I was hearing.

'You'll have a job proving it, photos or not. You know, you want to be careful where you go sticking your nose. I told you once before to stay out of our business. You like to think you're so close, you and Alison. But you know nothing about us.'

'Adam—'

'Bye, Fran.'

He hung up. Alison was looking at me impatiently. 'Well?'

I didn't know what to say – couldn't believe how horribly wrongly things had turned out. 'I – um.' I hesitated. 'The thing is, Alison. The thing is—' What was the thing? 'Adam knows. He knows we tried to set him up. I suppose Cheryl must have told him.' I swallowed. 'He's still with her. It seems they – he and Cheryl – well.' I was starting to perspire. 'I think they got along better than we'd anticipated last night.'

She didn't speak for a moment. Then she gave a harsh laugh. 'Bloody hell.' She shook her head angrily. 'Christ, I knew he was a shit. But you'd think he'd have a bit more class than this. I'm not even dead yet.'

I squeezed her hand.

'God, Fran.' She squeezed her eyes tightly closed. 'What the hell is going to happen to Erin? Is she nice, this Cheryl person? Suitable, d'you think?'

'What does it matter if she's nice or not?' I shook my head at her in astonishment. 'You'll be able to file for divorce and get custody of Erin. We've got photos, don't forget. We can use them to threaten Adam if need be. He doesn't know they're useless.' I thought with a lurch of the text Greg had sent Cheryl telling her we needed more photographs, and uttered a silent prayer that he hadn't given too much away.

She bit her lip and sighed. 'Bloody ironic, isn't it? All the hassle it caused, me trying to ensure he wouldn't be left on his own. Looks like I needn't have bothered. Bloody bastard.'

I studied her stricken face. All the spark I'd seen in her eyes earlier when she'd been talking about Erin had vanished. 'You okay?'

She made an effort to collect herself. 'I suppose my pride's a bit ruffled. It might have been nice if he'd put up a bit of a fight. Frankly, I haven't the energy to go getting upset any more.'

She leaned forwards and fingered one of the pictures I'd brought over, picking it up and studying it for a moment.

And then the same thought occurred to both of us at once.

'Greg,' we said together.

I tried his number now. There was no answer. It was like a repeat of my earlier attempts to contact Max. 'Please try later,' the automated voice on the other end of the line urged. I hung up in frustration and turned back to Alison.

'He's not picking up.'

Alison pulled a face. 'Maybe he's in the car or something.'

I shook my head. 'He has Bluetooth. He always answers his phone.'

'Oh, Fran.' Her forehead puckered in anxiety. 'You'd better get over there. See if he's all right. Imagine him sitting at home all night on his own waiting to hear from her.'

Tell her, said a small voice inside me. I ignored it and headed for the door.

'And call me!' she shouted after me as I hurried past her bewildered mother in the hall.

I made the twelve-mile journey across to Greg's apartment in just under twenty minutes, and took the stairs up to his front door two at a time.

There was no answer. I banged as hard as I could and kept my finger pressed on the buzzer for a good half-minute. I even tried calling through the letter box. Nothing.

Supposing he'd done something stupid? I grabbed my mobile from my pocket and called Alison.

'He's not answering the door.'

'Maybe he's gone round to your place?' Alison hazarded.

'He hasn't. His car's downstairs.'

'Oh, dear.' Alison's voice was anxious. Perhaps you should try a neighbour,' she suggested. 'Someone might have a key.'

'Okay. I'll call you back,' I promised.

After his wife left him, Greg had moved from their loft apartment to a smaller place in a block of six, on a development of similar properties that were stacked three storeys high, two to a floor, and marketed as executive living. I'd been here once before, when Greg had been off work sick and had asked me to stop by to collect a folder that Derek needed before the end of the day. I remembered observing how tidy it was, especially compared with the cluttered mess of my own home that was part and parcel of living with a six-year-old. His only neighbour, whose door faced Greg's on the opposite side of the small landing, was out.

Should I call the police? Or might there be a spare key hidden somewhere? I looked around the stairwell for inspiration. Nothing. No doormat. No milk bottles. No nooks or crannies to speak of. The public area was swept clean and smelled of polish. You couldn't have hidden a safety pin.

I tried the bell again and in sheer desperation I grabbed the door handle and rattled it.

It wasn't locked. The door swung inwards on silent hinges and invited me inside.

I stepped across the threshold and tentatively called his name. I remembered the layout of the place vaguely from my previous visit: a long hallway gave onto a spacious living-room with a kitchen off to the right. Both were empty, though the living room had lost that tidy, nobody-really-lives-here feel I remembered it having: the coffee-table had been upended, and on the floor in front of the kitchen door the remains of a mobile phone lay in pieces on the carpet. I picked up one of the bits and fingered it thoughtfully.

After a moment I crossed back through to the hall and tried the first door on the right. It gave onto a bathroom, the floor of which was covered in broken glass. I frowned and moved on to the last door, behind which lay a double bedroom that also bore signs of disturbance: the drawers in one of the bedside chests had been pulled out and upended, and the wardrobe looked as though it had been ransacked On the end of the bed sat an open suitcase containing a scattered assortment of objects: jewellery, a handful of books, some expensive-looking toiletries.

Was he being burgled? Perhaps he'd returned home and disturbed the thief in action, and given chase after the intruder had bolted from the apartment. That would explain the unlocked door, though not the time discrepancy: it was almost six hours since he'd left my house. Well, at least he wasn't lying unconscious in his apartment. I heaved a sigh of relief and turned to go back into the hall.

I never saw the ceiling coming down, but it must have caught me full on the shoulder, and I went crashing to the bedroom floor, banging my head hard as I hit the ground. Just before the world went black I heard a voice, so close to my ear it sounded as though it were right inside my head.

'Fran? Oh, fucking hell.'

Chapter 32

The first thing I became aware of as I opened my eyes was that my head hurt. A lot. The second was that my clothes were soaked. And the third was that Greg was leaning over me with an ice pack, and that confused me because it should have been the other way around, me holding the ice pack to his head, because Max had just come home and found us in the kitchen together, and had hit him right before walking out on me.

Greg's face sagged in relief when he saw I was coming round. 'Oh, thank Christ. I thought I'd killed you.'

I pushed away his arm and tried to focus on my surroundings. I was lying stretched out on the sofa in his living-room. The room swam as I struggled to sit up, and I sank back with a groan against the cushion he'd propped up behind my head.

'What happened?'

'I thought you were a burglar.' Greg bit his lip apologetically. 'I'd only nipped out for some milk, and when I came back I found somebody snooping around in my bedroom. So – I rugby-tackled you. You went down like a felled tree.'

'Did I?' I asked sardonically, and put a hand to my head. 'Ouch.' Something dripped from my sleeve onto my face, and I tried to sit up again. 'I'm wet. Am I bleeding to death?'

'It's milk. The carton burst when we fell down.'

'Oh, great.' I fell back against the cushion again and closed my eyes. Then I opened them again and looked at Greg sharply.

'You weren't answering your phone.'

'No: it's – um – not working.'

I glanced over to where the pieces of broken phone lay scattered on the carpet by the kitchen door, and raised my eyebrows at Greg enquiringly. The action sent a sharp stabbing pain through the back of my skull, and I winced.

'I take it you've heard from Cheryl, then.'

'Yep.' He pursed his mouth.

'Adam called me to crow,' I told him, and hesitated.

'He's said he can get her a role in a six-part drama the BBC are filming later this year.' Greg gave a harsh laugh. 'Two years, I gave us. Remember? Two years. And we didn't even make it as far as the register office.'

I put my hand over his. 'I'm really sorry, Greg.'

'Ach—' He made that dismissive sound I was starting to recognise. 'Best find out now, eh, before she buggers off with all the furniture.' He looked around at the disruption in the room. 'I must admit, I lost it when she told me. Threw the phone at the wall. Started chucking some of her stuff into a suitcase. Smashed her favourite bottle of perfume on the bathroom floor.' He grinned suddenly. 'Didn't mean to, but I must admit it made me feel a lot better. That's when I decided to calm down and make a brew. Only I'd no milk. So I nipped out to get some: the shop's just across the road. We must've barely missed each other.'

I shook my head and winced again. 'No, I think I can safely say we didn't miss each other. You couldn't have scored a more direct hit if you'd tried.'

He pulled a face. 'I'm really sorry. I don't know what came over me. I guess I'm knackered after last night. Your sofa's not the comfiest place to spend the night.'

I looked at him anxiously. 'How're you doing? Alison and I were worried about you.'

He didn't answer straight away. Then when he did, I wished I hadn't asked the question in the first place.

'Bit pissed off.' He gave me one of those looks I was starting to recognise too. 'But it's not like she was the love of my life.' Then the shutters came back down and he stood up. 'I'll go and find you something dry to put on. You'll be stinking if that milk dries in.'

After he'd gone I leaned back against the cushion again with a sigh. Life seemed to have become horribly complicated. In no small part thanks to me, my two closest friends were in the death throes of their separate relationships and were each mildly put out. Max had walked out on me, and my world had fallen apart. And the harder I tried to put things right, the further he seemed to recede from me.

I couldn't be making more of a mess of things if I tried.

Chapter 33

I awoke shortly after dawn on Sunday morning. The house was murmuring to itself: soft, unfamiliar sounds that were a far cry from the cacophony of silence that had greeted me when I'd woken alone on Friday. Beside me Max was still asleep, his quiet breathing melting into the whispering symphony of the house, and somewhere outside I could hear a dog barking: sharp, protesting, let-me-in barks, testimony to a too-early walk.

Soft tendrils of light were reaching into the room, sliding under the edge of the blind and stealing across the carpet onto the bed. It took me a moment of focusing on the way they stretched across the duvet before the realisation hit me that we didn't have a blind. Neither, if it came to it, did we have a mocha-coloured duvet cover. And of course Max couldn't be asleep beside me, because he'd left me – moved out, at any rate, though I couldn't be sure of the difference – and was away at his brother's house with Lottie, because he thought I was having an affair with Greg.

Greg, who was lying beside me in the bed, still fast asleep.

I hadn't set out to stay. I'd been desperate, in fact, to get back home, in case Max returned early from Penrith. The consequences of him turning up, if he did turn up, and finding me gone – worse, finding out *where* I'd gone – didn't bear thinking about. But Greg had called NHS Direct while I'd been out cold, and they'd told him I should go to hospital to get my head checked, and when I refused point blank, he'd called them back and asked what he should do, and they'd told him to make sure I had someone with me because I would need checking on every couple of hours through the night, just in case. 'So that knocks going home on the head. Sorry,' he added sheepishly at the look on my face. 'Bad choice of words.'

He swept aside my objections, saying it wasn't safe for me to be on my own, and it was all his fault anyway, and if he didn't keep an eye on me, who would? I was too exhausted to argue, and after I'd resigned myself to the situation I actually slept for most of the afternoon, stretched out on strange sheets in an unfamiliar bed and wearing an old shirt he lent me to replace my milk-soaked clothes. He came through a couple of times and shook me awake, and only when I'd grunted to show I hadn't slipped into a coma did he retreat back to the living-room and leave me to sleep some more. By the time the evening came I was feeling marginally better, though my head was still throbbing.

As the last of the evening light bled from the sky, he brought in a tray of supper and placed it on the mattress beside me. 'How're you doing?' he asked, leaning close and examining my eyes.

'Better than you, I think,' I said, holding him at arm's length and studying his face in return. The bruising around his eyes was starting to emerge. 'You look wiped out.'

He made a dismissive gesture with his head. 'I'm fine. I had a kip on the sofa.'

He'd made tapas, neat little dishes of self-contained delicacies that made perfect finger food. I shuffled along on the mattress and we ate together, the tray balanced companionably between us. 'This is delicious,' I commented, surprised. He'd never struck me as the kind of guy who cooked. He gave a self-deprecating shrug. 'It's nothing special. Tapas is just a fancy word for using up all the leftovers in the fridge.'

He picked up a remote control from the bedside cabinet and pointed it at a flat screen TV that hung on the wall opposite the bed. The screen crackled into life with some talent-spotting singing show where the emphasis seemed to be more on humiliating the untalented than on singling out the gifted. It was a favourite of Lottie's, I remembered with a lurch of sadness. She would watch it sitting cross-legged on the floor in front of the sofa, jumping up when a truly awful candidate came on and mimicking their performance, her head flung back and her eyes dancing with laughter. 'Lottie loves this show,' I said suddenly to Greg, and before I could stop them two fat tears squeezed out of my eyes and rolled down my cheeks.

Without a word he lifted the tray and set it down on the floor beside the bed. Then he hitched up beside me, leaning against the pillows, and put his arm around my shoulders. I must have hesitated for all of a nanosecond before giving in and letting the tears fall unchecked. It seemed to me that you could only sustain the kind of stress I'd been going through for so long: sooner or later it all got too much and you just had to throw in the towel. Besides, if I closed my eyes, I could almost convince myself that it was Max who was sitting there with his arm around me.

We remained like that for a couple of hours, watching Saturday-night dross while his thumb stroked the outside of my arm and the warmth from his body seeped through the thin cotton of the shirt he had lent me. Up on the TV screen somebody from Sheffield won £32,000 on *Who Wants To Be a Millionaire*; and 200 miles north of us Max tucked Lottie into a strange bed and promised her she'd see Mummy soon; and twenty minutes down the road my best friend hugged her daughter and refused to die, while her husband cavorted with the fiancée of a man who wasn't Max but who held me anyway until the tears finally stopped. And somewhere in the middle of it all I lay down in his arms and gave up the struggle to make sense of any of it, and – undeservedly, probably – slept like a baby.

The noise of the dog must have penetrated Greg's dreams, because he stirred sleepily and stretched out an arm, reaching for me, and drew me close against him, murmuring words I couldn't make out into the nape of my neck before subsiding back into sleep. I lay for a few moments, rigid with embarrassment, before easing myself from his arms and sliding from the bed, closing the bedroom door softly behind me.

In the kitchen I dropped my face into my hands and groaned. I felt a wave of nausea rise inside me, and I pushed open the window so that the cold morning air came spilling past me into the kitchen. Outside, the morning had an expectant feel to it, as though it were waiting for some audience appreciation before it got going properly. I took a few deep breaths and tried to work out how much more of a mess I'd managed to make for myself in the past twenty-four hours. If Max had paid a private investigator to follow me, as Alison had suggested we do with Adam, he'd have had enough evidence by now to secure a decree nisi before the ink on the cheque had dried.

I gave a sigh and filled Greg's kettle, still feeling dazed and headachy from the concussion. Someone must have let the dog in, because the persistent barking had stopped. I rummaged around in the kitchen cupboards, managing to locate teabags, and dropped one into a mug, remembering only as I fished it out and dropped it into the sink that there was no milk. I added a spoonful of sugar instead and carried my drink through to the sitting-room and curled up on the sofa with my hands wrapped around the mug.

Greg didn't emerge for another hour, stumbling through to the sitting-room rubbing bleary eyes and still wearing the same clothes he'd had on when he'd rugby-tackled me yesterday. 'God: sorry, Fran,' he said by way of a greeting. 'I must have crashed out.' He came over and crouched beside the sofa. 'How's the head?'

I prodded it tentatively. 'A bit tender. But intact, I think.'

He nodded. 'Good. Top-up?' He pushed himself to his feet.

'No, thanks.' I followed him out to the kitchen. 'I should probably get home. Max is due back tonight.'

He kept his back to me. 'Back home?'

'No. He's going to stay with his parents for a bit. I just

– I need to be there. Whatever happens. I can't—' I gestured helplessly around the kitchen. 'You know.'

He turned around, leaning on his hands against the worktop as though afraid of what they might do if he let them loose. 'Sure.'

We regarded one another for a moment. 'Right – well.' I gestured at my unconventional outfit. 'I'd better put some clothes on.'

'Oh – yeah.' He crossed to the radiator. 'I bunged your stuff in the machine while you were asleep yesterday afternoon. It's a bit creased, but at least it won't stink.' He pulled my jeans and jumper off the radiator and felt them. 'The jumper's still damp. But you can hang on to the shirt for now.'

I took the clothes from him, feeling awkward, and disappeared through to the bathroom to get dressed. When I came back he had taken up his station by the sink again, his hands gripping the worktop behind his back.

'Well—' I hesitated. 'See you tomorrow, I suppose. At the office.'

He pulled a face. 'I won't offer you a lift, if it's okay.'

'I think that's wise.' I gave him a lopsided smile, and turned to leave.

'Fran—' He dropped his hands to his sides. 'Look: I just wanted to say – well, I'm sorry. For what I said. The other day – you know. I was out of order. I just thought – anyway. I don't want things to be awkward between us. That's all. And I hope you manage to get things sorted out with Max. Really, I do.'

I walked over and placed the palm of my hand against

the side of his face, and then stood on tiptoe and kissed him softly on the cheek.

'Thanks.'

'Yeah.' He reached up and touched the place where I'd just kissed him. 'See you.'

As I drove home it suddenly dawned on me that in the confusion of yesterday afternoon I'd forgotten to call Alison to let her know how things had turned out, and I wondered why she hadn't called me. I pulled over and dug around in the pocket of my jeans for my mobile, which I found duly washed and radiator-dried along with the jeans, and quite dead to the world.

Chapter 34

Angela and I were never in any doubt, when we were growing up, that life was anything but unfair. Our mother would drive it home to us at any opportunity: when Angela told her she should never have had me, for instance; when I complained that everyone in the class was going on the school trip to Devil's Bridge except me; when the milk for our breakfast cereal was running low and we had to dilute it with water to make it stretch. Years later the milk marketing board would skim off all the cream anyway and sell what was left as the healthy alternative to full-fat, but at the time we felt keenly the injustice of our situation and were loud in bitter protest. 'It's not fair' became a kind of litany for us, uttered with brimming eyes and scowling brows, even though we'd known since we were old enough to talk that the only response from our mother would be a curled lip and a dismissive 'Life's not fair', accompanied depending on her mood by a cuff to the side of the head to drive home her point. You'd think we would have learned.

Now, even though it had been thirteen years since I'd lived at home, I still found myself railing at what life had thrown my way, and that five-year-old with the petted lip and the sense of injustice raging through her was back with a vengeance. The memory of the watery breakfasts might have faded with the years, but my mother's expression taunted me still, trapped as I was in a situation I seemed incapable of changing except to make it worse. I even think my lip began to curl.

The only consolation in the quagmire of uncertainty was the news about Alison, who moved in on Monday evening. I tried to keep reminding myself of this as I slowly accustomed myself to my new status as an abandoned wife. Periodically I would recall the last conversation between Max and me, when he'd told me he was moving out, and I would lie wide-eyed and sleepless at night wondering whether there was a difference between moving out and leaving someone. Was one more permanent than the other? Was it easier to move back than to come back? If I slept at all, I would have to go through the agony of waking up and suffering that lurch of sadness at how quiet the house had become.

I seemed to have a permanent headache. Work became an exercise in survival: holed up in my office trying to avoid seeing anyone and not answering my phone, I would push papers around my desk and fret. I felt trapped, held hostage by Max's refusal to talk to me, while the rest of the world got on with its life regardless.

True to his word, he had come round on Monday afternoon and packed up clothes for himself and Lottie. I stayed late at the office that evening, reluctant to confront the latest evidence of his abandonment, and took a circuitous route home via the supermarket, where I filled a trolley with groceries I didn't need. While I was filling the trolley, I found myself wondering how much stuff he would have taken; whether I'd be able to gauge from what he'd left behind how long he intended to stay away. By the time I reached the household products I'd started bargaining with myself: if he'd only taken a few essentials, that would be a good sign and I would call him after dinner. If he'd packed up lock, stock and barrel, I'd batten down the hatches on my hurt and give him a bit longer to come to his senses.

I pulled into the empty driveway and lugged the shopping through the front door, resisting the urge to call out, 'I'm home,' as I dumped the carrier bags onto the kitchen table. I stood for a moment listening to the now-familiar silence of the empty house, sure I could detect somewhere in the disturbed air faint traces of Max's visit, although there was nothing obviously missing.

Perhaps he hadn't come at all, I consoled myself as I went upstairs to change. Maybe he'd had time over the weekend to see sense and had decided he didn't need to move out after all. I took my courage in both hands and pushed open the bedroom door.

At first there was no obvious sign of his having been here. The book he'd been reading was still lying on his bedside table, and the papers I'd stacked haphazardly on the dressing-table appeared to be untouched. With a deep breath and a thumping heart I crossed to his wardrobe, running my finger lightly over the splintered crack down the front of the door before abruptly swinging it open.

The shock of what was waiting for me took my breath away, and I had to hold on to the edge of the wardrobe door to stop myself from falling. To say that he'd taken everything would have been an exaggeration, but only just.

A couple of dress shirts still hung disconsolately from disembodied hangers, but most of his casual clothes were missing, including the jumper I'd slept in the evening before the fiasco with Greg, the one I'd buried my face in, trying to take what solace I could from whatever lingering trace of him remained. I went over and checked on the chest of drawers where he kept his underwear and T-shirts, and gasped in dismay when I saw that they were virtually empty.

Lottie's room told a similar tale: he'd taken the bulk of her clothes as well, along with her dressing-gown and slippers and her favourite blue rabbit toy. The absence of the rabbit was like a knife-twist to the stomach, and suddenly the difference between 'left me' and 'moved out' seemed tautological: either way, he'd gone, taking Lottie with him, and leaving a great gaping hole in my heart. I sat down heavily on Lottie's neatly made bed and dropped my face into my hands and wept for the life I'd had before, the one where I'd taken Max and Lottie and bedtime stories about witches and ghosts for granted, and wanted it back so much I could hardly breathe.

Eventually I made myself get up and go back through to our bedroom. And it was then that I spotted the reason for the comprehensive packing. Draped across the chair beside the dressing-table back in our bedroom were the clothes I'd worn the previous day: the jeans and the jumper that had taken such a drenching when the carton of milk had burst all over them. And flung in the corner of the room behind the door, where I definitely hadn't left it, was the shirt that Greg had lent me, the one I'd had to keep on because the jumper hadn't been dry enough to wear.

No; my mother had been right all those years ago. Life was many things, but fair certainly wasn't one of them.

I was poor company for Alison that evening. Once I'd prepared the spare room for her and helped her arrange her barrage of bottles on the dressing-table, I fell into a melancholic funk. For some reason I felt irritable, though I couldn't put a reason to my irritability. We ate a dispirited supper together around eight, during which she probed for information about what had happened at Greg's apartment on Saturday afternoon and I gave her half-hearted non-answers, studiously avoiding mentioning to her that we'd spent the night together. Again. By nine o'clock she'd abandoned her questioning and proposed an early night for the pair of us, insisting I unplug the phone first to ensure I got a good night's rest.

I didn't bother telling her there was no point. I took my demons to bed with me these days; every time I closed my eyes they would creep out from the corners of my mind and pick over the spoils of my despondency, feeding off them like vultures feasting on carrion. They were insatiable; couldn't get enough of my misery. And I would lie there, sleepless, my head aching dully and feeling like I was about to throw up, and wonder when, how and if it was ever going to end.

Chapter 35

The week took on a rhythm that marched to the beat of my wretchedness like a metronome marking the tempo of a particularly tragic opera. At home I wandered disconsolately around the house tidying things that weren't messed up, while in the office I got Maeve to repel even the most persistent of would-be visitors by telling them I was updating the department strategy and couldn't be disturbed.

On Friday morning, however, she appeared in the doorway to my office looking harassed. 'Um – I'm sorry to disturb you—' she began hesitantly. I looked at her irritably. 'It's just that – well, your sister is on the phone, and she says if you don't speak to her she's going to come down to the office and make you.'

I sighed. The Exec meeting was due to start in under half an hour: I wouldn't put it past Angela to come barging straight in and start berating me in front of everyone there for not returning her calls.

'All right, Maeve – put her through.'

I could hear the tension crackling down the line even before she had spoken. 'Francesca, what the hell is going on?' She didn't wait for an answer. 'I have been trying to get hold of you since Saturday. You aren't answering the house phone, and I can't get through to you on your mobile. It's most inconsiderate: I've been worried sick. I said to Phillip, "Something must have happened," and of course he pooh-poohed it and said you were probably just busy, but I thought that not even you could be so spectacularly selfish as to have forgotten that I have been on tenterhooks waiting to hear from you for a week and a half.'

The niggling headache I'd been nursing since breakfast began to intensify, and I put a hand to my forehead. 'Angela—'

'I'm used to being ignored by you,' she swept on, 'but really, I thought in the circumstances you might show some consideration. Oh – I know you're very busy and important, and really, what's the point in keeping up with your family, who after all are *concerned* about you, nuisance though that is—'

'Max has moved out, Angela,' I said to shut her up.

There was a stunned silence. Then after a moment she cleared her throat tentatively.

'Oh – right. I see.'

'I unplugged the phone on Monday evening, and I forgot to plug it back in. And my mobile has been put through the wringer, quite literally, and quite frankly I know how it feels; and I haven't had a chance to get a new one yet. But you're right: I should have called you – I could have rung from the office. I've been horribly selfish: completely wrapped up in myself.'

There was a moment's silence from the other end of the line. 'Yes: well, it's not surprising,' she said eventually, somewhat mollified.

'Anyway—' I ran a hand through my hair. 'I really have to go: I have a meeting starting—' I checked my watch '—in twenty minutes.'

She tutted impatiently. 'Francesca, I will not allow you to just – dismiss me like one of your minions in the office. Twenty minutes is plenty of time to update me. Either that or you can come over this evening and we'll have a proper talk. Phil is driving the kids up to his parents for the Easter weekend, so the house will be quiet.'

'Angela, I can't.' I thought guiltily of Alison. 'I have someone staying at the moment.'

'What?' The conciliatory tone was gone in a blink. 'Oh, for goodness' sake, Fran. I would have thought you had enough on your plate without inviting house guests. I don't know how you can think of entertaining at a time like this. Have you no sense?'

I ground my teeth, as was my habit after exposure to my sister's sharp tongue. 'I'm not entertaining.' I gave a sigh. 'If you must know, it's Alison.'

'Alison? But I thought she was at death's door in hospital. Honestly, Fran, sometimes I despair, I really do.' She tutted into the phone. 'Let me get this absolutely clear. Max has moved out, and Alison has moved in. Yes?'

'Yes,' I answered in a tired voice.

'And when did you last speak to Max?'

'Last Saturday. When he phoned from his brother's house to tell me he was leaving me.'

I could feel her frowning into the telephone. 'You're going to have to backtrack. The last thing I knew about was that he'd stood you up that night when I was babysitting Lottie.'

'Max didn't stand me up, Ang. It wasn't him on the dating site. It was Adam, Alison's husband. He'd used Max's picture because he was too cowardly to put his own up.'

The confusion in her voice deepened. 'But – you mean – he was messing around on dating sites while his wife was sick in hospital?' She sounded aghast. 'Well. That's – that's disgusting.' She drew in her breath sharply. 'So when he turned up at the restaurant—'

'He'd come in answer to my email, yes,' I finished. 'He said he was there on business, remember? But then I made another date with Max, and Adam turned up for that as well. And that was when I realised what was going on.'

Angela reflected for a moment. 'Right. So then you rushed home and told Max everything, and the two of you fell into each other's arms and lived happily ever after.' She paused expectantly, and I sighed.

'Adam set me up,' I told her. 'He went to see Max, and told him I was seeing someone. A colleague from work.'

'Well, that's ridiculous.' Angela's tone was dismissive. 'Max wouldn't believe that for a minute.' She waited for me to concur, and when I didn't she tutted. 'No, sorry. We might not see each other all that often, but even I know that you're not stupid enough to put your marriage on the line.'

'Of course I'm not!' I said hotly.

'So how come Max thinks you are?'

I cringed inside. We were back at the point where I was trying to explain to Greg why Max had just thumped him. It had been bad enough then, when it had just been Greg and me. Now, with my sister waiting to hear what I had to say, it was positively mortifying.

I gave a nervous cough. 'Greg and I – well, we're good mates. More than just colleagues.' I hesitated. 'When his wife left him, he confided a lot of how he was feeling to me. And so when all this trouble started with Max and the dating site and everything, I suppose he wanted to be there for me, too. That's what friends do, right?' I waited for her to say something to show she was keeping up to speed, and when she stayed silent I ploughed on. 'So he came with me on the second date. For moral support. And Adam saw us together. I don't know if he genuinely thought we were up to something, but he went and told Max.' I broke off for a moment. 'I suppose I can't blame Max for jumping to the wrong conclusions. Circumstantially, it didn't look good.' A tear spilled over and trickled down my cheek as I spoke, and I wiped it away impatiently. The last thing I needed was to turn up blubbering at another Exec meeting. 'But that's what it was: a wrong conclusion. There's nothing going on between Greg and me.'

There was a heavy silence, and finally Angela spoke. 'Finished?'

I sniffed. 'Mm-hmn.'

'Right. Well, first of all, I just want to say this. I know I'm a bossy cow, and I give you a really hard time sometimes – well, most of the time, probably. But I'm your sister, Fran. I don't care what you've done, or how much of a mess you're in: I'm here for you. And yet I feel like I'm getting half a story here.' I glanced at my watch surreptitiously, and as though she were sitting in the room with me Angela cut across my thoughts. 'I don't care what meeting you're supposed to be at – they can wait ten minutes, can't they?'

I took a deep breath. 'I suppose so.'

'Right. So spit it out.'

And so I did. As briefly as possible, I told her about how Greg had come round to take me to work, and how Max had appeared when he'd been giving me a supportive hug and had taken a swing at him, and then I had to backtrack and explain that Max had thought I'd always been a bit sweet on Greg. Eventually I got around to telling her what Greg had admitted to, pausing to give her a chance to comment so that I could gauge her reaction. When I got none, I told her about how we had ended up spending two nights together, the first because we'd been in shock over what Cheryl had done and the second because Greg had knocked me unconscious and I couldn't be left on my own. And finally I asked her if she still thought that I wasn't stupid enough to put my marriage on the line.

She didn't answer straight away, though I could hear some odd muffled noises from the other end of the line. 'Angela?'

'Sorry.' Her voice was still muffled. 'It's just—' She broke off again, and then a small snort escaped down her nose and she started to laugh.

'Angela, this is not funny,' I said indignantly. 'I am going through the most traumatic time of my life, and there is absolutely nothing to laugh about.'

'I'm sorry,' she said again, before dissolving in another snort of laughter. 'It's just that the thought of him rugby-tackling you – no.' She coughed suddenly. 'Of course you're right. It's not funny.' Another curious whining noise echoed down the line.

'Angela, did you hear any of what I just said? Greg actually admitted to having feelings for me. And then I ended up spending the night in his bed. With him. And I'm supposed to be trying to save my marriage.'

'Fran.' Angela's tone was brisk. 'Fran, listen to me. Don't you get it? Of course this guy Greg has feelings for you. He wouldn't be human if he didn't. Everyone that knows you falls a little bit in love with you: that's just the kind of person you are.'

'That's rubbish,' I protested. 'Of course they don't.'

'They do,' she insisted. 'Look at Alison. You just don't do casual friendship, Fran. You do a hundred per cent commitment. Once you let down your defences and actually allow someone to get close, you're like a bloody Labrador.'

'I'm not!'

'You are! Why d'you think I'm so sure you'd never cheat on Max? The word isn't in your vocabulary. It's one of the things about you that drives me so mad. You're the Labrador, and I'm the bloody porcupine. Nobody dares get too close to me, but everyone wants to tickle your tummy.'

A wave of relief washed over me. If Angela felt like this about me in spite of our having spent so little time together over the past few years, maybe there was hope for Max and me after all.

'For God's sake, stop beating yourself up about what happened with Greg.' She made a snorting sound. 'Even if he is a bit sweet on you, that's his problem. He'll get over it when he finds out what a complete flake you really are. Anyway, obviously I can't leave you to sort this out on your own: you've already made an unholy mess of things. If you can't make it round this evening, how about if I come to you? I'll bring supper,' she added as an incentive.

My head gave another throb, and I capitulated. 'Okay, then.'

'Eight o'clock? I'll make a moussaka.'

'Lovely.' I squeezed my eyes shut as the pain behind my temples increased.

'And Fran?'

'Mm-hmn?'

'Don't worry. It will all work out. With Max, I mean. You know what drama queens men can be.'

I smiled in spite of myself. 'Thanks, Ang. See you tonight.'

I hung up and began to gather up the papers I needed for the meeting. I'd been dreading it all week: it would be the first time since the previous weekend that I'd be face-to-face with Greg. The thought of seeing him now made me cringe with embarrassment. I dawdled at my desk for a few moments and then arrived at the meeting deliberately late, so that there wouldn't be time for any pre-meeting chit-chat. I took the only remaining chair at the table, opposite Greg, and avoided catching his eye as I sat down.

Happily, the bulk of the meeting was taken up with the fallout from the O_2 fiasco, so I was able to keep my head below the parapet while Brian bore the brunt of Derek's wrath. A couple of times Greg tried to catch my eye, but I managed to avoid anything too heavy in the way of non-verbal communication. At twelve Derek dismissed us all with a fresh set of objectives for the following week. I shuffled my papers together and pushed my chair back to leave, and it was then that Greg spoke directly to me.

'Fran? Got five minutes? I need to run through something with you.'

I looked nervously around the rapidly emptying boardroom, but couldn't think of anything feasible to say that wouldn't sound like I was making excuses. Reluctantly I took my seat back at the table, blushing furiously, and tried a half-hearted smile.

'Sure.'

He waited until everyone had left, and then picked up a pen and fiddled with it. It was seeing him do this that made me realise he was as nervous as I was.

'So – how've you been?'

I tried to look positive. 'Oh – okay.' Another nervous smile.

'How's the head?'

I touched the back of my head tentatively. 'Still attached.'

There was an uncomfortable pause, and then I cleared my throat.

'What about you?'

'Sorry?'

'I just wondered – after Cheryl and everything—'

He made a dismissive gesture. 'Ach – ancient history.'

'Right.' I nodded sagely.

'Well: I should probably—' He gave a half-nod in the

direction of the door. 'I just wanted to make sure you were okay.'

I stood up and gathered up the papers I'd brought to the meeting, and then gave a sigh and dropped them back onto the table.

'This is ridiculous.' He looked up at me enquiringly. 'This – skirting around each other.'

He gave a half-laugh of relief. 'Yes – yes, it is.'

'I mean, we're both adults.'

He nodded in agreement. 'We are, yes.'

'And it's not as if anything – I mean, we never – even if we—' I blushed again and broke off with another sigh. 'I just want things to go back to the way they were between us. Before any of this happened. God knows, the rest of my life is a pig's ear. It would be nice if you and I could just—' I gestured helplessly.

'Get over ourselves?' he finished for me.

'Yes! Exactly.' I looked at him hopefully. 'So can we, do you think?'

He pursed his lips, and examined the end of his pen thoughtfully. 'You know that stuff I said to you in the kitchen after Max had left?'

Oh, God. Not this again. 'Greg—'

'I never meant it, you know.' He forced himself to look at me. 'I only said it to try and cheer you up.'

'Sure you did.' I eyed him sceptically.

He nodded. 'You're not even my type. You're too – too—' He looked me up and down. '—clumsy,' he finished lamely.

My lips twitched involuntarily and I looked at him properly now. I looked hard into his eyes, where there lurked a thousand unasked questions, and saw the concern, the worry, and, yes, maybe a glint of something more, but nothing I couldn't handle, surely? He was handing me a way out of the awkwardness that had sprung up between us: for once in my life couldn't I just stop digging around for the truth and accept it for what it was?

'Want to come round for supper this evening?' I asked after a moment.

He looked at me in surprise. 'Wow. Well – that's a bit of a turnaround.' Then he gave me a knowing smile, and suddenly the old Greg was back. 'I knew you wouldn't be able to resist me for long.'

'Don't flatter yourself.' I grimaced at him. 'My sister's coming over. I need all the reinforcements I can get.'

The rest of the day passed in a haze. At lunch time I took some painkillers that did nothing to ease my throbbing head, and eventually around five-thirty I decided to call it a day and try to squeeze in a nap before Angela and Greg arrived for supper. Sleep hadn't brought much refreshment latterly, I reflected grimly in the car on the way home. The sooner we got things sorted out, the better. I'd had enough of this half-life. My head gave another agonising throb, making me gasp aloud.

As I pulled out onto the roundabout that fed onto the dual carriageway a car cut across my bonnet blasting its horn angrily, and I hit the brakes hard, my heart thumping along with my head. I sat there for a moment on the roundabout, my palms sweating, while cars streamed past on either side of me. Then I wiped my hands across my eyes and pulled away slowly.

For some reason the traffic around me seemed to be moving in slow motion. There was a darkness spreading across the corner of my vision, eclipsing the evening inch by excruciating inch. I peered over the steering wheel feeling disorientated: where was it I was supposed to be going? A steady stream of traffic coming down the opposite side of the dual carriageway pierced my skull, and the pain inside my head intensified. From some distant place I registered a dark shape looming in front of me. And then a cloak came down over my eyes, and everything went black.

Chapter 36

Somewhere close to my head a lorry was reversing. I could hear the insistent beep-beep-beeping as it inched past, and wished it would hurry up and finish its manoeuvre as the noise was waking me up and I wanted so much to sleep. And then somehow I must have climbed onto the lorry, because I was being borne along on its back down a brightly lit tunnel, and a woman was looking down on me and saying something. It wasn't Alison, or Angela, or anyone I knew. I tried to focus on the face, and then gave up the effort and closed my eyes again. Eventually we came out of the tunnel and back into the darkness and the lorry stopped, although that couldn't be right because I could still hear the beeping noise. Then it, too, faded, and I descended back into the deep pit of unconsciousness and slept.

I dreamed, as well. Someone was crying: I could hear them trying to say something, the words breaking and falling from their mouth in incoherent gasps. Then in the dream Alison came to see me and told me all over again that her cancer was gone, and Lottie gave a shout of laughter and announced that she was a Daisel Fly before sprouting wings and flying off through the open window. After that everybody disappeared and someone told me to rest, and so I did.

When I next woke, sunlight was streaming in through the window, making me blink myopically. A figure was silhouetted against the bright square of light, and a second person was slumped in a seat next to my bed. Above my head a metal arm held a bag containing a clear liquid, from which a tube ran all the way down its stand and into my arm, and on the cabinet alongside the bed, a vase of snowy-white freesias spilled their delicate perfume into the room. I blinked again and turned my head a little, noting as I did so that the pain that had been plaguing me for so long had finally gone away, and the figure in the chair straightened and leaned across to me.

'Fran?' My mother reached out and lightly touched my cheek. 'Oh, Max, I think she's waking up.'

The other figure detached itself from the window and crossed to the bed. 'Hey,' he said in that soft way he had. And then he smiled at me, a lopsided, sad sort of smile. As he reached out and took hold of my hand I realised that it was him I'd heard crying across my dreams, and I covered his hand with my own.

'Hey,' I said back to him, and I began to cry as well.

My mother pushed herself stiffly to her feet, muttering something about topping up the water jug, and tactfully withdrew, leaving Max and me to explore the fragile beginnings of a reconciliation. He spent a full five minutes telling me he'd been an idiot who didn't deserve me, and I thought to myself that it had been worth almost dying just to hear him say that. And then, because he couldn't stop apologising and reproaching himself, I asked him to fill me in on what had happened to me from the point when I'd blacked out in the car.

I'd suffered an acute subdural haematoma, he told me – fancy words for the blood clot that had formed following the knock on the head I'd received at Greg's apartment, and that was responsible for the headaches and confusion I'd been suffering all week. I'd only survived thanks to the sharp observational powers of the on-call registrar, who'd spotted when I was brought in by the paramedics that one of my pupils was dilated and had carried out an immediate CT scan. Even as the surgeon was cutting a neat circle in my skull and irrigating the blood clot, the police were tracing the registration number of my car and ringing at the door of the house. Max had been at his parents' home when the call had come through from Alison, and had come straight to the hospital, running into my mother in the hospital lobby in a flurry of unanswered questions.

'She hasn't left your side for three days,' he told me now. 'We've had to draw lots for the chair. She wouldn't even leave you to get something to eat. I've been bringing sandwiches in.' He gave me a remorseful grin. 'Now I know where you get your stubborn streak.'

A warm feeling began to steal across the dark recesses of my heart. 'Daft streak, you mean.' I drew in a deep breath. 'I can't even remember now why we stopped speaking in the first place. Maybe it took that blow to the head to knock some sense into me.'

'Into all of us,' Max corrected. 'You weren't the only one. I reckon the past few weeks will go down in the family history book as the worst on record.' He shook his head ruefully. 'All the hurt. The imagined offence. Most of the time the only place it existed was in our own heads.'

'Such a waste of energy,' I agreed. I fingered the waxy petals of one of the snowy freesias in the vase beside the bed, and smiled suddenly. 'Alison bought these, didn't she? She always had a bunch of them nearby when she was in hospital. She says there's nothing like them for combating the smell of antiseptic.' I lifted one of the delicate blooms from the vase and inhaled its sweet perfume. 'I expect you've heard her news, haven't you? Hard to believe, after all the weeks of worry.'

The air in the room grew suddenly still, and beside me Max stretched out a hand.

'Fran—' He swallowed.

I inhaled sharply. 'It's like a miracle,' I went on, battening down hard on the thin tendril of despair that had begun to unfurl somewhere inside my chest. 'Isn't it? Amongst all the shit that's been going on? Don't you think so, Max? Such wonderful news.'

Max covered my hand with his own, and I concentrated on examining more minutely the fragile flower I was holding.

'She's going to be staying for a while,' I said, desperation causing my voice to crack. 'If that's okay with you? Just until she's on her feet properly?' I lifted my eyes from the bloom, and looked into his anguished eyes. 'It *is* okay, isn't it, Max?' My mouth wobbled, and a tear spilled unchecked down my cheek. 'If she stays with us? It wouldn't be for long. You wouldn't mind, would you?'

'Fran—' he said again, and then he shook his head, his own eyes glistening. 'Of course I wouldn't have minded.'

Chapter 37

We are parked on a bench at the fringes of the little graveyard, my mother and I, sheltered by the timeless solidity of the churchyard wall from the implacable November weather. Around us the feathery branches of denuded trees dip and curtsey apologetically as though lamenting the relentless wind that has stripped them of every last vestige of foliage and strewn its plunder across the Berkshire countryside, where it lies mulching itself into a disconsolate carpet of fading splendour. Our faces are tilted towards the leaden sky, seeking out comfort from a recalcitrant sun. The air is sharp, crisp with the smell of wood smoke and a presage of the harsh winter forecast for the months ahead.

'Thanks for coming.' I keep my face lifted upwards, and feel rather than see my mother's eyes upon me.

'That's all right.'

I have been weeks – months, rather – harnessing the courage to come here. Reproaching myself endlessly as I crawled one infinitesimally small step at a time back to health. Chiding myself for every manner of selfishness. Loathing the self-absorption that had left me blind to what had been there so clearly, right under my nose if only I'd had the humanity to see it. And somewhere in the midst of it I'd been angry too: raging, even, at my best friend for pulling off such a comprehensive deception; at myself for falling for it. And suddenly it was November, and Alison's birthday – or would have been – and I realised that if I didn't do this thing now, I never would.

It was Max who had telephoned my mother and asked her to come with me, Max who had bought the bunch of white freesias that lay on the bench beside us, tied together with a tangle of ribbon. She is unruffled, a splash of colour in her chirpy red coat against the greyness of the afternoon, while I sit and wrestle with a thousand demons and try to find the courage to confront the sense of betrayal that is threatening to overwhelm me.

'She would have stayed if she could,' my mother says unexpectedly, cutting into my thoughts. 'She didn't have a choice.'

I shake my head and make no answer. I have never spoken about this before, and my mother has never asked. On the ground a few feet away a lone bird – a sparrow, I think it is – hops amongst the tumbled leaves looking for food.

'She had a choice about lying to me,' I say after a moment. I am shocked at the bitterness in my tone. 'Lying about a thing like that, knowing she had so little time left. Robbing us both of the chance to say any kind of goodbye.'

My mother looks as though she is about to say something and then changes her mind. 'You're right,' she agrees unexpectedly. 'What kind of a friend would do that? She must really have hated you.'

She smiles at my crestfallen face. 'Did she hate you, Fran?'

My tongue grows thick in my mouth, and I swallow and shake my head.

'You know, when you were growing up you were always so – *categorical* about life,' she tells me. 'And I used to say to myself, that child will have her heart broken if she doesn't learn.'

'Learn what?' I ask.

She smiles at me again. 'To bend with the wind, Fran. Life isn't black and white, thank God. It's every colour imaginable. Maybe your friend just had something so important to do in what little time was left to her that she couldn't risk you trying to stop her. As she no doubt knew you would.' She looked at me searchingly. 'You want the truth about your friend? Maybe she just plain loved you enough to lie to you. Maybe that was her parting gift to you.'

She reaches out and takes hold of the lapels of my jacket lightly in her fingertips, smoothing them against my chest and patting them into place. 'Now: how about we go and say those goodbyes?'

I nod mutely and collect the flowers from the bench, and the two of us begin to make our way along the path. Around us the wind whips up another pile of fallen leaves before bringing them gently to rest in a whispering pile about our feet. As we round the corner by the church I see two figures ahead of us. The smaller of the two is kneeling at one of the graves, arranging something in front of the headstone. At the sound of our approach, the taller figure reaches down to touch his companion on the shoulder, and she straightens.

'Adam.'

'Fran.' He inclines his head slightly.

The eight months since his wife died have taken their toll on Adam. Gone is the cocky self-assurance: he looks defeated, these days. Defeated and old. His hair is peppered with grey, and his face, thinner now, is crossed with lines. He couldn't look less like Max if he tried.

'Hello, Erin.' I crouch beside her so that we are on a level.

'We brought flowers too,' she tells me, spotting the bunch I am holding. 'And a card. I made it with Daddy yesterday.'

'That's lovely, sweetheart.'

'It's not a birthday card,' she goes on. 'It's just a card to tell her how much we love her. Isn't it, Daddy?'

He swallows. 'Yes.'

'D'you want to see it?' She reaches down and plucks it from the ground for me, and I study the picture of flowers she's drawn on the front for a moment. I can't bring myself to look at what they've written inside.

'It's lovely, Erin.'

She spends a moment or two rearranging it amongst the flowers, and then Adam speaks again.

'Come on, you. Time for lunch.' He meets my eye again as he turns to leave. 'I'll be a bit earlier dropping her off this Monday.' His face is puckered in a frown. 'I have a breakfast meeting in Marylebone at eight.'

Not *Can I drop her off early,* I note. There's still a hint of the old arrogance in amongst the fragile truce we have negotiated that allows Erin to come and stay with us during the week while her father is busy with work, though now I see it for the defence mechanism it is. *I never really thought she would actually die*, he'd told me the first time we got together after the funeral, after he'd read the will she'd written and found her request for Max and me to help out with Erin. *She was always too alive for that.* Gone now are the easy affairs, the casual deceptions: these days the only girl in his life is his daughter. It took losing Alison for him to realise, too late of course, that she was all he'd wanted in the first place. I acknowledge the request with a small nod. 'Bring her over on Sunday night if it's easier. Save her getting up at the crack of dawn.'

'Yes!' Erin gives a whoop of delight, incongruous in the quiet of the graveyard, and in that moment of unguarded exuberance I see her mother in her smile, in her infectious enthusiasm. From the way his face clouds over, so does her father. 'Can Lottie and me watch *Madagascar* before we go to bed?'

'Of course you can,' I answer, never taking my eyes off Adam's stricken face, watching him struggle to negotiate a path through his loss. 'As long as it's okay with your dad.'

He collects himself. 'Right.' He nods once or twice, distracted again, then catches my eye briefly. 'Yes, it's fine.' He hesitates. 'Thanks.'

I raise my eyebrows at this rare acknowledgement. 'See you Sunday, then.' I lift my hand in farewell.

We wait until the two of them have disappeared around the side of the church, and then I kneel to add my own fragrant offering to the small collection already gathered at the graveside, frowning over the inscription on the headstone and wondering why it is that I have been so reluctant to do this earlier.

Beside me, my mother stretches out a hand and lays it gently on my arm.

'All right?'

I consider the headstone for a moment longer, and then turn away. 'She isn't here.' I look around me at the wind-tumbled graveyard, at the trees bowing and dipping in the lowering afternoon, and suddenly a break appears in the dark sky and a low shaft of sunlight spills across the fields in front of us.

'Did you ever see anything so beautiful?' I ask.

My mother shakes her head at me, and tucks a rogue tendril of hair behind my ear.

'Never,' she answers.

She threads her hand through my arm and we turn to leave. As we retrace our footsteps back to where we parked the car at the gate to the little church, a fresh gust of wind snatches at my hair, and somewhere in amongst it I feel my grief being caught up and borne off with the leaves, tossing and pitching in the fading light, before being laid gently to rest on the ground behind me.

Afterword

Jane Phillips was my friend for fourteen years. She taught me to speak Franglais, and didn't like too much butter on her crumpets, and loved her kids, Rhiannon and Josh, her husband, Haydn, and her dogs, Charlie and Peanut, in equal and wholehearted measure. She had a way of seeing the funny side of a situation that saved my sanity on too many occasions to number. She rocked at Pictionary and was lousy at cleaning, and she could create anything from anything: give her a roll of tin foil and some double-sided tape and she'd conjure up fancy dress costumes for an entire school production before you could turn around. After I moved up to Scotland with my family, she sent up a Christmas wreath she'd made, decorated with miniature Bonio biscuits for the dogs, and a length of home-made bunting for me that read 'We love Susy' across its tiny flags. Even over a distance of more than 400 miles, I basked in the warmth of her love, her generosity of spirit and, above all, her unconditional friendship.

Jane died of bowel cancer in 2002. Her legacy, aside from the two beautiful children who carry their mother's courage in their eyes, is the zest for life that she communicated to those who knew and loved her as I did and do.

Alison is not Jane. Jane never asked me to fix up her husband after she'd died. She never tied me in to promises

I couldn't keep. She didn't even tell me she was ill. Jane, you see, was all about living. She was the most alive person I ever met. Amongst all the crumpets and the tennis games with the dogs and the fears and triumphs that young mums bringing up small kids share, I was proud and deeply honoured to call her my friend.

I still have the bunting.

Ebury Press Fiction Footnotes

Turn the page for an exclusive interview with Susy McPhee …

What was the inspiration for HUSBANDS AND LIES?

My friend Roz was on a dating site, showing me the photograph of someone who'd invited her on a date. We started window-shopping, giving the ads marks out of ten for presentation, wit, etc. and I said to her, 'Wouldn't it be awful if you saw someone you knew here? Your boss, say, or your husband, ha ha. After that the idea just wouldn't go away.

As a writer one of your great talents is being able to seamlessly blend humour and pathos, but who makes you laugh? And cry?

My dog Mishka makes me laugh. She's such a clown; she keeps me sane. There's a dog in my next book inspired by Mishka. If we're talking about people who make me laugh, it would be my kids – especially my youngest daughter Lauren. She doesn't take life – or herself – too seriously, and can usually raise a smile from me even when I'm in a real strop. (She's often responsible for the strop, too, so the ability to make me laugh has probably saved her from all manner of dire consequences.)

I don't often cry these days. I was a right cry-baby when I was growing up. There were four of us kids: my twin sisters, then me, then my brother Simon, all vying for our mum's attention. The twins were cute and always being photographed, and Simon was the youngest and a boy to boot, so I was lacking in novelty features. I got it into my head that if I snivelled enough, Mum would like me best. She didn't.

Have you ever been on a dating website?

Apart from that time with Roz, only when I was

researching for *Husbands and Lies*. I've never gone on one looking for dates. I met my husband about a hundred years ago at university when he was studying Maths and Computing and I was trying to break into the world of espionage, and we married straight after graduating. I would use a site, though, if I were single and wanted to meet someone special. I think they're a great way for people to get together.

Which book are you reading at the moment?

I suppose I should say something intellectual so that I sound really intelligent and educated. Truth to tell, I am between books, having just finished a rather boring one – I won't tell you the title, because it wouldn't be fair on the poor person who spent all those hours writing it.

Who are your favourite authors?

I really like Marc Levy's work. He's hard to categorise, and I like that. Some of his books are quite off-the-wall – he wrote one story about a girl whose 'ghost' goes back to haunt the apartment she lived in before a car accident put her in a coma, and then last year he brought out *Les enfants de la liberté*, which was a pretty grim account of a group of young resistance fighters in France during the German occupation. Amélie Nothomb is brilliant as well – *Sulphuric Acid* is spine-chillingly good. And I recently read *The Vanishing Act of Esme Lennox*, by Maggie O'Farrell, which was terrific.

Which classic have you always meant to read and never got round to it?

Silas Marner. I know the story upside-down and back-to-front, but I've never read the book.

What are your top five books of all time?

I can't limit this to five! So I'm not even going to mention *To Kill a Mockingbird, The Catcher in the Rye, Nineteen Eighty-Four, Lord of the Flies, Gatsby, Pride and Prejudice, Animal Farm*, or anything by Shakespeare or John Irving (especially *A Prayer for Owen Meaney*) as they're all too obvious (well, maybe not the Irving, but Owen Meaney made me laugh out loud).

I love *Anne of Green Gables*. My friend Mandy and I used to act the book out on the school bus. We took it in turns to be Anne and Diana, and our friend Carol was coerced into being a reluctant Marilla. We used to drive her nuts. *Brat Farrar* by Josephine Tey is another favourite: full of twists and turns and unexpected alliances. Ira Levin's *Stepford Wives* – horrible! A nugget of a read, much darker than the film versions would have us believe. *Never Let Me Go* by Kazuo Ishiguro – so, so sad. Jon McGregor's *if nobody speaks of remarkable things*, though I found the structure hard to handle and the lack of capital letters in the title put my teeth on edge. Paolo Coelho's *Veronika Decides to Die*. I know that's six already, but can I have one more? *Frankenstein*.

Do you have a favourite time of day to write? A favourite place? What's your writing process: are you a planner?

I like to get started as soon as I can prise my eyes open in the mornings, and will often sit in bed for an hour with my laptop and a cup of tea. The minute I come downstairs there's usually a whole heap of chores waiting for me, so if I've already done some writing I feel more in control. Once I've run round after my messy family, cursing them roundly and vowing to make them do more to help around the house, I make some coffee and Mishka and I get stuck in for a good few hours, either in the study where it's warm or in front of the fire in the living-room. When she thinks I'm in danger of atrophying she drags me out for a walk up the hill behind the house, which is a great opportunity for working on the plot of whatever I'm writing. I think I probably talk to myself during these walks – I get some funny looks from other walkers sometimes – so having Mishka with me is a great cover.

As for my writing process – I start with a really broad idea and live with it for a few weeks. I like to let a character brew for a bit before putting anything more than a few notes in writing. It's a little like having a house guest around the place. Then I jot down some ideas for the plot, although these are a moveable feast and tend to change and evolve as the characters and storyline develop. And then one day I just think, right, time to get going, and I sit down and write the opening line. I love opening lines: all that potential in a sentence or two. After that I'm fairly disciplined: I have a target word count I have to hit each week, otherwise I feel guilty. I never get writer's block. I get writer's laziness sometimes, or writer's too-much-washing-and-ironing-to-do, or writer's it's-a-sunny-day-I'll-do-the-garden-for-an-hour-or-so, but not writer's block. I think you have to write through any block, on those grunged-up days when you don't feel you've got anything to say. Just sit down and write – anything. Even if you think it's a pile of mince. You can always go back and revise it later, and nine times out of ten you discover that it isn't mince at all, or at least not all of it – it was just your mood that particular day that made you think it was.

Which fictional character would you most like to have met?

Depends on my mood. Ma Larkin from *The Darling Buds of May*, on those days when I feel like a sympathetic ear, though my sisters are pretty good listeners. Boo Radley – I'd love to know what he got up to all day in that house. Ophelia – poor girl. We could have had a G&T together instead of her going off and drowning herself like that.

Who, in your opinion, is the greatest writer of all time?

I used to think Enid Blyton couldn't be beaten. When my sister Dale sat the Eleven-Plus, one of the questions was, 'What is the most famous book in the world?' And she answered, 'Enid Blyton's.' I think she was probably right – she passed the exam, anyway. *The Famous Five*! Brilliant. Every book was exactly the same, and I couldn't get enough of them. These days – I hate to be predictable! – I would have to pick the bard.

Other than writing, what other jobs have you undertaken or considered?

When I was growing up, I wanted to join a circus. I still have a story somewhere that I wrote when I was six, illustrated with a picture of me underneath a circus horse in a tutu, clinging on to its belly. In my head it was much more glamorous than the picture. Then I wanted to be Samantha, the woman off *Bewitched* who could wiggle her nose and do magic. When I hit my teens I dreamed of becoming a vet. A stint with the RSPCA after my 'O' levels killed off that ambition – anyone who's been as close to a cat's blocked anal glands as I have will confirm it's not all it's cracked up to be. I worked in Liverpool University Science Library for a year before I went to uni myself, and then after graduating and not getting taken on by any of the big spy houses, I got sucked into I.T. Don't ask me how: I didn't even know how to turn on a computer in those days. Scattered in between all of this I've worked for a butcher (great for titbits for the dog, though my sister Kerry once cooked them up for dinner by mistake), a grocer, and a tobacconist. I've also been, amongst other things, a barmaid, a lecturer, a supermarket assistant, a tiler, a wine merchant, and a karate instructor. I can milk a goat, though I never seriously considered this as a career option. I've trained rocket scientists in the former Soviet Union. And I once found myself advising the Deputy Prime Minister of Israel on how to improve standards in the construction industry. In Russian. Eat your heart out, MI5.

What are you working on at the moment?

My next book – *The Runaway Wife*. It's about a woman – Marion Bishop – who is mugged on the the night she goes out to buy paracetamol to kill herself. So a nice cheery subject.